Sam to the Ends of the Earth

— THE —
SEA WITCH

Sam to the Ends of the Earth

— THE —
SEA WITCH

By M. P. Ward

LANG
BOOK PUBLISHING

langbookpublishing.com

Cover design by Blair McLean
Photography by Mike Ward

National Library of New Zealand Cataloguing-in-Publication Data
Lang Book Publishing 2017

ISBN 978-0-9941417-4-3 – Paperback
ISBN 978-0-9941417-5-0 – Hard Cover
eISBN 978-0-9941417-6-7 – ePub
eISBN 978-0-9941417-7-4 – Kindle

Published in New Zealand
A catalogue record for this book is available from the National Library of New Zealand.
Kei te pātengi raraunga o Te Puna Mātauranga o Aotearoa te whakarārangi o tēnei pukapuka.

For Karen

A boy will come from War,

a joining band and heavy weight.

He has no one friend, but a friend to enemies is he,

A hag's child, and a servant to the sea.

Beware land lovers for he is the hope of all who sail,

The outsider is coming. Hail the true king of Cornwall

Before the telling book is full,

The boy must come or all will fail.

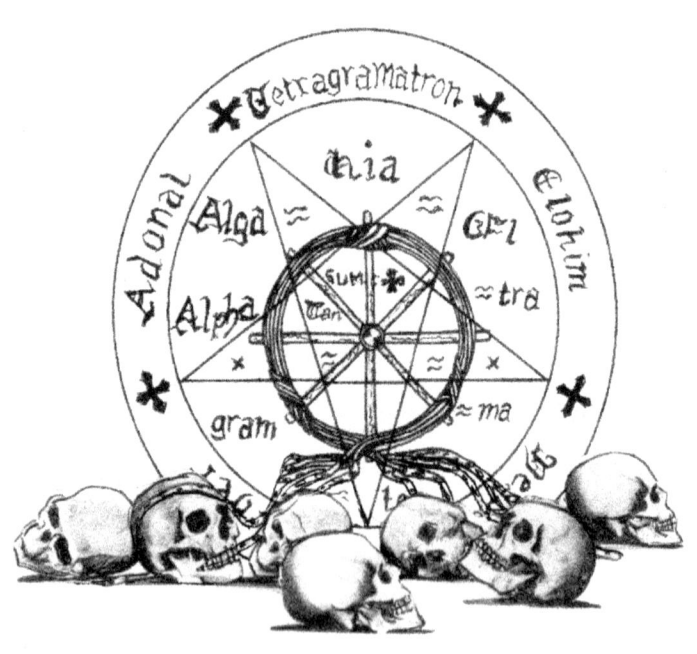

Did you know, hundreds of years ago there really were sea witches.

They lived in villages around the coast of Britain. Each day combing the beaches, they searched for long strands of seaweed. Gathering five strands together in their hands, they would tie three knots in them.

Down at the harbour, where the ships were moored, the sea witches would sell them to the boat captains for a few coins.

When the ships were out at sea and the captains wanted the wind to blow, they opened one of the knots, and the wind would blow ... or so they believed.

PREFACE

The Cavern

Larson flew across the cavern, lightning fast, like he had that day in the woods. Striding up, trying to get between Jenny and Sam to hastily separate them. There was no time for words, Jenny knew that for sure. She gasped. An immediate, frantic assault was being forced upon her by the large, bulky man, whom she had thought was her friend; he wasn't anymore – she despised him for it.

Much as she tried, in the end she knew her efforts would be useless. There was nothing she could do to stop him, but still she tried. *Maybe his resolve isn't as powerful as his strength, just maybe.*

'No, please, let me go, Frank. I don't want to leave him. No... No... No!' Jenny turned trying to slap him away for a second. 'I cannot go with you,' she cried, gripping Sam tightly around his neck again with both hands. Tears began sliding, snake like, down her pale skin and a salty taste entered the corner of her mouth. *No good could come of this, no good at all.*

Larson suddenly yanked on her arm, reeling her body to the side. 'We've got to go, Jenny; leave him.'

Oh my, we're going to die. Her eyes remained fixed on Sam's

11

emotionless face. 'I don't care if this is the way it is meant to be. If Sam's finished, then I am too. I don't want to live anymore, not without him.'

'Live today, fight tomorrow,' Larson breathed into her ear.

Jenny wouldn't listen. Hollowness opened up in her heart. *Poor Mum, how I will miss her, with her cups of tea and fussing. How she'll miss me too. I hope she'll be okay. I know she won't. Oh, don't think that.*

She couldn't believe it. The pain was too great. Gripping Sam even tighter, she pulled his head alongside hers, kissing the side of his face. She was determined to stay, willing him back from the dark place in his mind. 'He's trapped in there, Frank, unable to escape, like a coma. But sometimes they come back, don't they? All it takes is something to jar him, a voice or music he likes... Oh, Sam, follow my voice and please come back to me.'

'There's no time for that,' Larson shot at her. 'He's gone and we've got to get out of here.'

Sam's cold, wet jumper oozed sea water between Jenny's fingers as she squeezed it, desperate to hold on.

But Larson was undeterred, throwing his arm around her waist, tugging at her, determined.

Jenny, filled with panic, cried out, 'No… No…' once again. 'He's not, Frank. I can bring him back.' Her fingers began to straighten under the pressure. She was losing her grip; then a haunting, terrible scream echoed around the cavern. *Oh God, help me.*

Larson wrenched her free and stumbled back a few paces.

'No, you can't do this, Frank. Let me go. I'm not leaving him… I won't, please, please,' she cried out in a jittery, sobbing tone, whilst reaching out her long narrow fingers, yearning to pull Sam back into her arms, but she could not.

Ashen faced, Sam remained unmoved, like a porcelain figure knelt upon the cold sandy ground. He appeared to be totally unaware of what was going on right in front of him.

Larson didn't seem to care, slinging Jenny unceremoniously over his broad shoulder like a bag of sand.

Fury and frustration spilled from Jenny like molten lava pouring from a jug. Her fiery tongue lashed at him and she writhed, kicking and punching him all over. 'Put me down you big oaf or I'll kill you, I'll kill you, I'll kill you,' she cried, her voice becoming weaker with each word.

Larson wasn't interested in words; she knew that also, and his strong powerful limbs pressed her even tighter against him. There was nothing she could do. Her last-ditch efforts had failed. Suddenly, her chest was struck by a sharp physical pain, as if Larson had stabbed her with a knife, ripping the heart from her shattered body. He left it on the ground, as he did Sam, at the mercy of the sea witch and the wolves. Sam would find no mercy there, of that Jenny was certain.

But why is Larson leaving Sam and carrying me away? Why me and not him? Jenny had lost the fight to remain, and nothing made sense anymore. She cried out to him, through rolls of tears, hoping that somehow Sam would hear her, in denial that this would probably be the last time she would ever see him. 'I will find you, Sam. No matter where she takes you, I will follow… to the ends of the Earth if needs be, remember, Sam, to the ends of the Earth.' Tears streamed down her hot flushed cheeks, and Larson callously whisked her away.

Sam remained slumped for a moment on the damp stone and dirt, his dark glazed eyes staring blankly towards the beautiful woman in the long black robes. Oblivious to his surroundings, he rose up, stepping the short distance to her side like a puppet. She allowed him to move only towards her and to see only what she wanted him to see.

Larson ran frantically around the cavern boulders towards the dark passage. Jenny sensed his fear. The wolves which had sat for so long, like good dogs, watching and unmoved by her emotional outburst, turned into savage, snarling beasts. They raced across the cavern and leapt over the giant stones, biting at the air. One of them came within an inch of Jenny's face. She yelled at the sight of its horrible gnashing fangs trying to latch onto her dangling hair.

Suddenly, the wolves stopped at the narrow passage entrance and began prowling back and forth, hesitant to go in. Jenny knew why, and she could see the frustration in the dogs' eyes. The last time they tried to enter here, they were met by a hail of gunpowder and shot. It may not have killed, but it certainly did hurt enough to render them unconscious.

Dogs like these are not easy to kill. Jenny discovered this the last time she was here. Only by losing their heads did they die.

Into the darkness flew Larson with Jenny still bent over his shoulder, and then with an almighty thud, they came to a sudden halt.

Someone slammed into them, running around the bend, almost blind in the dim torchlight, from the opposite direction. He fell backwards, moaning, onto the cold ground. Jenny recognised his voice before she saw his face.

'What are you doing here, Mr Camponara?' asked Larson.

'Where's Sam?' he yelled back, ignoring Larson's question and glaring up with terrified eyes. He sprang to his feet, trembling, fear and desperation emanating from him.

Larson ignored it; pushing him back with his huge hand, passed

Mr Booty and moved further away from the cavern entrance. 'I'm sorry, but you're not going out there,' he shouted, dangerously. 'I won't let you. Lichen throats are about to enter, and they'll kill you for sure.'

He looked like he was about to cry, his face contorting. 'Is Sam dead? Is he out there?'

Mr Booty knelt poised over his red detonation box. 'Better be quick, Mr Larson,' he said, in a very nervy tone. 'They'll not wait forever.'

Mr Camponara wasn't listening. Jenny could see he didn't care; his only concern was for Sam. 'Have you left my son in there with those beasts?' He gasped at the thought, and then frantically he tried to force his way around Larson.

'You give me no choice,' shouted Larson, grabbing him by his shirt collar and dragging him, like a dog, deeper into the darkness. There he stopped for a moment in its darkest depths.

Jenny's friend, Johnny, hopped on ahead of them, bouncing off the walls with short, shocked breaths, the horror of what was happening written across his gaunt face, his eyes wide and black.

Larson yelled back down the tunnel, 'Okay, Mr Booty, let it blow.'

'No, please, you can't,' screamed Jenny, kicking out again in an attempt to escape his vice-like grip.

Mr Camponara barged into Larson, also, and this time Jenny felt his powerful body much more determined. She glanced around. His face had changed, filled with fury, knocking Larson and Jenny back, but Larson stood solid like an iron girder, forcing Mr Camponara onto his back foot again.

'For God's sake, Frank, let him pass, will you' cried Jenny, still folded over his shoulder.

'That's my son out there; I have to save him,' yelled Mr Camponara, barging into Larson for the sixth time, but Mr Booty, ignoring his pleas, pressed down on the detonation handle.

Immediately there was an almighty explosion, and the ground rumbled beneath Larson's feet. Jenny thought he was about to drop her, as he fell reaching out to the cavern wall. Stumbling against the sides, Larson tried to press on, deeper and deeper, as rocks fell from the ceiling onto the wolves, blocking the tunnel's entrance into the cavern and filling it with blinding, choking dust.

Through gritted teeth, Jenny sobbed, 'No, no, I can't believe it; you've killed Sam. I'll never forgive you for that, never.'

Larson appeared to be unaffected by Jenny's emotion, but finally he released her slowly to the ground. 'If I have, then think about all the other children I have saved, all the people, hundreds, maybe thousands. It's not nice to say it, but sometimes there has to be some collateral damage.'

'My son's not collateral damage,' cried Mr Camponara, his eyes blazing up from the ground into Larson's, through a film of tears.

Larson sighed. 'Yes, well, what's done is done.' Calmly he slipped his hand into his pocket and pulled out an A5 book. He turned the pages until he came to a black-and-white sketch of a boy standing over a sea witch. 'I don't think Sam is dead. I think he is fulfilling the prophecy here in *The Book of Black Magic and Revelations*, and when this cavern is cleared, we'll know for sure.'

'What do you mean?' asked Jenny.

'Well, if Sam and the hag aren't here amongst the rubble and the wolves…?' He stared for a moment at the page with mild excitement. 'Then, we'll know, won't we?'

CHAPTER ONE

The Book of Black Magic and Revelations

Two days later

Although the sun shone down on the grass-covered hill, there was a definite autumnal dampness in the air. Jenny pulled her thick coat up tight around her neck. She gazed down the hillside and through the trees to the campsite with dread. All around her and down the hillside, large clumps of thistle grew in pockets everywhere except for the place where the biggest clump had stood. It was hacked back to almost nothing by the emergency services, revealing the tunnel entrance.

Jenny, Johnny and about fifty other people watched with interest from the police cordon tape a metre or so back. On the other side, three large bulky men, each wearing orange boiler suits, oxygen tanks and carrying compressed air drills, pulled masks down over their faces as they entered.

'Who are they?' asked Johnny.

'It's the *Confined Space Rescue Team*,' Jenny told him.

Johnny remained blank.

'Have you never been over to the Geevor Tin Mine Museum?'

Johnny shook his head. 'Never been anywhere before I met Sam.'

'They've got pictures of men dressed just like them in there. You should ask your dad to take you; it's really interesting, and you get to crawl through some really tight tunnels.'

'Narr, I don't fancy that; this one was bad enough for me.'

A few minutes later, one of the rescuers appeared, and the police superintendant walked over to talk to him.

'He must be the team leader,' Jenny told Johnny. 'Usually two go in, and the team leader stays on the surface, giving instructions on his radio. They mustn't think it's a big job, though, because sometimes they have two teams or more.'

Suddenly, Jenny heard a rumbling engine and then the screeching of wet brakes. Everyone turned around to see what it was. A big canvas-back khaki-coloured truck came to a halt in front of them.

'Ah, good,' said the superintendant to his colleague, 'reinforcements.'

Johnny tried to smile. 'It won't take 'em so long to clear it, not now the army's arrived, will it, Jenny?'

'I dunno; there's a lot of rock needs moving in there.'

Suddenly, Jenny felt a large hand pressing down gently on her shoulder; she turned around and looked up.

It was Larson. 'I reckon we should get out of here whilst we can; nothing much to see anyway,' he breathed, looking very nervous.

'No, I want to stay to see if they bring anyone out alive.' Jenny was thinking about the promise she had made to Sam. Nothing else mattered now, and as long as the tiniest glimmer of hope remained, she intended to keep her promise. Even after everything Larson had said, it did not completely dispel all that – he might be wrong. Sam might be in there alive, but if the worst thing had happened – if Sam was dead, crushed by falling rocks and stone – she will have fulfilled her promise and she will have found him.

'They won't, and it's going to take them at least another day before they get close to entering the main cavern.'

Larson was right. Jenny noticed he had the red book inscribed with the words *The Book of Black Magic and Revelations* in his hand. 'Frank, can I take another look at that, please?' she asked, pointing to it.

Jenny had seen the book, very briefly, two days earlier, but she was too upset and angry to absorb anything. Even now she hated what Larson had done, and if Sam was brought out of that cavern dead, then she was determined the police, and all those other people, would know exactly who had killed him.

'Okay, but not here; back at Mr Booty's shop,' he whispered into her ear.

Jenny touched Johnny's arm, pulling him away. 'Come on, we're going.'

'Why?' asked Johnny, disappointed. 'What about Sam?'

'You heard Frank; nothing's happening. We'll come back tomorrow.'

Larson gave a little hoot, mimicking a wood pigeon sound.

Jenny noticed Johnny's and Sam's Dads shoot their eyes to him immediately. They, along with the rotund Mr Booty, drudged from the cordon tape towards the car.

'They'll not get into the cavern today; we'll try again tomorrow,' Larson told them before they had time to ask.

Sam's dad glared hatred at Larson, accusing; then he drove off down the hill in his rented car.

Jenny and Johnny jumped into the Land Rover with Larson.

From across the hill, scowling, angry faces were staring at them. Jenny knew they were the families from Saint Cleer, waiting to see if their loved ones were still alive inside the cavern, and she imagined this is how it must feel for people when miners get trapped in a pit collapse.

A cold chill ran through her, so she turned away from their gawking, accusing eyes. It was obvious from their expressions; they knew who it was that caused the cavern to cave in, she was sure of it.

Larson noticed them too. 'And there's another good reason for us not hanging around here too long, don't you agree?' he said in a serious, sullen tone.

Jenny nodded her head.

The Land Rover bounced down the hill over the thick tufts of grass and into muddy puddles, then between the trees and off to the left onto the dirt track, which led to the main road.

'Here,' said Larson, pulling the book from his pocket and handing it to Jenny. 'You might as well take a look at it now, whilst I'm driving us back.'

Jenny forced a smile. 'Thanks, Frank,' she said, flicking through the pages. She stopped at the picture of a boy, on the seabed, standing over a sea witch. On the page opposite there was a riddle which read:

A boy will come from War,
a joining band and heavy weight.
He has no one friend, but a friend to enemies is he,
A hag's child, and a servant to the sea.
Beware land lovers for he is the hope of all who sail,

The outsider is coming. Hail the true king of Cornwall
Before the telling book is full,
The boy must come or all will fail.

'A boy will come from War,' Jenny read out loud, her eyebrows furrowed. 'I don't understand.'

'Well, it's not Sam, is it?' Johnny pointed out. 'He's not been in any war, born in a war or anything like that.'

'*A joining band and heavy weight,*' Jenny went on. 'Oh, I just don't know.' She turned to Johnny. 'What do you think it means?'

'Not sure. Sam was interested in weights though. He said he wanted to look like Swarzenegger. I thought you would know that.'

'Why?'

'"Cos you know everything about everybody,' said Johnny.

Jenny smiled and blushed a little. 'You cheeky thing,' she said, staring down at the book reciting again. '*He has no one friend, but a friend to enemies is he.* What does that mean?'

Larson stopped at the main road, turned right onto the tarmac heading towards Liskeard and home. 'Mr Booty and I were talking about that, and we reckon Sam is possessed by the sea witch. The poor lad's an imp, the hag's servant.'

'Yes, it says that here, *A hag's child, a servant to the sea.*' Jenny started thinking about the last time she saw Sam. She was hauled over Frank's shoulder screaming for him to stop. He carried her away into the tunnel, but just before they entered, Jenny saw Sam sleepily writhing, intoxicated in the witch's grotesque arms. Jenny pulled away from her thoughts, shuddering and feeling very peculiar.

'Well, we reckon Sam is a tortured soul now. He's torn between the sea witch and you and Johnny; he's batting for both sides. Can't help himself, see, because he has loyalties to all of you,' said Mr Booty.

Jenny could not deny there was something there between Sam and the sea witch. She had seen it for herself; in fact, now she remembered that in amongst the trauma of leaving Sam behind, she had also felt jealousy. Now she experienced shame, *'jealous of an ugly old sea witch.'* 'Okay,' Jenny conceded, 'I'll give you that one, but what about the next bit.' She started to read again, *'Beware land lovers for he is the hope of all who sail.'*

'Don't know,' said Larson.

Mr Booty said from the back of the Land Rover, 'Maybe the witch is going to try to destroy all the ships.'

'Maybe Sam is going to save the fishing fleet,' Johnny chipped in.

Larson laughed, but Jenny knew he wasn't laughing, not really, and his eyes remained fixed to the road. 'It's pure speculation; now let's not get carried away.'

Jenny continued, *'The outsider is coming. Hail the true king of Cornwall.* Well, that fits the bill; Sam is definitely an outsider. I never saw him as a king, though.'

'He's a king to me,' Johnny's dad piped up. 'I'll do anything for that boy. Saved my son's life, he did, so there's nothing I wouldn't do for him, even if it means following him to the gates of hell, and if that means losing my life, then so be it.'

Larson's and Jenny's eyes met for a second, and Jenny was sure they were both thinking the same thing. Johnny's dad, Mr Pothelswaite, didn't think Sam was dead, and secondly, maybe the book is not talking about a literal king, but a people's king. Someone that Cornish people will follow and give up their lives for. Maybe Sam is the king of Cornwall.

Jenny said nothing, but she knew in her heart of hearts that she also would not think twice about giving up her own life for him.

She read on, '*Before the telling book is full...* Well, that is obviously the 'Register of Berserkergangs, Lichen Throats, and Imps'. *The boy must come or all will fail.*'

'Like I said before, Jenny,' Larson breathed calmly. 'I think the boy has come, and it is Sam. Now we need to watch the register to see what happens next. If Madema writes another name there, we'll know the witch isn't dead.

Jenny closed the little book and handed it back. Larson slipped it into his pocket, and everyone sat quietly thinking about the prophecy, as the car grumbled and creaked down to the coast.

CHAPTER TWO

The Wall Witches

The following day it rained heavily, and it was grey and muddy on the hillside. Still Jenny stood by the police cordon tape waiting for news of Sam. The weather had not deterred anyone else either. The people from Saint Cleer, mainly women and children, all waited, sopping wet, in an atmosphere of apprehension and terrible trepidation.

'Look, they're bringing somebody out.' Jenny's heart thumped in her chest.

Johnny stared at the rescuers and then at Jenny. 'I knew they'd start bringing them out today,' he said. 'That's why the ambulances have turned up. I wonder why Frank and Mr Booty aren't here.'

Jenny saw deep-seated worry in Johnny's eyes. *It has to be more than them two louts not arriving. He must be thinking about Sam being carried out dead. His lifeless, crushed corpse, slumped on one of those stretchers being taken, one after the other, into the tunnel.*

She reached out slowly, squeezing Johnny's hand to comfort him. He tried to force a smile, and then the first of the stretchers came back out of the darkness. Two soldiers were carrying a burden of weight, and Jenny was sure there was a body hidden beneath the orange blanket.

Suddenly, gasps and haunting shrills rang out into the heavy morning rain. A woman collapsed over the stretcher and another, older lady, tried to pull her back. This was the moment reality really gripped Jenny. Her stomach dropped at the thought. The cavern roof had collapsed and killed everyone and everything, including Sam. She had been deluding herself; he could not have survived the blast. 'It's a good job Larson and Mr Booty aren't here. If they were, I'd kill them both for this.'

'Hold on, Jenny. Let's just wait to see what happens. They did it to save people; you heard what Frank said.'

'But all this pain, it can't have been worth it. I hate them for what they've done. Look, Johnny, they're just people like you and I.'

She was referring to all the mourners crying. The men who had not come home the previous night were almost certainly dead. Husbands, fathers and sons, crushed to death in the cavern.

Another stretcher appeared from the tunnel. It was quickly followed by the next.

'The rescuers must be in the main cavern,' said Johnny.

One after the other, the bodies slid into the back of the waiting ambulances. None of the bearers, who now wore dark-green nylon ponchos over their uniforms, paid attention to the sobbing crowds. They looked uncomfortable and straight-faced, their eyes lowered to the ground, as if they didn't want to look at anyone. Jenny sensed they were trying to keep a distance between them and the emotions emanating from the desperate families kept back and separated by cordon tape and a police line.

'Oh, I hope Sam isn't one of them,' breathed Johnny.

Jenny squeezed his hand tighter. 'Don't think that. I'm sure he won't be.' Jenny didn't believe what she was saying. Logic suggested that he must be there, crushed to death by the fallen rocks. Everything happened so fast; there was no time. Why should he have escaped when all of those people did not? It was very unlikely. However she held on to one hope, *The Book of Black Magic and Revelations*. Could what Frank told her be true? Had Sam been taken by the sea witch to the bottom of the bay? Was he the boy in the riddle? It was Sam's best option now because no one was coming out of that tunnel alive.

'So where is Frank?' asked Jenny, her thoughts finally slipping through her lips.

'And Mr Booty; I can't believe they're not here?' Johnny sounded distressed.

Jenny let go of his hand and folded her arms. 'I can. It's just typical of them. You trust people and they always let you down. They knew the bodies were coming out today, and I bet they know I'm going to grass them up if Sam's one of them... Oh, they make me so mad.'

'They're probably thinking those people wouldn't let them get out of here alive, not once they knew their loved ones were dead. I wouldn't if it was my family.'

'Yes, that will be it. Bloody cowards, I'd kill them too.' Jenny sensed Sam's dad standing on the other side of her. She felt embarrassed for being so insensitive and gazed up at him. 'Sorry about that Mr Camponara... I... I...'

'Don't worry, I know what you mean.' Mr Camponara looked tired and sad. 'There's no good outcome with all this, no matter what happens. Sam's either dead in there, or he's at the bottom of the sea. I'll tell you this though: Mr Larson, he ain't no coward.'

Jenny blinked, as the cold rain pattered her face. 'Don't give up, Mr Camponara. Johnny's been down there and he survived.'

'What do you mean?'

'Last year when the witch held Johnny prisoner, she kept him at the bottom of the sea for fifteen days.'

Johnny looked up, nodding slightly in agreement.

'Yes, but that was different,' replied Mr Camponara.

Jenny stared up at him. 'No, it's not. If Johnny could survive down there, so can Sam.'

Mr Camponara was quickly distracted as the next stretcher came out of the tunnel carrying yet another body. 'Well, let's hope he isn't in there then.'

Suddenly, Jenny had the most awful thought: 'What if Frank and Mr Booty are dead. Yes, that would account for them not being here if some of this lot went over to Mr Booty's shop during the night and killed them?'

Johnny face filled with fear. 'Oh, Jenny, don't say that.'

☆ ☆ ☆

A couple of hours passed before the last of the bodies was brought out of the cavern. Jenny barely spoke another word, worrying about what might have happened to Frank, and she had an urgency to rush back to see if he and Mr Booty were alright. But she could not go. Sam was her first concern. Was he in there crushed to death or was he at the bottom of the bay?

The two cave rescuers in the orange suits came out of the tunnel. Mr Camponara reached out, grabbing one of them by the arm as he strolled by. 'Is that it? Are there no more?'

'No more?' The man looked at him confused.

'Yes, a young lad fifteen years old. Is he in there?'

'No, there was no young lad. They were all older than that.'

'Then what about an old woman, in black robes?'

The rescuer stared at Mr Camponara, puzzled by the question. 'No, sorry, there were no women either. Just men, all men and all naked; I don't know what they were doing in there, but it looked very odd to me.'

The man started to walk away and Mr Camponara gripped him again.

He turned sharply, glaring into Mr Camponara's eyes.

'Are you sure?'

The rescuer snatched back his arm. 'Yes, there's nobody else down there.' He turned and walked off towards his colleagues, clearly disgruntled.

'That's it then,' said Jenny.

All around her people wept and held onto each other. Some sobbed onto stretchers laid out on the ground, but at least the rain had finally stopped, and the clouds were breaking up.

Mr Camponara looked around at the carnage. 'Come on, kids, let's get out of here.'

Slowly Jenny and Johnny followed him back to the rented car. Nobody said anything on the way home. Jenny did not know what to say; Sam was gone, but it wasn't much consolation for his dad. There was no end to it. At least when you're dead, that's it, final, and you have no choice but to move on or die with grief.

For Jenny that was enough for now. Sam was still alive somewhere, but she realised for Mr Camponara, it must be awful knowing his child is at the bottom of the sea and there is nothing he can do about it.

'I want to call at the house before I take you home. I'm picking up Sam's mum and we're going into town.'

'Mr Camponara, can I ask you a question?' Jenny didn't wait for him to reply and went on, 'Where do you come from, originally I mean?'

'We're from Warrington in the northwest. I'm sure I've told you that before?'

'Have you? I don't remember.'

'That's okay; it doesn't matter,' Mr Camponara continued, whilst focusing on the road ahead. 'Sam was the reason we came to Cornwall in the first place. He was always in trouble back home, but he didn't want to move. I made him. I can't believe I brought him here. Oh, how I wished we'd stayed there. If we had, then none of this would have happened.'

Jenny and Johnny said nothing as the little car turned right onto the dirt track leading up to the house. It felt strange. She had never been along the track without Sam being there, and she wondered if she would ever have reason to come along it again.

'Might as well jump out for a minute. Mrs Camponara won't be ready, she never is,' Mr Camponara told them, as the car pulled up next to the front porch.

Jenny watched with Johnny through the car window as Mr Camponara opened the front door and went in, leaving it ajar.

Sam's mum was visible in the kitchen window wiping her hands on a towel. Her eyes looked puffy. She'd been crying. The cloth fell out of sight, and then Mrs Camponara disappeared.

Suddenly, Jenny's heart was aflutter. Sam's little sister, Ellie, stepped out onto the porch, smiling. It was the first time Jenny had seen her since her escape from the cavern. She was excited and relieved she was safe. Big Billy Beaumont had rescued Ellie by dragging her into an underwater tunnel which came out in Polperro. Jenny stepped out of the car and ran, falling to her knees, wrapping her arms around

Ellie's shoulders, hugging her tight.

'Oh, Ellie, how are you?' asked Jenny, pulling back a little from her face, meeting her eyes. She didn't wait for an answer. 'Tell me, how did you get back?'

Ellie looked a bit overwhelmed at first, and then she smiled. 'Billy was amazing. He held onto me, and his underwater scooter took us into an air pocket. He handed me a mask and told me to put it on. I could breathe through it, and we went under the water again for ages before we came out onto the beach. Billy brought me home; he was really great.' Ellie's face became sad and serious. 'Where's Sam?'

'I don't know,' Jenny mumbled, 'but I'm sure he'll be okay.'

Ellie leaned forwards and whispered into her ear, 'Come on, I want to show you something.'

Jenny stood up intrigued. Ellie gripped onto her hand and dragged her into the house. She looked around the room at the familiar setting. To the right, a door into the kitchen; in front, the large white dining table with the stairs behind it. Ellie's mum and dad were no longer in the room, and Jenny stared down questioning. There was nothing unusual.

Ellie gazed up silently, her finger beckoning Jenny to bend lower. She whispered into her ear again, 'Look at the wall.'

At first, Jenny couldn't see anything.

'Keep looking,' whispered Ellie, her breath held in anticipation.

Suddenly, they both jumped back and looked at each other giggling, shocked by the suddenness of it. The wall moved in a superfast wave from right to left, and then it was gone.

'Did you see that?' Ellie said, in her quietest voice then she smiled. 'I told you.'

Jenny smiled back. 'Yes, what was it?'

'It's a wall witch. Sometimes it moves slower than that, and I can see it better.'

'Is there more than one?'

Ellie nodded, still smiling. 'Yes, I think so.'

'Wow, that's really strange.' Jenny thought for moment; then she said, 'Can you bring me a sweeping brush?'

Ellie nodded and smiled again before running off into the kitchen. A minute later she reappeared with a feather duster. 'Is this okay?'

Jenny took it from her. 'Yes, that's even better.' They both stood staring at the blank wall. Suddenly, it moved again and Jenny swung the duster at it, slapping the wall. 'Did I get it?' Jenny laughed.

'Quick, it's there,' Ellie pointed up to the right.

Jenny hit the wall again and they both laughed out loud.

Suddenly, Jenny's thoughts were taken away from the wall witch by Mr Camponara's entering from the lounge on the other side of the room. 'Hey, what are you two doing?'

'Just trying to get at that cob web,' Jenny told him. She and Ellie looked at each other and laughed again.

Sam's dad ignored them. Nothing could make him laugh today. 'Are you ready to go?'

Mum followed him in and opened the cupboard under the stairs. She pulled out a small brown coat from a hanger on the back of the door. 'Here, Ellie, put this on,' she told her.

As the car travelled down towards the town, Jenny thought about what she had just seen. It took her back to the night Sam returned from Schooner's house in the middle of the night. The two of them freezing cold in a little boat, the air around them drenched in thick blackness, and Sam was clutching five strands of weed in his hand. Witches swam through the walls in that house he had said. Schooner was completely possessed, and the witch leapt forwards out of his chest. Then only a few days ago, Sam admitted making a wish on it, but now he was gone. Why were the witches still here? Surely the debt was paid; she had taken him to the bottom of the bay, for heaven's sake.

Jenny returned from her inner thoughts. 'Are you okay?' asked Johnny.

'Yes, I'm fine,' she replied, shivering.

The little car crossed the estuary bridge and pulled over near the car park.

'Not parking up, Mr Camponara?' asked Jenny, as Johnny opened the door and started to get out.

'No, we're going to report Sam missing at the Police station, now that we know he's not in the cavern.'

'But we…'

'I know, they're not going to believe that, are they, so he'll have to go down as a missing person for now.'

Jenny heard Mrs Camponara wince; then she wiped her nose on a tissue. 'Right, well, I'll see you later then. Thanks for the lift… Bye, Ellie,' she said stepping out onto the pavement.

The little car drove off and Jenny rested her head on Johnny's shoulder. 'Oh, what are we going to do?'

'I don't know, Jenny, I just don't know.'

'Well, I'm going to find out what's happened to Frank and Mr Booty; are you coming?'

'I think it's better if we don't. They won't want you asking questions. It's bound to annoy them.'

'But they might be dead. Do you not want to know?' Jenny could see he didn't. She pulled away from him, her brows furrowed, annoyed. 'Suit yourself,' she said sharply. 'I'll go on my own.' She turned away and marched off across the car park towards Mr Booty's shop.

Johnny scurried after her. 'Okay, wait for me!' he shouted.

Jenny ignored him and hurried on.

'I'm sorry, what more can I say.' He reached out touching her arm.

Jenny stopped and spun around angrily. 'You don't need to worry about me, if that's what you're thinking. I can look after myself.'

'Yes, I know you can, but…'

'Look, Johnny, you need to get some bigger balls if you're going to help Sam get out of this mess.'

Johnny stared at her for a moment saying nothing. 'Okay… well… err, from now on I will. I'm going to be much braver.'

Jenny melted into his worried puppy-dog eyes. She touched his hand and smiled. 'Come on then, let's see if they're alive, and if they are, they better have a good excuse for not being there.' She grabbed Johnny's arm and pulled Johnny across the car park.

A few minutes later, they were walking up the two foot-eroded steps into Mr Booty's shop.

Mr Booty looked up from behind the counter. His face looked strained as if he was half expecting trouble.

Jenny glared as if she hated him.

Mr Booty put out his hands before she had a chance to speak. 'Now, Jenny, I know what you're going to say,' he fumbled. 'Too busy, see; too much to do.'

Luckily for Mr Booty, the shop was empty, but Jenny didn't care. 'Too busy…'

'Yes, Gwen's off today and…'

'Then you should have closed it,' Jenny told him, angrily. 'You should have been there for Sam.'

'But that's it, see. No point being there 'cos we already know…'

Just at that moment the little bell chimed, the door opened and an old lady dithered her way into the shop. 'Good afternoon, Mrs. What can I get yer?' asked Mr Booty, turning his attention from Jenny.

But Jenny stared at him unmoved, her chest vibrating confrontational breaths. She tried to calm herself.

'I'll have two of your loveliest baking apples, half a dozen eggs and a bag of flour, please, Mr Booty,' replied the old lady, barely noticing Jenny with her stern face.

Mr Booty did, and he looked very uncomfortable. He placed the apples into a white paper bag and turned to meet Jenny's eyes. 'Mr Larson's upstairs. Would you like to go up and see him?'

Johnny shook his head, but Jenny shot him an angry glance, and he began to nod.

'Yes, we would,' Jenny said, sharply.

Mr Booty lifted the hinged worktop and gave the old lady a nervous smile, as Jenny closely followed by Johnny stomped past and through the door which led into the back.

The door closed behind them.

Jenny instantly remembered the last time she had been here: the dark, dank silence, the stacked wooden boxes and the smell of fresh strawberries. Sam was with her then. He had led the way, determined and brave. Oh, how she wished he was with her now. Jenny breathed, 'It's this way, come on.' She led Johnny by his hand across the blackened room to the door at the bottom of the stairs.

Slowly she pulled it back, and light shot in and across Jenny's face. She stepped forward onto the stairs, which led up to the flat where

Larson slept. Jenny remembered clearly the nice clean wallpaper and carpets, and Larson in his blue-striped pyjamas, slippers and flat cap, looking very strange.

'Frank,' Jenny shouted up to him.

'Jenny, is that you?' Larson replied instantly.

'Yes, it's me… and Johnny.'

'Come on up.'

Jenny thought he sounded pleased, so relieved, she raced to the top of the stairs and peered from the door into the lounge. Larson was sitting in the arm chair. This time he was dressed, and it took her back to the first time she had ever met him. It was behind the back of the cabin on the campsite. How it seemed such a long time ago now. Sam was holding Ellie's hand and Johnny stood behind her. Larson appeared from out of the ground wearing the same old brown suit and dusty flat cap he was wearing now. 'Don't go into the woods,' he had told them. *'If only we had listened, maybe none of this would have happened?'*

'Come in children; don't stand at the door.' Larson smiled up at them.

Beside him on a small cup table was a large book: 'Register of Berserkergangs, Lichen Throats, and Imps'. It was open on the page where Sam's name was written in the column of imps. It made Jenny shudder. Below Sam's name, two more names were entered in the column Berserkers.

Larson noticed where Jenny was looking, and he followed her eyes to the page.

Suddenly, Jenny gasped. Black writing was appearing, as if from an invisible pen, in the column Lichen throats. 'It… it…'

'Yes, Jenny, it goes on. As you can see, the witch isn't dead.' Jenny said nothing. She felt her way to the sofa and slumped onto it, the colour draining from her face. Johnny sat next to her speechless then Larson stared into Jenny's eyes. 'Sam's body wasn't in the cavern, was it?'

'No, we waited 'til everyone came out; there was no sign of him.'

'Then we have failed to kill her. That much was already clear to me when Madema continued to write people's names in the book. The witch is still changing them into berserkers, werewolves and imps, but now we know Sam is with her, and that is to our advantage. It's up to Sam now; only he can save us.' Larson held the leaves of the book between his fingers. 'Look, Jenny, only three pages left.' He sounded defeated and extremely worried.

Jenny wasn't, not yet. 'So how can we help?'

'You cannot; only Sam can do it,' said Larson, grim.

'Then his family. How can we help them? We must do something?' Jenny continued.

Larson looked confused. 'What do you mean?'

'There is something in the house with them, I've seen it. Something is moving through the walls, and Sam's little sister, she's seen it too. We need to help them.'

'Oh, yes, that. I know already. It's an entity sent by the sea witch,' he said, frivolously.

Jenny frowned.

'It's just an energy carrying a little bit of her wicked soul. I told you… Sam is batting for both sides. He took something to the witch. He wanted something from her, you Johnny, and she gave it to him. That's why Mr Booty and I have stayed away from his house; she knows everything that's goin' on there.'

Jenny started thinking out loud, 'No, that's not it; he made a wish.'

'What?'

'That's not why the entity is there. I think Sam made a wish on the witch's pendant.' Jenny's heart sank. 'I asked him and he swore to me he hadn't, but just before you dragged me away from him, in the cavern, Sam told me.'

Larson sat forward in his chair, surprised and very interested. 'You're telling me Sam held the pendant in his hand and made a wish?'

'Yes, on the night we came back from Lamorna cove and God knows how many times before he gave it back.'

Larson's eyes flitted between Jenny and Johnny. 'And what would he wish for?'

'The house… he wanted to give his parents, the loveliest house in Cornwall. But his dad won a competition; he gets money from that, so the house has nothing to do with Sam?'

'If there's a wall witch in Sam's house, then something's fuelling it. Maybe the witch concocted this nonsense of a competition so that she could fulfil Sam's wish, and no one would know.'

Jenny was at a loss with it all. Sam had lied to her – she knew that now – but she could not give up on him. 'Oh, Frank, there must be something we can do?'

'Just pray, Jenny; pray that Sam can fulfil the prophecy.'

CHAPTER THREE

The Sea Witch

It was the fifth of September. A year had passed, and Jenny stayed home and cried over breakfast. Mum understood why, it was clear in her sympathetic face. The anniversary of Sam's disappearance, not death, oh no, she couldn't cope with the idea it might be that. Jenny was so depressed that Mum allowed her to have the day off school. Jenny could not think of anything but Sam, alone out there in the sea, and she was filled with despair because she could not think of any way to follow him without drowning or to bring him back.

She sat in the big chair by the fire, sobbing. Mum put the television on and left the room, but Jenny barely noticed the news reporter talking about a trawler from Newlyn that had gone missing.

Suddenly, the house began to shake and the ground rumbled beneath her feet. It lasted only a few seconds before everything became still once more, but it was long enough to make the hairs on the back of her neck stand up.

The next day, Jenny and Johnny sat on the quay, dangling their legs over the side, licking vanilla ice creams.

'Hey, did you feel that earthquake?' asked Johnny.

'Did I, it scared me to death. Thank goodness, it only lasted a few seconds, the whole house was shaking. Mum ran into the room screaming, get under the table. I don't know what good that would have done if the house fell down on top of us. Anyway it stopped before I even got out of my chair.'

'I know. My house was shaking too. It's a strange feeling, isn't it?'

At that moment the children were distracted by a dark shadow passing overhead then something swiped Johnny's ice cream out of his hand, and it tumbled into the sea. A second later, a gull swooped down and scooped it up into the air. The disappointment on Johnny's face instantly made Jenny feel sorry and concerned for him. *What was it?*

They turned quickly to see what had hit him. 'Hey, you,' Johnny shouted.

Johnny's face became angry, and Jenny knew he was about to say a lot more, but when he saw who it was standing over him, his anger and voice shrivelled to a murmur, and he remained locked to the ground.

Jenny was expecting to see one of the kids from school, but it wasn't. It was a bull of a man, six-foot tall and equally as wide, wearing navy blue overalls and a flat cap.

The man gave Johnny a kick with the side of his foot. 'Zoo little vrunt,' he snarled. 'Move or I'll kick zoo into ze zea.'

Johnny jumped onto his feet shocked and moved to the side quickly. 'Von Strictum, I… I thought you were dead.'

Von Strictum sniggered at him, 'I bet zoo and zor little frind here vud have loved zat, vudn't zoo?'

Jenny stood up behind Johnny then she stepped forward, unafraid. 'Yes, that's right; I can't think of anyone who deserves it more than you.' Von Strictum snarled at her, but Jenny didn't care. 'So where's your horrible son? Why's he not with you?'

Von Strictum's face filled with despair for a second. He bent down breathing into Jenny's ear, 'Ztay out ov my vay, or I vill be coming vor zoo before zour time.' Then he shoved her to the side and marched off down the steps towards the small mackerel-fishing boats.

'Aye, Johnny, are you two all right?'

Jenny turned around. It was Big Billy Beaumont, riding up to them on his black Fire Flame lowrider bike.

'Yes, we're fine,' said Johnny, as the bike came to a halt.

'It's just, I saw that guy hassling you.' Billy's eyes pointed towards the steps.

'That was Von Strictum. He caused all that trouble we had last year. I don't know what he's doing down there though? He's a pie-van driver from Piermont's, not a fisherman.'

The three of them moved closer to the edge and stared down at him. He was stood in *The Enchantment*, proudly wiping over the engine cover with a cloth.

'Hey, Von Strictum,' shouted Jenny. He looked up instantly, stern faced. 'What yer doin' in Old Whiley's boat?'

'It'z not Vhiley's, it'z mine; I've bought zit now.'

'You've bought it… but why? You're not a fisherman. You're a pie-van driver,' Johnny sniggered.

'Yez, vell, maybe I've dezided to try my hand at zomzing elze. Anyvay what'z it got to do wiz zoo, zoo nozy kid? Go on, get out ov here before I give zoo a good thrazhing.'

'You'll have to get past me first,' said Big Billy, spreading out his chest, making him look even bigger.

Jenny turned away, disgusted. 'Come on let's get out of here.'

'That'z vight, goez on chicky, chicky, chickiez,' Von Strictum goaded.

Jenny stamped her feet trying to hold back her frustration. 'Arrg, I hate that man!'

Billy turned around sharply, pushing his sleeves back and clenching his fists. 'Right, that's it; I'm going to have 'im.'

Jenny grabbed Billy's arm quickly, fearful. Billy did not know what Von Strictum was capable of, but she did. 'No, Billy,' Jenny screamed, staring up into his eyes. 'He's not worth it.' A tear welled onto her cheek and she slowly released him.

'Okay… this time,' said Billy, scowling at Von Strictum then they turned away and walked off together. Jenny was feeling humiliated and knew the boys were feeling it too.

It was at that moment Jenny realised the clouds were gathering over the bay. The air became cooler, a light breeze raced past her face, the smell of salt filled the air, and black storm clouds gathered on the horizon.

'It looks like the rain's coming,' said Johnny.

'Yes, I wouldn't like to be out there in a boat right now; it's going to be rough.' Then Billy changed the subject, but it was probably looking at the stormy sea that made him think of it. 'Have either of you seen Marcus or Sennen, today?'

'No, why,' asked Jenny?

'They never showed up at my place this morning, that's all. I was expecting them around ten, and they've never done a no-show before, so I thought I would come looking for them. They're not at their houses, and their mums said they never came home last night. Now that's pretty worrying, don't you think?'

Jenny and Johnny looked at each other, shocked. Jenny said, 'Oh no, not again.'

'What?' asked Big Billy, sounding really concerned.

'Yesterday was the fifth of September. Tell me, Billy. Tell me, they didn't take one of the boats out last night.'

'They might have?'

'Which one,' asked Jenny?

'Not sure. It was pretty dark, and they all look the same to me, why?'

'I don't know,' said Jenny. 'It shouldn't matter, not now that *The Sea Witch* has been burned. It doesn't make any sense, but what if…'

'Come off it, Jenny. You could be adding two and two and coming up with five,' Johnny told her.

Jenny smiled. 'Yes, you're right; I'm sure they'll be okay.' But she didn't sound convinced.

'I know what you're thinking,' said Billy. 'When Johnny boy went missing for a couple of weeks, summer before last.' He met Johnny's eyes. 'And we went down to watch Old Whiley's boat being burned on the beach. Everyone said the boat was cursed.'

'It was, but it looks like things haven't changed,' Johnny told him.

Billy smiled, uncomfortably. 'Narr, Marcus and Sennen, they'll be all right.'

I hope so, Billy, I really do,' replied Jenny.

'See you later, dudes,' said Billy, looking very concerned as he rode off and away from the quay.

The rain started lashing down on the harbour. At first for a second or two, there was the sound of slow tapping on the stone and Jenny's feet. It quickly turned into a very fast patter, patter, and then stronger slapping and splashing, followed by an almighty roar of thunder. Jenny was soaked through to the skin, rain running from her long auburn hair and down her pretty face in a matter of seconds. She pulled her pink cardigan up over her head, but it was too late – her hair was already drenched.

She walked to the edge of the quay and looked back to where the boats were tied to the rusty metal wall ring by long blue frayed ropes.

Nearly everyone had run for shelter, away from the sea front, and the harbour was instantly deserted. But there in the little mackerel fishing boat, *The Enchantment*, stood Von Strictum. His pale, rugged face looking up at the dark clouds, his arms and hands outstretched, as if he welcomed it. The rain slapped him all over, like a cold power shower, and he laughed and laughed and laughed, crazily into the air, which sent Jenny the eeriest frightening shiver.

Johnny grabbed a hold of her hand, pulling her away. 'Come on,' he shouted, 'let's get the hell out of here.'

She turned and ran; she could not get away from that horrible, wicked man quick enough, and it left her with the most chilling thought of all.

After a few minutes, Jenny stopped near the car park, pulling Johnny closer to her. The rain continued to lash down on them as she whispered into his ear, her plump lips almost touching his cold, wet cheek. 'Tonight, we must come back, when everyone's asleep. I want you to bring a bottle of paint stripper and a cloth from your dad's shed.'

'Okay.' Johnny smiled, lingering close. 'But why?'

Jenny felt his hot breath on her face. His slate-grey eyes penetrating hers more than usual or maybe she just hadn't noticed it before. She smiled at him, shivering slightly from the cold and rain, perhaps, and still he too held her there pressed against him. 'You'll see; now don't let me down,' she told him in a serious voice. 'Be here by eleven.' She released her grip, pushed him away and ran off towards home.

Everywhere was dark and eerily quiet. Not a soul anywhere and the only sounds were the salty breeze whipping the shop fronts and the sea lapping against the side of the harbour wall.

Jenny pulled her grey duffle coat up tight around her neck. It was cold, very cold, but at least the rain had stopped. The cobbles felt slippery under foot, and small puddles had gathered in the dips and crannies between the stones.

Cautious not to be seen, she moved silently in and out of the shops' dark spaces, until she saw a sign about ten feet away which read, 'Old Whiley's Mackerel Fishing Trips'. Jenny thought how that was about to change, and how Von Strictum's Mackerel Fishing Trips just didn't have the same ring to it.

Quiet footsteps, gradually getting louder, tapped on the cobble stones behind her; then a boy's grey shape came into view. 'Hey, Johnny, I'm over here,' Jenny whispered to him through the thick darkness.

Johnny rushed to her side, throwing back the hood of his coat. 'Hi, Jen,' he breathed.

'Hi, Johnny, did you bring the stuff?'

'Yes, of course, I did. I nearly got caught by Dad though.' Johnny lifted up a plastic bag. 'Now what's this all about?'

Jenny smiled and grabbed Johnny's arm. 'I'll not tell you, I'll show you,' she said, pulling Johnny across the walkway and down onto the first step.

He immediately shook his arm free and stopped. 'Whoa, hold on, what are you doing? I'm not going down there.'

Jenny was furious. She put her hands on her hips and scowled. 'I thought you said you were going to be brave from now on.'

'I know, but…'

'Just give me the bloody bag.' She snatched it from him and marched down the steps to sea level. It was so dark the boats were barely visible, but Jenny could just about see five of them, all tied to the wall by long, frayed ropes.

She leapt from the step into the boat closest to her. It shifted dramatically, rocking from side to side for a minute. Jenny stumbled and grabbed its wooden side until it stopped moving.

Johnny rushed to the bottom step and breathed in an anxious tone across the water, 'Jenny, what are you doing?'

'I'm looking for *The Enchantment*. It's got to be here.' After checking the name plate at the back of the first boat, and to no avail, she leapt into the second and bent down over the back as before. 'Hey, Johnny, this is it.'

Jenny was excited and a bit frightened by what she might find. Hurriedly, she pulled the paint stripper and a rag out of the bag then she began plying the cloth. It smelled strong and repugnant, but she did not delay, rubbing up and down on the name plate very vigorously. After a few minutes *The Enchantment*'s name began to blister, smudge and then flake off. Beneath it, her worst fears were realised – she could clearly see a large S and part of an E. 'Oh my God, I knew it,' the words fell unexpectedly from her lips.

'What is it, Jenny? What have you found?' breathed Johnny, from the steps.

But before Jenny could speak, a massive dark figure descended from the harbour towards them, and another figure was close behind.

Jenny gasped. She had been caught and *'Von Strictum'* ran through her mind.

Suddenly, a deep voice bellowed, 'I told you to stay away from here; it's not safe.'

'Frank,' Jenny breathed a sigh of relief, recognising his voice instantly. 'I was right; come and see for yourself; it's *The Sea Witch*, just as I suspected.

'Okay, you've proved your point. Now get your bones back onto dry land, quickly,' said Larson.

Jenny suddenly felt extremely vulnerable; there was a trickling sound like popping bubbles beside her. She gazed down hesitant, nervous into the cold inky blackness.

'Careful now, Jenny. Just make your way over here to me – there's a good girl,' Larson said again.

Jenny stared across the darkness at Johnny, Frank and Mr Booty for a second, their dark shapes set against the sea drenched steps and the harbour wall behind them.

Then she jumped, her whole body tingling, and her eyes shot back into the water, shocked by a hissing sound behind her. It snarled and whispered, 'Get away from that boat!'

Eyes as black as coal blazed up from out of the icy sea, and a white, tired face covered in long black sea-drenched hair scowled and hissed again.

Jenny could hardly believe it. 'Sam,' she cried. 'Quickly, get into the boat.' Unable to stop herself, her fingers reached out to touch him. She wanted to pull him from the water and save him from the evil witch, but his face was filled with anger, and he hissed dangerously at her like a lion about to pounce.

'Get out of the boat, now,' Sam warned her again.

It wasn't the Sam she knew, but a fierce beast of a boy. Violence seared through his voice like a killer, cold, calm and dangerously chaotic.

Jenny feared for her life. *Is he going to kill me?* Sam was threatening, and her thoughts were filled with him dragging her in and drowning her in the icy, black water. Fear was thick around her; a sense of evil consumed the boat. Something else was rushing towards her; she sensed it was much more evil than Sam. He had preceded whatever it was.

Jenny knew everyone else had felt it too because at that moment, even though Sam remained unseen by the others on the steps, Frank shouted to her again. His voice filled with terror. 'Run to me, Jenny, run now, run, or it will be the end of you!'

Sam's emotionless face sank slowly beneath the waves, disappearing into the blackness once more.

Jenny was desperate and terrified she wouldn't reach the solidness of stone steps, so she ran and jumped across the boats, filled with panic of what might happen to her.

Suddenly, from behind, there was a splash. She turned to quickly see what it was, shocked. A black panther leapt from the sea into the boat. Its yellow eyes shone through the darkness, and it prowled dangerously along the boat, snarling ferociously at her.

But Jenny knew something much scarier than the black beast was coming, and it wasn't going to let her go near to the cursed boat again. *'Oh my God, she's coming, the sea witch.'* Jenny took one last leap from the side of the first boat, and she was on the stone steps next to Larson.

He grabbed her hand tight. 'Quickly, to the top, run, run,' he shouted, pulling Jenny up the stone steps.

Within seconds, Jenny was looking down at *The Sea Witch* filled with relief and thankful to be alive. 'Frank, the boat, it wasn't burnt on the beach, it's down there.'

She turned to Johnny, holding him to her. 'Oh, Johnny, I thought I was a gonner. I thought Sam was going to kill me, and I thought I'd never see you again.'

'Sam... What do you mean?'

'He appeared in the sea beside me. He told me to get away from the boat... I think he was protecting it. Oh, Johnny, we've lost him.' Jenny cried onto his shoulder.

The black cat still prowled back and forth along the little boat, but made no effort to scale the steps.

Larson stared into Mr Booty's eyes, concerned. 'Well, at least we can do something about that ruddy boat and the imp that's in it, can't we?'

Jenny gazed up at him. *'What does he mean?'*

'Now you two get off home and leave this to me,' Frank told her.

Mr Booty pulled three sticks of dynamite, fastened together with black insulation tape, from under his coat.

'No, don't do that. You might kill Sam.'

But Mr Booty wasn't for listening. 'God damn imps, scum of the earth they are.' He scowled, slipping his hand into his pants pocket, retrieving a silver flip-top petrol lighter. The flint sparked, and a second later, he lit the fuse and threw it down into *The Sea Witch*, twenty feet below. 'Run children,' he shouted, and they all disappeared into an alley between the 'Tackle and Bait shop' and the Butchers. There was an almighty *boom* and the black sky behind them filled with orange, and splintered wood flew up and out in all directions.

Jenny didn't know whether to laugh or cry. *The Sea Witch* was gone that was for sure, but had the blast killed Sam? Jenny prayed he had escaped and was safe even though he had threatened her. *'It wasn't his fault,'* she told herself. *'He was possessed by that wretched witch.'*

She thought about Big Billy's friends, *'they weren't coming back, they were the last victims of* The Sea Witch*, thank God for that at least.'*

'Quickly children, go to your homes, climb into your beds and say nothing of what has happened tonight to anyone. The police will take but a few minutes. We were never here. We are all sleeping and awakened by the loud bang. Goodnight children, goodnight… hurry now,' said Frank, as he disappeared into Mr Booty's Fruit and Veg shop. Mr Booty smiled reassuringly at them, and then he followed Frank in, closing the door.

CHAPTER FOUR

Witches are Everywhere

The following morning, the sun shone down from a blue sky. Jenny knocked heavily three times on the door. Johnny opened it and left quickly, pulling his arm into his black cotton jacket as he closed the door behind him.

'Oh, Johnny,' said Jenny. They began to walk the narrow, cobbled street down to the harbour. 'I did see Sam last night. His head came up out of the water by the side of the boat. He's alive or at least he was. I cannot believe it's been more than a year since I last saw him. He gave me such a scare, I nearly screamed, and at first, I thought he was going to pull me into the sea, he looked so angry. But it wasn't me he was after. I think he was protecting *The Sea Witch*, keeping its secret safe, doing the witch's deeds. But I had already seen her name plate; it was definitely her, and I guess he was still there when Mr Booty blew it up.'

'No, that was just an imp. We don't know it was Sam. It could have been Peter Von Strictum or anybody. I tell you, Jen, I've never seen anything like that before, a naked boy leaping from the water, changing before my eyes, and by the time he landed in the boat, he looked like a huge cat, but that just can't be right.'

It reminded Jenny of the time she sat next to Sam, sipping tea, in Frank's cottage. When Sam asked him what he looked like as a werewolf, he changed right there and then. Johnny hadn't been there, so for him it was much harder to believe in changelings. 'It was Sam, alright. I saw his face. He changed into a black panther.' Jenny hesitated. 'I don't like calling him an imp, but when he leapt out of the sea, I was sure he was going to kill me.'

'Okay, so let's say it was Sam, although I didn't see him clearly enough to be sure myself. Do you think he was killed when Mr Booty blew up the boat?' Johnny looked very concerned.

'It was him, Johnny, I promise you. After what happened, I don't know why we are even bothering to try and save him. If I hadn't leapt onto the steps when I did, I would be dead. On the other hand, I doubt he was blown up, not if the prophecy is true, and we have to believe it is, especially now, with all that has happened. But poor Sennen and Marcus, we'll never see them again, I'm sure of that.'

Johnny stared at the ground, glum. 'That's going to be awful for their mums and dads.'

Jenny was thinking about Sam's mum and dad and what they went through after losing Sam in the cavern. 'Well, I think we should go over to Sam's house and tell his mum and dad we have seen him alive. It will, at the very least, give them some hope.'

The narrow street opened up, and in front of them was a very congested car park. People were busying themselves around the fire engine and police cars, looking to see what had gone on during the night. The air-sea rescue helicopter flew from above the houses and hovered over the end of the harbour. The noise was instant and deafening then it mellowed as the *Sea King* hovered further away over the bay.

Jenny looked to her left, only to see Mr Booty standing outside his shop. He gestured to her with his hand, touching his white trilby hat, and he nodded a little.

He shouted across the road to the car park, 'Hey, Joe, what's been going on there?'

A bulky, middle-aged fireman was rolling up his hose on the side of the engine. He turned around and smiled. 'It's Whiley's boat, *The Enchantment*, blown up it has, taken chunks out the *Padstow Lady* and a couple of others too.'

'Oooo, that is bad.'

'Well, we've done what we can, and they won't be going anywhere soon. I guess it's down to the insurance companies to sort it out now.' He walked to the door and climbed aboard the fire engine. 'Right, well, I'll see yer when I see yer,' he said, smiling and pulling the heavy door closed.

Mr Booty waved him off; then turned to Jenny, smiling. He winked before disappearing back into the shop.

He thinks it's just a game. Jenny gave a deep sigh. 'Come on, let's get our bikes out and ride up to Sam's house. I want to tell his mum what we saw.'

☆ ☆ ☆

It was a hard ride, uphill all the way. At one point Jenny had to get off and walk; it was just too steep for pedalling. They passed the giant white rock, which stuck out over the other side of the road, and a short time later, they turned left onto the dirt track, which led to Sam's house. Here the ground levelled off, and the children were able to ride the rest of the way over the muddy bumps.

It had been a year since Jenny last came up to the house, but the house had not faded at all; in fact, it looked newer, whiter, cleaner and even more elaborate. They rode round to the side, towards the patio and front door which faced out to sea. A large swimming pool had been built since the last time she had been. Blue sun-glistening water, beautifully tiled and a veranda, where once stood a washing line across some dry patchy grass.

'Oh, Johnny, look at the house. Now it is truly the most beautiful house in Cornwall. If only Sam could see this.' Those words sent a shiver down Jenny's spine because as soon as she said it, she remembered Sam saying the same thing, and now she dreaded climbing up the two pristine white steps and knocking on the door.

Johnny stood astride his old bike not wanting to go any closer either. Jenny gave him a nudge. 'Go on, Johnny, you go,' she told him. *'What would it be like in there, and more importantly, what would Sam's mum and dad be like after a year of having wall witches in the house and no Sam? The house had certainly changed on the outside, so it is bound to have changed on the in? I hope Mr and Mrs Camponara are alright.'* Jenny's mind was running away with her.

Johnny said, 'No, you go', whilst gripping tightly onto the handlebars, as if he thought she was going to pull him off.

'Go on, Johnny, get to that door.'

'No, I don't want to. You go.'

'Knock on the door, you baby.' Jenny was getting really angry with him again.

But Johnny just stared at the ground and said nothing.

Suddenly the door clicked open slightly.

The children stopped bickering instantly and stared in the direction of the sound. They gazed at each other, uncertain what to do; then they stared back at the thin line of open door. No one spoke and there was no sound. An atmosphere of fear started to build around them. *What was it beyond the door? Who had opened it? Was it a trap? Were the witches waiting to pounce, or Mrs Camponara, insane and clutching a bread knife, ready to run out and stab us to death.* Jenny thoughts were getting crazy.

She had to know. Looking at Johnny, who was about to ride away with a fearfully worried expression, she shot him a firm, angry stare and waved him to her.

He lowered his bike to the ground and skulked up behind her. They crept up the steps slowly, cautiously listening intently, but still there was no sound. She reached out her finger to touch the door, her intention being to push it open. Her long slender finger lightly pressed upon its white, smooth plastic surface, and she was about to push hard to see what was beyond it.

Suddenly, the door flew back, almost scaring Jenny to death, and she cried out, 'Oh!' and jumped back into Johnny, shocked.

'Hello, Jenny, what are you doing here?' It was Sam's dad, sounding really loud and boisterously jolly.

'Mr Camponara, you gave me a fright.'

'Oh, sorry about that,' he said, turning around and shouting into the house. 'Hey, come and see who's at the door.'

Mrs Camponara came rushing to them. 'Hello, Jenny. My, haven't you grown,' she said, in a flighty tone. 'Come in… come in, and you too, Johnny. It's been such a long time since we've seen you both.' She paused for a moment, and then asked, 'What do you think of our new swimming pool?'

'Yes, it's lovely,' Jenny told her, as she followed her into the main hall.

'Come in, sit down.' Mrs Camponara sat on a chair, guiding Jenny to the one next to hers and sliding her finger lightly across the polished table. 'Would you like a drink?'

'Oh yes, please, a cold one.'

'Lemonade?' asked Mrs Camponara.

Jenny smiled and nodded.

'What do you think of my beautiful house?' she said, gazing around it, as if for the first time then she looked at Mr Camponara. 'Can you…'

'I know; two lemonades,' he said, closing the front door and disappearing into the kitchen.

'Yes, I love it. Everything looks so new and clean and expensive,' replied Jenny.

Mrs Camponara's face told Jenny she liked what she was saying. Vacant, bimbo smiles, finally capturing a seeping negative thought and her face straightened. 'I have to clean it all myself, you know. Can't get a cleaner for love or money.'

'Oh, and why's that?' Jenny wasn't really bothered, but she was just trying to be polite. It was difficult to feel sorry for someone with so much, especially when she thought of Mum.

'I don't know. We hired a few, but they all left within a matter of days. I've given up now and just do it myself.'

Jenny smiled, touching her hand. 'And how's Ellie?'

Mrs Camponara stared at Jenny with a blank expression for a long time before finally breathing very slowly, 'Ellie, Ellie?' It was as if she didn't remember her own daughter. 'Arr, yes, Ellie's just fine.' She paused again then a switch seemed to go on in her head and her eyes came to life. 'So what brings you up here after all this time?'

'Well, I don't know how to tell you this, but I have some good news for you.' Jenny sensed her eyes sparkling with excitement.

Mrs Camponara smiled back. 'We could do with some of that. Ellie's been full of a cold for days, and I've been under the weather too.'

Jenny couldn't help frowning for a second. *How odd a minute ago she said she was fine? But never mind that, I need to focus, not sure how Mrs Camponara's going take the news. Will she be pleased or will she be angry, call me a liar and throw me out? It's good news, the best I could give them and they deserve to know.* 'It's about Sam,' Jenny said, searching for her reaction.

Mrs Camponara's face remained unchanged. 'What is, dear?'

'The news I've brought you, it's about Sam.'

Suddenly, the wallpaper fluttered dark shadows. Jenny knew what it was, *wall witches.* There were two of them now, much more pronounced than the last time she had been. The shapes were clearly visible, gliding across the wall beneath the red flower pattern paper. It was just like Sam had described in Schooner Stevenson's house when he went in to retrieve the witch's pendant.

Jenny was very concerned for Sam's parents. After all, Sam had told her that Schooner was completely possessed by them, and one even leapt forward out of his chest. For a moment, Jenny was repulsed by the idea that Mrs Camponara might have one inside her, lying there dormant, waiting to leap out.

No, that's just nonsense, she tried to dismiss it. *It couldn't be, not when they have been through so much already.* Her heart felt for them and for herself. They had all lost him, Jenny too. She grieved. That's what her mum had told her, that's what the aching pain was.

Jenny reached slowly, gently touching her hand. Sam's mum didn't resist, but Jenny saw the worried look appear in her eyes.

'What is this, Jenny?' she said, letting out a little embarrassed giggle.

Jenny felt her eyes filling up. 'Do you think we could go outside, please?'

'Yes, of course, we can. Why, whatever is the matter?' she replied, rising from the chair and putting her arm around Jenny to comfort her. As they reached the door, tears began streaming down Jenny's face.

Mrs Camponara pulled a tissue from her cardigan sleeve, offering it to Jenny whilst shooting Mr Camponara a wide-eyed glance.

He stepped back from the doorway into the kitchen immediately. Mrs Camponara ignored him and they stepped out onto the patio, Johnny shuffling along behind them.

Outside was almost as bad inside. Everywhere Jenny looked, something seemed to be moving, staring at her, listening; she was almost too afraid to speak.

Sea witches fluttering just below the surface, along the front of the house, along the garage and even in the pool.

'I'm sorry, Mrs Camponara. It was a mistake, my coming here.'

'Why, Jenny, whatever is it?'

How can I speak to her? I might as well be talking directly to the witch. The thought made Jenny shiver. She started to feel hot and flushed. *I've got to get away.* She pulled free, still sniffling and lifted her bike from the ground.

Mrs Camponara looked surprised and Jenny was embarrassed by that, but what could she do – the witches were listening. 'I'm sorry,' she said, as starting riding away.

Jenny could see Johnny didn't know what was going on, pulling his face and lifting his shoulders.

The last thing Jenny saw was Mrs Camponara staring after her. It gave her a cold shudder then she disappeared out of sight, and Jenny became surrounded by trees.

Johnny rode up alongside her. 'Hey, what was all that about?' he said angrily. 'We've got to see Sam's mum, you said, tell her you've seen Sam. What a waste of time.'

Jenny met Johnny's eyes. 'I couldn't say anything. Things are worse there than I ever imagined they could be. Didn't you see it?' Jenny wanted to cry again, thinking about Ellie living in that house. 'It might look like the most beautiful house in Cornwall, but it's not, is it? Did you see all those witches?' Jenny could see by his face that he had.

'What are we going to do? They aren't aware of them, I'm sure. They think they're living the dream, and they can't see they are possessed just as much as Sam.'

'I don't know what we can do. See how Sam's mum wanted to show us all their possessions. Have you seen the pool, come and look at this, come and look at that, and the way her hands slid along everything, as if nothing else matters? Even the bloody lemonade glass looked posh.'

'They did appear to be happy though, didn't they? I hope my mum and dad were that happy, when I went missing,' said Johnny.

'Are you stupid or what? I can assure you they weren't.' Jenny was angry at the idea. *How can they be like that, knowing Sam is at the bottom of the sea?* 'Clearly, all they care about now is their material possessions.' Jenny had acquired a sudden distaste for Sam's mum and dad.

CHAPTER FIVE

The First Clue

It was just after four, the following day. Jenny and Johnny turned the corner from Ridgemont into Harbour Road. It curved round to the left quite steeply, and it was the main road back into town. Jenny stared down at the harbour car park in the distance. To her left, rows of cottages led the way into town. Further away, out over the sea, dark storm clouds filled the sky.

'School hasn't been too bad today, has it?' said Johnny.

'No, I thought the remembrance assembly for Sam was nice.'

'Yes it was, but for a minute I couldn't help thinking, it could have been my remembrance service.'

Jenny looked at Johnny for a second. She was grateful for that at least, and she smiled, acknowledging that she was pleased he was there with her. 'I see the police are out again.' Jenny was referring to the officer, knocking on the cottage doors further down the road.

'Just like last year and the year before. This time they'll be making enquiries about Marcus and Sennen.'

'No point.'

'They probably know that, but I suppose they've got procedures to follow.'

'How do you reckon *The Enchantment*, I mean, *The Sea Witch*, got back to her moorings? It wasn't like last time when I was taken. Sam brought it back, but this time both Sennen and Marcus went missing.'

'I think both you and Sam would have been goners too if it wasn't for the witch thinking your granddad had escaped with her pendant.'

'He didn't escape with it. He didn't even know it was there.'

'I know, keep your shirt on… I'm just saying. Anyway, back to your question, there can only be one answer to that: Von Strictum.'

'You mean?'

'Yes, Von Strictum was expecting it to happen. He knew *The Enchantment* was *The Sea Witch*, and he waited for the sea witch to come and snatch Marcus and Sennen before he towed the boat back in.'

'It's all a bit presumptuous.'

'Maybe, but who else could it be?'

'I don't know; possibly the witch or it might have a mind of its own.'

Jenny gazed up and down the road; then touching Johnny's arm near his elbow, she herded him across. 'Hey, it's my mum's birthday, soon. Do you want to help me find a present and choose a cake?' Jenny started smiling and skipping backwards in front of him. *Something nice at last*, 'Well… what do you say?' she said, tugging at his jacket.

Johnny laughed, whilst holding his hands up, as if surrendering. 'Okay, I'll come with you.'

Further back up the road, a car engine rumbled into life. It hummed for a few seconds, and then the tyres screeched like a banshee on the tarmac. Jenny screamed out, shocked, and her eyes shot in the direction of the sound, but it was too late for her to react. The engine roared like a lion and the car hurtled down the street towards them, crazy as a black bull completely out of control.

Jenny gasped in horror, frozen to the spot. She closed her eyes; she didn't want to see what it was about to do to her. Johnny's arms closed around her body protectively, but she knew it was the end for both of them. In that split second, Johnny cried out also, 'Arrg.' The solid metal was about to strike. Jenny put out her hand instinctively towards it. The car was so close she could almost touch it. Her breath held still. *Solid metal is about to hit the most powerful blow and trample over me or throw me into the air. It's about to knock the wind from my lungs and crush my bones. I feel numb.* Then it came, not from the side Jenny had expected but from behind Johnny. His body hit her so hard that she flew backwards off her feet and into the air, landing with a heavy thud on the curb.

Instantly Jenny's shoulder filled with pain where it hit the cobbled stones; then Johnny landed on top. She yelped like a puppy, her body squashed under his weight. He rolled off to the side, moaning.

'Get off me, you big lump.' Jenny pushed him aside, and the black car glided past, as if in slow motion.

Inside the car, Von Strictum's angry face stared at her through the side window, his eyes burning furiously into hers.

She shivered terrified by what she saw. *Von Strictum must really want me dead!*

The car sped off, turning right at the bottom of the road and disappearing behind the houses. He had crossed the estuary bridge and driven away from the town in a matter of seconds, leaving Jenny trembling on the floor.

Where are the bloody coppers when you need one? The police were here only a minute or two earlier, but as soon as something happens, they've gone into someone's house for a cup of tea and a chat. That is so infuriating.

Then she was distracted from her thoughts by a woman's voice saying, 'Hey, are you two alright?'

Jenny gazed up from the cobbles. It was Bersaba Daniels, Frank Larson's daughter, staring down and offering her hand. Jenny took it and Bersaba pulled her onto her feet. 'Orr, that bloody hurt,' moaned Jenny, rubbing her shoulder.

Bersaba laughed. 'Nothing broken, though.'

Jenny smiled and shook her head. 'No, I'll be fine.'

Johnny struggled to his feet and started rubbing his elbow. 'What the hell happened?'

'It was Von Strictum; he tried to kill us,' Jenny told him angrily.

'I bet that's because we blew his boat up.'

'Shush,' Bersaba smiled naughtily, putting her finger across her lips.

Jenny smiled back, and then winced at the aching in her shoulder. 'You don't say,' she whispered sarcastically before focusing on Bersaba. 'Anyway, thanks for saving our lives, Miss Daniels; I owe you one.'

'No, you don't, Jenny. I was just glad to be in the right place at the right time.'

Jenny smiled and shook her hand.

Suddenly, a Land Rover screeched to a halt beside them. It was Larson, all fired up about something. 'Come on, children, get in and you too, Bersaba.'

'Why, what's up?' asked Jenny, concerned.

'We're going back to the cavern. All the work men have left, and we need to check it out.'

'What? I'm going for my tea,' Johnny told him.

'Never mind that; this is much more important. Quick, get in. I'll tell you all about it on the way.'

Bersaba climbed into the front, and Jenny and Johnny jumped in the back. Larson put his foot to the floor, and they shot off across the estuary bridge and up the steep road, past the dirt track leading to Sam's house, and on towards St Cleer.

The old four-by-four creaked and whined constantly, much to Jenny's annoyance, especially as she had to listen very carefully to catch the conversation in the front.

So, what's this all about, then?' asked Bersaba.

Larson put his hand in his coat pocket and pulled out a small A5 book. Jenny recognised it instantly. It was *The Book of Black Magic and Revelations*. He handed it to Bersaba. 'Turn to page twelve,' he told her, hardly able to catch his breath.

Bersaba stared at it for while, then none the wiser, she said, 'I can't see anything that I haven't seen before?'

Jenny leaned forward staring down at the book over Bersaba's shoulder. Almost immediately she saw what Larson was so excited about. *But what has this to do with the cavern?* 'Look at the skulls.' Jenny pointed to them. 'There's a distinct line and change in tone cutting across at a diagonal, both at the upper and lower outer edges of the page.'

Larson smiled. 'I knew you would see it, Jenny.'

'Yes, but why haven't I noticed it before?' Jenny was annoyed with herself. She had flicked through the book on two previous occasions: once in the land Rover, on the way back from the cavern after Sam had been taken, and before that when she discovered it in Larson's cellar.

'Well, you wouldn't, would yer? I only just found out and by chance,' Larson told her.

'Found what? It doesn't tell us anything that we didn't already know, except there's a fault in the printing.'

Larson smiled and looked rather pleased. 'I was reading the book, looking for answers, clues, anything that might help, and after a while, I guess I fell asleep. When I awoke, the book was closed, but I still held it on the page with my thumb between the leaves. When I opened it, at first I was disappointed – no more than that, annoyed with myself. I have damaged the page. Hundreds of years of being carefully looked after, and then one mistake and the corner of the page was creased forever.'

Jenny reached over, touching the creased corner. On all the pages throughout the book, cherubs faced outward in the four corners. Jenny had thought they represented God's angels, the innocents, turning away from the witch's evil wheel. But as she turned the page along the crease Larson had made, the cherub faced inward. Jenny felt excitement rush through her and she understood why Larson could hardly catch his breath. The cherub's held little bows and arrows, and when the corner turned over, the arrow head pointed straight at the centre of the wheel.

Bersaba's eyes lit up at the discovery.

'Sorry, Frank, I've got to bend the other corner,' Jenny told him.

Larson shouted out, 'No.' He clearly felt obliged to keep it in as perfect a condition as possible.

His abhorrence sounded involuntary and Jenny understood why, but she had to be sure. Before the word had finished slipping from Larson's lips, the second corner was creased along what appeared to be a printing error. It too pointed to the centre of the wheel. Now two arrow heads pointed there. Instantly, two faint zigzag lines, like lightning rods, magically appeared to travel from the arrows to the centre of the wheel.

Jenny sensed her skin tingling, amazed by the magic she had seen.

It was a clue, and Jenny dared to think it might be the first step to saving Sam in over a year. 'So we're going to the cavern to discover what is at the centre of the giant ship's wheels.'

'Yes, exactly, and to see what this has to do with the sea witch's revelations.' said Larson. His eyes remained fixed on the road ahead, and it wasn't long before the sign for the campsite came into view.

Suddenly, Jenny was afraid. She had seen so many terrible things already, most of them connected to this place, and she also knew how much the people there wanted her and Johnny dead. That became apparent with Von Strictum's trying to run her over only twenty minutes earlier. *Where had he gone when he sped away? He might be at the cavern right now, and we are about to walk straight into his trap.*

Larson's face appeared serious and determined. Jenny slumped back into the seat, unable to disclose her thoughts. The car turned left, off the main road and onto the dirt track.

In front, on either side, dark trees were coming closer, like spindly black giants looming over her. Jenny feared that beyond them was the camping field, where people had been snatched from their tents in the middle of night the previous summer. She remembered the decaying cabin, which would now be lifeless and alone. The nasty, evil people that lived there having crawled away to hide in the dark spaces under the nearest rotting stump when the emergency services arrived. It sent a shiver down Jenny's spine, imagining they were like ugly, hairy spiders, hiding and waiting for their chance to shoot out on unsuspecting victims as they passed. She imagined them dragging their drained corpses back into their new, secret lair so they could suck the souls out of them.

Johnny noticed her shudder. 'Somebody walked over your grave too,' he said, grim.

They entered the trees and everywhere became much darker; then they turned right and up a steep incline, towards the cavern entrance.

'Frank,' said Jenny, anxious. 'What if some of those people are here protecting it, because surely if the witch's wheels are of any use, they will be?'

Larson reached down the side of his chair, lifting up his sawn-off shotgun so she could see it; then he carefully rested it again. 'I'm hoping they don't know. I didn't, so why should they? The sea witch will, of course, but she ain't getting back in there, not with all that stone in the pool. And if I was her, I wouldn't go telling anyone because then she would have to trust 'em.'

Jenny was feeling a little more at ease. *Hopefully, no one will be there and we can sneak in and out without being seen.*

The brakes screeched and the boxy car ground to a halt. Jenny jumped out into the long brown grass. From the top of the hill, she could see for miles. Larson, Johnny and Bersaba joined her, taking in the view for a moment and a few deep breaths of clean cool air.

'Bodmin looks beautiful from here. It's not dissimilar to my own country,' said Larson.

It was barren, brown, marshy and boggy, and Jenny had a dappling of dread at the idea of being out there alone, but nevertheless, it had something very special that was hard to put a finger on. She knew what he meant.

Jenny picked up on a certain tone in Larson's voice, sad, regretful. 'Do you miss it, where you come from?'

He smiled at her for a second, and then cast his eyes back over the view. 'No, I don't regret it. I love West Wales, Cornwall; it's my home and everyone I care about is here.'

'Father, don't you think it odd that the duke has done that?' Bersaba asked, pointing towards Caradon Hill. A gust of wind blew and she pulled her long black coat tight around her neck.

'Aye, I do. It must have cost an absolute fortune to get them up and running again,' Larson replied.

Jenny followed Bersaba's gaze to the engine house, some way off in the distance. 'It's amazing that people could build stuff like that all those years ago, don't you think so?'

A very tall stone-built house with a chimney stack reaching high above the top of it, bellowing plumes of white smoke into the air. Jenny had read about the engine houses that encircled Caradon Hill. They were relics from the past, an age of boom then bust for the area which lasted only fifty years and had more or less ceased by 1890. The newly covered roof hid the steam-engine shaft, or bob as it was called, which pumped water out of the ground so the miners could work. Dig a hole in Cornwall and it will soon fill up with water. Other engine houses worked the mining machinery.

'Them?' asked Jenny, confused. She could see only one restored engine house and that came as a surprise to her. Why had she not heard about this before now?

Larson stared down at Jenny and smiled. 'What, have you not heard? I thought you knew everything. The Duke of Cornwall paid for all the old mines to be put back to the way they were originally. That was more than two years ago.' Larson tittered, a little, inappropriately. 'If I was a younger man, I'd have been asking for my job back.'

'But why?' asked Jenny again. 'There's not going to be enough copper or tin left in the mines to make it pay.'

'My thoughts, exactly,' Bersaba agreed, 'and I should know.'

'What do you mean?'

'That's my job; I'm a geologist. Dad paid for me to go to the university to study rocks.' Bersaba laughed. 'I think he wanted me to go off and find him an oil field.'

Larson cleared his throat and reset his flat cap tighter around his hairy ears.

Jenny wondered if he was feeling the cold chill too.

'Not necessarily,' Larson interjected, ignoring her folly. 'If they advertise them as working mines, it will attract more revenue from tourists and some additional income from the bits of metal they get out. In fact, I bet more tourists would be interested in visiting if the mines were working, and some that have already been will return for a second look, you know – see how it was done? It's a win-win.'

'Yes, maybe,' said Bersaba, changing her point of view.

'Can we take a ride over there to get a closer look at what they're doing?' asked Jenny.

'Yes, I think that's a good idea. We should have done it before now.'

It seemed like anything changing these days was suspicious. With all that had happened, everything was held in a dark corner of fear and concern that it might be connected to the sea witch. Copper and tin mines did seem improbable though; they have nothing at all to do with the sea, but neither did a campsite on the middle of Bodmin Moor, until now. That just proved how far into this land the sea witch could actually go, if she wanted to.

A white-and-grey washed sky remained still above her, but out to the coast, Jenny feared the dark-blue storm clouds and the flashing white lightning. Something was building up out there over the sea, something massive, devastating and it felt like a ticking bomb ready to go off.

Larson, noticing Jenny's concern, stared at them too. 'The book is almost full, Jenny. I think we're talking a matter of days, not weeks; then something cataclysmic is going to happen. God help us all.'

Jenny knew he was referring to the storm. 'The witch has brewed it up, hasn't she? And it's only going to get worse unless we can stop her.'

'Yes, I think so. We'd better get moving,' Larson said bravely.

Suddenly, the ground began to shake, and loose dirt tumbled down the hillside in front of them. Jenny's feet shook and her legs wobbled. Johnny shouted out, and a wave of terror came over her. *Is this it, is it the end?* They fell about like drunks grabbing hold of each other, trying to steady themselves, but the earth's rumbling continued, and eventually, they all fell hard onto the heather and wet grass.

'What's happening?' shouted Johnny.

'It's another earthquake, but this time it's much worse,' replied Jenny. She stared at Larson, searching for something, anything telling her it would be okay.

But Larson's face looked drawn, his glaring orange eyes reaching out across the moors below. 'Oh my God, I don't believe it.'

'What is it?' cried Jenny. 'What can you see?'

Still shaking, Larson's arm came up, his finger pointing into the distance, following his gaze. Jenny saw what he was talking about. A huge hundred-foot wave swept across the land from the southwest towards them. The rumbling stopped, the earth became still and the low thunderous tone of rolling water, eating up the land, filled Jenny's ears.

'It's a tsunami,' yelled Johnny, 'and it's heading this way.' He leapt to his feet and pulled Jenny up from the ground next to him. 'Quick, we've got to go.'

'Woah, now you just hold on there, young feller,' Larson told him. 'We're okay up here. It's them poor souls down there that need to worry.'

It was terrifyingly beautiful, a wall of blue and green rising up into the air with white froth and surf bubbling along the top, pushed by the force of water behind it. At the same time it was deadly, sweeping through the fields and across the moors, smashing houses, trees, everything that stood in its path. Suddenly, the white surf came crashing down, sending wood, stone and earth high into the air. Jenny knew amongst it would be people – lots of people and animals – but they were too small for her to see in the turmoil.

A strong whiff of sea salt passed under Jenny's nose. 'Is this it, is it the end?' She had though it, and now the words fell from her lips. She was horrified and defeated by what she saw. Nothing human could stand up to the power of the sea. If the sea witch can do this, then no one can stand up to her, and the presage can never be fulfilled.

'I don't think so,' replied Larson. 'Not for us at least, but it's not natural for sea water to travel this far inland, not even from a tsunami. Something really bad has happened out there. God save them poor people's souls.'

Jenny knew what he meant. Lots of village folk were drowned and smashed by the torrent, but it had lost its momentum and rolled forwards around Caradon Hill and across the moors like it does on a beach just before it slides back out.

Larson looked at Bersaba, touching her arm. 'That's just paddling water. The people at Saint Cleer, they'll be alright.'

'I know, Dad,' she replied.

CHAPTER SIX

Berserker's Rising

Larson lifted the shotgun from the car, slammed the door shut and marched over to the tunnel entrance.

Sticky candyfloss webs tickled Jenny's face, as she left the fresh, light breeze to still, damp and stale musty smells. The black walls touched her shoulders and the top of her head, and she sensed an overpowering feeling of everything collapsing in around her. *It wasn't this small the last time I was here, surely I would have remembered.* But she could not go back. Jenny heard Johnny's loud breathing close behind her. Not loud under normal conditions, but in here it was deathly quiet, and everything stood out, breathing and shuffling feet.

Larson continued on, his back arched low like a hunch. The light from his torch spread out across the muddy web-covered walls in front of him. Nobody had been there for a long time, Jenny was sure of that. Debris had fallen from the walls; she saw it in Larson's torchlight and felt it crunching under her shoes. Clumps of vegetation had started growing in the corners too. *If anyone was still using this place, they would certainly have kept it in better condition than this.*

Jenny's mind was eased by that thought. It was possible they could get in, find what they were looking for and get out, without seeing a soul.

Then she heard Johnny whimper, 'I want to go back.'

There were shuffling feet; then Bersaba said, 'Can't go back, Johnny. There's no room to pass; just keep moving.'

Jenny thought she heard Johnny being pushed. 'Stay close to me,' she whispered to him; then everywhere went quiet again.

A little way on, the walls parted to the sides and above, and Jenny was able to straighten. In the torchlight, she saw the massive stone wheel, which had previously blocked the tunnel. It had fallen to the floor and broken in three. *Maybe the rescue team had done it. Their only concern would have been getting in and trying to save people.* She was inside the first chamber. In front, the second tunnel, its curved top shaped like a gravestone, lit up by the torch, and inside, where Jenny had to go, there was only thick blackness.

Larson wasted no time, bending down as he entered. Jenny's fingers touched the damp, gritty mud at the sides. It slipped under her nails, and a shiver ran through her once again. She hated the feeling of grit separating the nail from her skin. Using her thumb, she started to frantically scrape it out as she scurried on through the darkness.

The narrow passage went round to the left; then gradually it widened so that Larson was now marching on, upright. Jenny could see from his stance that he only had one thing on his mind. Torch in one hand, gun in the other, he stepped out of the passage into the huge cavern.

Giant shards of rock had completely filled the pool. Jenny gazed up the wall and into the canopy. She saw white sky peering through a large jagged hole. It was surrounded by green moss, hanging down like ripped curtains mingling with thin spindly tree roots.

Larson immediately headed to where Jed and Pauline had been shackled. One of the giant wooden wheels of the ship still hung there above the inverted five-pointed star.

Jenny ran to his side, and together they began to examine the centre. Larson's fingers followed the cornice around, searching for something, anything. He tried to unscrew it, but it wouldn't budge.

'God damn it, Jenny, there's nothing here that I can see,' shouted Larson.

'Where's the other one? There were two; somebody must have been and taken it, but why?' Jenny stared up; twelve feet at least to the top of the wheel. It still had five very thick, long strands of greenish brown weed wrapped around it.

She was pondering on it when Larson said, 'Jenny, step back. I'm taking the middle of this wheel with us, and if it won't unscrew, then I'm blasting it off.' He lifted the gun and pointed it at the wheels spars. Jenny ran back to Bersaba and Johnny, some distance away; then Larson fired at it. Splinters of wood flew in all directions. Quickly, he released the barrel, loaded two more shells and fired at it again. After his third attempt, the centre of the wheel fell to the earth.

'Well, that sorts that out. We can inspect it more when we get home,' said Larson, lifting it from the ground by his feet.

Jenny ran back to the wheel, staring at its outer section and the weed surrounding it, which remained firmly fixed to the wall. 'I was just thinking, the weed has three knots and the knot at the top is bigger than the other knots. Why is that?'

Larson started thinking and rubbing his bristly grey chin. He said, 'I don't know. I never noticed.'

Jenny smiled. 'I think we need to take down this weed and have a look at that knot, as well.'

Larson grabbed a hold of the weed. 'Yes, I think you're right; well done, Jenny.' He placed the gun down on the ground and started to tug at the weed.

'It's not going to move that easily,' said Jenny.

After a couple more yanks on it, Larson nodded and smiled, defeated. It hadn't moved at all. 'I know, this should do it,' he said, opening his long coat and pulling out a short-handle axe.

'Bloody hell, Frank, are you carrying a full arsenal in there, or what? Come on; show us what else you've got?' asked Johnny.

Larson tittered. 'No, lad, that's about it; well, except for this.' He pulled out four sticks of dynamite from an inside pocket on the other side of his coat. 'Now, you climb up there, and try to unhook the weed over the top of the wheel.'

Johnny stood staring at him for a second.

'Go on then, we haven't got all day.' He cupped his hands with his back to the wheel. 'Put your foot in here and I'll give you a pog up.'

Jenny could see Johnny did not want to do it. It frustrated her terribly, *what a wimp*. 'Move it,' she told him, sternly.

Johnny moved closer.

'Right, foot in and grab the top off the wheel when Frank lifts you up.'

'Here we go,' said Larson. 'One, two, three, up you go,' and he lifted Johnny into the air.

Johnny grabbed on to the top and wrapped his arm around it. With his other arm, he tried tugging and pulling the weed over the wheel. 'It's too heavy.'

'Hold on a minute,' Larson told him. 'I'll cut the weed off, as high as I can.' Larson swung the axe, slicing through the weed and into the curved wooden edge. Two cuts and Johnny was able to lift the piece of weed with the large knot over the wheel, and it slid down to the ground by Jenny's feet.

'Right, jump down and I'll catch yer,' Larson told him.

Jenny dropped to her knees, excited. She picked it up, surprised; it felt cold and wet. 'You think it would have been bone dry by now, wouldn't you.' But then she remembered the first time she ever saw the witch's pendant. Sailing out of Lamorna, Sam held it across his palm. She remembered how disappointed she had been. Five strands of weed, three knots. Sam had even said if it wasn't for saving Johnny's life, he would have thrown the worthless thing back into the sea.

'Aye, Jenny, but that ain't no ordinary weed, is it?' Larson pointed out.

'No, I guess it's not.'

Johnny was dangling from the wheel and shouting out, afraid to let go.

'Jump, boy, jump,' Larson breathed, but he sounded harsh and frustrated.

Suddenly, Jenny gasped. Shuffling feet sounds were coming from the next cavern. Hers and Bersaba's eyes shot to it, but it was dark, very dark, and she could not see anything. 'Quick, Frank, hand me your torch,' Jenny shouted, her heart racing.

Larson threw it to her, still concentrating on Johnny.

Jenny immediately pointed it towards the sounds. *'What is that?'* The torch lit up shapes moving about very slowly and low to the ground. Small grey and whitish smooth pebbles, perhaps, but they do not move? Jenny's breath held still. A momentary glance at Bersaba, her eyes looked like they were popping out of their sockets in disbelief. 'What is that Bersaba?' She did not speak, but the smooth grey shapes continued bubbling in waves. Slowly they became larger and more distinct; then the pebbles rolled upward. They were not pebbles at all, but bald grey heads, hundreds of them with horrible white eyes staring out of the darkness.

Jenny screamed out, 'Berserkers', terrified by what she'd seen. Another voice screamed also, *Bersaba, it has to be.* 'Oh my God, quick, Frank; we've got to go; there's no time to lose,' Jenny shouted, frantically.

'Berserkers,' shouted Larson, confirming what Jenny had said. 'Johnny, get down here, now,' he said in a vicious, threatening tone.

Johnny stared down, terrified. 'What the hell are berserkers?'

'They'll scratch out your eyes and rip off your head if they catch you, boy; now jump.'

Johnny let go immediately. Larson caught him as he fell, and the Berserkergang charged towards them from out of the darkness.

'Run children,' Larson shouted over the roar of the oncoming chaos from the slaughter horde.

Jenny scooped up the weed and ran as fast as she could towards the passage. 'We must have awakened them.' Into the blackness, heavy breathing, her painful shoulders bouncing off the muddy sides, a lump hammering out of her chest, and her skin shivered, prickling with electricity. Blackness surrounded her; only a single beam of light emanated from the torch, and it flashed up the walls and in all directions. Jenny had no time for that. She stumbled on as fast as she could, praying she would not fall over, knowing that if she did, someone, Johnny, Bersaba or Larson, would fall on top of her, and she would be ripped apart by those frenzied creatures.

'Faster, faster,' Larson shouted, causing Jenny to scream out again.

The screaming noises echoed through the passage. Screaming madness filled her ears, loud and overwhelming, like a steam train racing into a tunnel, blowing its high-pitch horns. Jenny gasped knowing the berserkers were in there and gaining on her fast.

She continued to bounce off the walls; then suddenly in front, daylight. Her heaving chest burned, legs wobbled, but now she was close and sensed she could possibly escape the tunnel.

Wham! As fast as that, out into the low evening light, the Land Rover in front of her. She flung the door open and threw herself in. Johnny too was in before she had time to turn around, and he slammed the door shut. Clunk... bang. Clunk... bang. Bersaba and Larson were in the front seats.

Larson threw the wheel centre down by Bersaba's feet and fiddled frantically with the chinking keys.

'Oh, oh, quick, they're coming,' Jenny screamed, as the berserkers piled out of the tunnel, like water bursting from a pipe, and headed straight for the car.

Suddenly, the key turned and the engine fired into life.

They all screamed out as hands banged on the doors, and scraped and clawed at the windows. One of the berserkers flew onto the bonnet and grabbed a hold of the wiper blades. His face smashed into the windscreen, as the Land Rover rolled, careering down the hill and between the trees. Still it held on, the Berserker's body bouncing up and down violently on every bump. It yelled at them, dangerously, in some incoherent tongue through the glass, its eyes mad, fiery and filled with hatred, like a starving animal trying to get at its prey.

Jenny sobbed with fear; she had escaped the cavern and most of the horde, but this one alone could tear them apart then she realised something even more terrible. The berserker on the car bonnet, which was terrifying her so much, was Jed.

'Oh, no,' Jenny cried out. 'It can't be! Look, Johnny; look at it.'

She couldn't stand it anymore, seeing him like that. Jed was a crazed animal, scratching at the glass and trying to kill her.

She remembered him and his wife, Pauline. Come this way every holiday for the surf, he said. They had been camping on the site the previous summer and spent the evening together around a campfire talking about Jed's passion for surfing, and Sam told them about his bat-catching net, which was really for the Beast of Bodmin Moor. They sat laughing and eating Pauline's biscuits. Jenny remembered feeling a little jealous. She was sure Sam had a fancy for Pauline. Later that night they disappeared, and their car was gone. Jed was kind and handsome. *Oh God, look what the witch has done to him.*

She buried her tear-filled face into Johnny's neck, not wanting to look at Jed anymore. All the other berserkers were now fading into the distance, and the Land Rover bounced away down the hill. Suddenly, Larson slammed on the breaks, and Jed flew off the bonnet onto the ground in front of them.

The growling crazy screaming sounds stopped. Larson set off again, bouncing twice, first the front wheels and then the back, and Jenny knew Larson had run over Jed's body. Each time she screamed out, and then she cried over Johnny's shirt.

The car turned right onto the smooth tarmac road. Bersaba and Larson gave a sigh of relief, and they smiled at each other, visibly shivering.

Jenny knew they were just glad to be alive. It had been a close call. If the berserkers had got them, it was certain death. She lifted her head off Johnny's shoulder, staring into his slate-grey eyes. Her face felt warm and her eyes were stinging from salty tears.

'Are you all right?' asked Johnny quietly.

Jenny tried to smile, but she could not speak. Yes, they had escaped, but at what cost? Jed was dead. A feeling of guilt and despair swept over her, and she thought back to the previous year. The day Sam went missing, the day everything changed and brought her to this point. Jed and his wife, Pauline, strapped to the witch's giant ship's wheels. The witch had taken Jed's soul that day and made him into the animal they had just seen and killed.

If only they had tried harder, maybe they could have saved him – if they could have captured him and kept him safe somewhere, until all of this business was over. Maybe doctors could have helped him, even if it meant going to a sanatorium; surely it would have been better than death. And poor Pauline, they had not seen her. Was she there mingled in amongst those crazy beasts? Jenny feared the worst and wondered what could have possibly happened to her?

'Oh, Frank. Why did you have to kill him? Jenny cried.

'The berserker, you mean? What does it matter; he was trying to kill us,' Larson replied, oh, so matter of fact.

'That maybe so, but he couldn't help it… Frank, we knew him,' Jenny sounded really low.

'Oh, I see… Well, I'm sorry about that, but if it's any consolation, we did him a favour. Your friend, he's been gone for a long time. That was just his body, an empty vessel controlled by the witch.'

Jenny knew what Larson meant. 'It was like old Mr P, Johnny's grandfather. He had a heart attack on the harbour wall and fell into the sea. His soul escaped from his body before the sea witch got to it, so he lived on and helped Sam get Johnny back from her. If the witch had captured his soul, she could have used his body too. But this was different. The sea witch took Jed's soul out of him using a spell, and it was probably eaten by Hades, or that's what the witch said.'

Larson agreed. 'It makes sense. If the witch takes your soul then she controls your body, and if she doesn't, then you can do what the hell you like, fly away somewhere and your body just rots in the ground. That's the way it's supposed to be innit?'

Jenny stared down at the large knot made from five strands of weed. She pushed her thumbs into its cold, wet crossover and carefully pulled it apart, just a little.

She met Johnny's frightened eyes, without saying a word.

He whispered in her ear, 'You know, you could be opening Pandora's Box.'

It was the first time Jenny had truly smiled since nearly getting run over. Her eyes dropped and very cautiously she peered in.

CHAPTER SEVEN

Mirror Shavings

'Don't do that!' Larson shouted so loudly Jenny nearly jumped off her seat. 'Pull that knot together tight quickly, come on... come on.'

Jenny was suddenly filled with fear. Not because she was afraid of Larson's shouting, but he actually sounded frightened, and if he was fearful of it, then she most definitely should be.

Johnny snatched the weed, grabbing a hold of it quickly by both ends and pulling it tight shut. 'Okay, Frank, it's done,' said Johnny, breathing heavily.

Johnny was scared of most things, including what might be inside the knot, but not half as much as hearing Larson shout.' That was Jenny's first thought. Her second was one of curiosity. *Maybe Johnny was not so much afraid of Larson, but believes in him. He gave the order and Johnny reacted instantly to his command.*

'Bersaba, take it from them. Something like that, we don't know what harm it can do.'

She reached out her hand and Johnny gave it to her willingly.

Jenny scowled, but Bersaba smiled, reached over and stroked her hair. 'Come on, dear, don't take it like that. Frank's only thinking about your safety.'

'That's right, I am. Sorry for snapping. Anything could be in there? It might be a booby trap or it might be a curse.'

'We're not babies, and we don't need looking after, either, so don't go telling us what to do. That weed belongs to me; it was my idea to take it from the giant ship's wheel, and Johnny got it down.'

Larson was still watching the road most of the time, but his eyes kept flitting to Jenny as he spoke, 'I know. I'm sorry. We're nearly back now. When we get into Mr Booty's flat, we'll have a proper look at it, together.'

'So you're not taking it from us then?'

'No, of course not. Like you said, you're not babies, and you have as much right to know what is in there, as anybody else.'

Jenny was feeling much better. She smiled at Johnny and he immediately grabbed her hand. *He does have unusually lovely eyes.* Jenny allowed him to hold onto her hand, and after a few moments, she rested her head on his shoulder.

Before long, the car pulled onto the car park over the road from Mr Booty's shop. Jenny jumped out, eager to get into the flat, so she could examine the contents of the knot. *There was definitely something in there, something sparkly? Maybe it is filled with diamonds?*

Suddenly, there was a rumble of thunder in the distance. Jenny stared up the cobbled street, through the town and above the roof tops. Angry storm-filled clouds, dark blue and black rolled ever closer to land. Occasionally, flashes of white lit up the sky, as if the witch was flicking a light switch on and off.

Jenny shuddered. *It's her alright; the sea witch is coming.*

Johnny stared up at the sky, his face looking as worried as she felt. 'Come on, Jenny, there's nothing we can do about that.'

'That's her, isn't it? Her power is increasing and she's affecting the weather.'

'Probably,' agreed Johnny, glum.

'Hurry, children, quickly into the shop.' Larson pushed on the door. The bell chimed and they all stepped out of the cold evening chill into the smell of citrus fruits.

Mr Booty was counting up cash behind the till. He looked up very pleased to see them.

'Prosperous day?' asked Larson, giving reason for Mr Booty to be so happy when things were really extremely dire.

Jenny knew it was the relief that they had returned safely that had put a smile on his chubby, red face. After all Mr Booty had been friends with Larson for hundreds of years.

He hurried around the counter, quickly bolting the door and turning the key. 'Up the stairs, my friends; the kettle's on.'

Larson led the way between the fruit boxes and through the door which led up to the flat. They all piled into the lounge and sat around a smoked-glass coffee table, as Bersaba placed the weed on it. Jenny and Johnny sat on the carpet as close as possible.

Larson placed the wheel on the carpet, peeled off his coat and threw it down over it before slumping into his armchair.

Suddenly, Jenny was distracted by an unexpected voice coming through the kitchen door.

'Hey, thank goodness, you're back.'

'Dad, what are you doing here?' Johnny jumped to his feet, surprised.

'Whoa, slow down; you'll knock the tea over,' said Mr Pothelswaite, both hands holding a tray with cups, a pot of tea and digestive biscuits.

'But how did you know?' Johnny asked.

'Mr Booty,' he said with a smile.

Johnny couldn't contain his excitement. 'You wouldn't believe what we've just seen back at the cavern. First of all, there was another earthquake.'

'I know. I felt it too. Much worse than the last one, and they're happening far too often.' Mr Pothelswaite looked very worried.

'It was... much worse,' Johnny agreed, 'and then there was a tsunami which covered most of Bodmin and as far southwest as I could see.'

Mr Pothelswaite glanced at Larson. Larson nodded in agreement.

'We went into the cavern, you know, where the people from Saint Cleer died and Sam went missing. Hundreds of crazy people chased us out. I tell you, Dad, we're very lucky to be alive.'

Jenny could see, Mr Pothelswaite had already been told where they had gone. He was not surprised at all, but by the look on his face, as he now stared angrily at Larson, he had not expected them to be in such danger. Jenny thought he was about to go mad when Johnny mentioned the Berserkergang, but considering everything he'd just been told, he was extremely calm. *I guess after losing Johnny twice, the sea witch and everything else, he's not so easily shocked anymore.*

Larson lifted the weed from the table and Mr Pothelswaite placed the tray on it. He gave out the tea and biscuits, whilst Larson examined the green strands tied in a knot.

He appeared to be judging its weight with his hand, after that, he ran his finger along it, searching and sniffing like a dog looking for a bitch's scent.

Jenny waited with eager anticipation. 'Well, what do think?' she said eventually.

Larson continued to examine it. 'It has no smell, except for fresh salt. It weighs about the same as a bag of sugar, and the surface feels damp and smooth. Hmmm, I guess we'll just have to take a chance and open it up.'

'Let me do it, Frank; I found it,' Jenny told him.

Larson gazed up at her for a second. 'Are you sure?'

Jenny smiled, taking it from him. She held the five strands in both hands and slowly pushed them together, loosening the knot again. It felt springy as if it was trying to stay closed. But Jenny pushed hard and the weed separated. She gazed at Larson, and then peered down into it, sensing everyone around her was eagerly waiting with anticipation.

'What can you see, Jenny?' asked Johnny.

Her first instincts had been right; there was something shiny in there, but it was disappointing. 'It isn't diamonds,' she told them. 'It's silver and reflective like mirror glass, but it's in thin curly strips like wood shavings.'

'Mirror shavings,' said Johnny.

'Yes, that's the only way I can describe it; see for yourself.' Jenny stared at Johnny with an excited glint in her eye.

He peered inside. 'I've never seen anything like that before. I wonder what it does.'

Suddenly, distracted, Jenny's eyes shot to the side of Larson's chair. Something was vibrating under the black coat; then she saw it – the wheel hub was rocking rapidly on the floor and slowly edging out from under the coat towards the coffee table.

'Quickly, pull the weed tight together; something is happening,' shouted Larson.

At the same time the curtains blew, as if caught by a strong breeze. A horrible screeching voice laughed wildly, whirling around the room like a cyclone, knocking over the lamp. Pictures flew off the walls; then Jenny's hair whipped up from her neck as it passed, and she felt goose pimples prickle on the back of her neck.

Johnny shuddered and hastily pulled the weed firmly shut once again. Suddenly, the gale stopped, leaving a stench of sea weed and stale fish.

'Phew that stinks,' said Jenny, holding her nose. 'And where did that icy wind come from? You had better shut the window; it pongs out there.'

Everything went quiet again, a sense of eeriness filled the room and Larson breathed, pointing his finger, 'Look, Jenny, the window is already closed.'

Jenny was unable to take her eyes off Larson. He looked so afraid, twice in one day and he was supposed to be the rock. *Who will lead us, if he doesn't? Oh God, I guess we are done for.* But Jenny fought her weakness. She had promised Sam, she would save him, and by God, she was not willing to give up now. 'What is it, Frank? Why are you looking like that?'

Larson rubbed his hands over his face. 'She was with us in this room. Now I know she can get to us whenever she wants to, and here we are, only days away from our destruction, and we're messing about with these stupid trinkets; it's useless.'

'It's not useless,' Jenny retorted. 'It's something… it's all we have.'

Larson's head dropped into his hands. 'The sea witch was in this room.'

Jeez, Larson really is losing it. Then she remembered Sam's mum and dad. 'Listen to me will you, Sam's mum and dad have been living with the witch in their house for over a year. What I don't understand is why she's still there. Why did she not move on, once she had Sam?'

Larson shook his head. 'I don't know… I don't know,' he cried.

'You had better find out, hadn't you? Look in the book,' Jenny told him sternly.

'I've looked and there's nothing.'

Jenny was filled with determination. 'Then you've missed something – look again.' She slumped back onto the carpet trying not to cry. Her hand dithered around the cup, and she sipped at the sweet tea.

The room was consumed by silence for a long time until Jenny finally had had enough. 'Come on Johnny, let's get out of here. I can't stand being around these defeatists any longer.' She marched out of the door, filled with anger because of their lack of furore. She turned around, flushed. 'I'll tell you this. Sam would not want that house, not anymore. Beautiful as it is, he would burn it to the ground, rather than let his parents live with those witches swimming through it. So here's what I'm going to do, I'm going to go over there, and I'm going to torch it to the ground for him.'

Larson jumped up and marched across the room, grabbing her arm.

'Let go of me,' she screamed, trying to yank free.

Larson's dark-brown eyes were wide and alive and changing again. 'Wait, I know what to do,' he said, in a surprised voice. 'You're right, Jenny; it is in the book and has been staring at me all along. Wait here whilst I get it from my coat.'

'Stop it, you deceitful old man; you're just trying to obstruct me.'

'Why would I, we're all done for anyway. It doesn't matter to me what you do. But wait one minute and I'll show you.'

Jenny sighed as Larson left and went into his bedroom. A moment later he returned, flicking through the pages. He sat back into his chair.

'Arr, here it is,' he said, pushing back the page.

Jenny stepped up behind him, so she could see the book over

his shoulder. Larson's finger followed each word as he read it. Jenny thought this was for her benefit, and she could see that the words he read out were true to the page.

'Our Mother Earth lives because of the Sea of Life.' Larson went quiet for a few seconds and then said, 'It talks about the gods of the sea and the gateway between the world of Mother Earth and the sea of souls. It talks about life coming from the sea, adapting to land, and later returning to the sea.' Larson's finger moved down the page quickly. 'Ha, here it is; this is what you made me think of, Jenny. It says: "In order to find passage to the sea of souls, the owner must give up the one thing he or she holds most dear."' Larson closed the book. 'When the witch came tonight, I thought we might have made a gateway, a porthole, right here by opening the knot, but no, I sense the room is clear once again. However, the witches have continued to swim through Sam's house. I believe we may find a way to the witch through there, but only if the owner gives up that which he or she holds most dear.'

Jenny was terrified at the thought, and the words unintentionally fell from her lips, 'Ellie.'

'No, that's not what I'm thinking,' Larson sounded agitated.

Then Johnny revealed, 'Sam's house.'

Larson rose from his chair. 'Yes, yes,' he said, pacing the room. 'Mr Camponara must destroy the house on the edge of the rocks.'

'But how can we persuade him, he's not going to give that up is he? When I last went there and mentioned Sam, it was as if they didn't care anymore. I came away not liking them at all, but what if it's not the house? What if it's Ellie?'

'Then he must sacrifice her.'

Jenny gasped.

'It's been done before, the slaying of one for the lives of many. People have killed their children, whom they loved more than their own lives, in order to save this world or just to please their god.'

'Frank, that's just not going to happen,' Jenny told him. 'Could you do that to Bersaba?' Jenny expected him to agree. She could not imagine it was possible, even for him, to kill his own daughter.

Larson turned around and his eyes fell to the floor, as if ashamed. 'Well, I'm afraid if I must.'

Jenny stared at him in disbelief, and she wondered what Bersaba must be thinking about her father, knowing he was willing to kill her. 'Okay, putting all that aside, Mr Camponara, is under the witch's spell, so there is no way he would give up the house, either, not for anything.' She felt queasy at the thoughts that he could love the house more than his own son or daughter, although right now, she prayed that he did. 'Can someone do it for him?'

Larson sighed. 'No, the porthole will not open, so it would be a pointless.'

'How on earth can this work? If he loves it more than a parent loves his child, there's no way he's going to destroy it.' Jenny was at a loss with the whole thing. 'We're all doomed.'

Nobody spoke, but Larson placed the book on the table and lifted the wheel hub from the floor. He looked it up and down, front, back and around the sides, where broken spokes stuck out all around it. Jenny watched curiously from behind the chair.

'Hmm, I just want to try something,' he said, staring across the table at Johnny. He lifted the wheel round so that the back of it faced towards Johnny. 'Open the weed again, Johnny.'

Johnny did as he was asked. Lifting it up, he carefully prised it open, so that only a thin line showed the tiniest glint of mirror shavings.

'I can feel its pull. Aha, the blighter is pretty strong.'

Jenny watched Larson's arm straining to hold it there. It pulled forward and Larson held it back with all his might.

'Don't let go of the weed now, Johnny,' Larson warned.

Johnny actually smiled. 'I won't. It doesn't even feel like it's pulling at my end.'

Jenny could hardly believe it. He was enjoying something he didn't understand, and that was not like Johnny at all.

Nobody could take their eyes of the magical objects and Jenny's head filled with questions. *Where does it get its power, what is it for, why does it pull like that, on one end and not the other, it just doesn't make sense, and what is it doing?* The last question was just about to be answered.

The curtains whipped up again and a wind began to howl like a banshee. Jenny's hair flew back, and objects around the room started falling and clattering to the floor.

Johnny quickly lost his smile and his eyes stared, terrified, at the hub. 'Frank, it's doing something.'

The wind grew even stronger. It was like a tornado blowing around the room, and then Jenny spotted a sea witch, white, almost transparent, circling above them.

'That's okay, just hold it there,' Larson told him very calmly, ignoring everything.

Jenny moved around the chair and knelt down on the carpet next to Johnny. She could not see what Johnny was talking about from the back of the chair. And why Larson thought it was okay to continue this little experiment, when everything in the room was being smashed to pieces, was beyond her because Larson definitely could not see what was happening to the hub. She stared at it and smiled with excitement, 'Oh, Johnny, real magic.'

The wooden centre of the hub, about the size of a teacup saucer, was turning. Round and round it went very slowly, gradually unscrewing.

Jenny giggled with excitement and anticipation, clapping her hands together nervously, ignoring the sea witch entity. 'I wonder what's inside it.'

Johnny was back to his old ways, horrified. 'I'd rather not know if you don't mind. Anything that belongs to that witch has got to be bad for us,' he yelled over the horrendous sound of the wind and the witch.

Larson smiled, his eyes never parting from Johnny.

I don't think he's bothered anymore and I don't blame him.

Suddenly, the hub's centre shot out from the wheel, flew across the table and stuck onto the side of the weed.

'Close it, Johnny,' shouted Larson, barely audible in the wind.

Johnny pulled the weed tightly together again, and the hub centre fell clattering onto the table.

The wind stopped immediately and the witch disappeared.

'Well, that was interesting.' Larson tittered, 'I guess we're still here and alive.' He placed the wheel on the floor, picked up the wooden object and explored every inch of it intensely.

Jenny could barely wait for him to announce something wonderful.

His fingers routed around inside it and then he began to pull something out. 'What is that?' It looked like clumps of long strands of black hair. Larson did not reply; his fist was full of the stuff and his beady eyes peered back inside the hub. Jenny sensed he was expecting to find something more. 'There's nothing here,' he said, sounding very disappointed.

'What?' Jenny could not believe it; there had to be.

'Here, see for yourself.'

Jenny snatched it from him. *There's got to be, it's magical.* But Larson was right; it was just an empty chamber and the black hair, still clenched in Larson's hand, told her nothing at all.

Filled with exasperation, Jenny said, 'Well, there's nothing more for me to do here. I'm going home before Mum phones the police again. And don't worry, I'm not going to burn Sam's house down; there's no point, now, is there?'

'Wait for me, Jen. I'm coming with you.' Johnny jumped to his feet and chased after her down the stairs.

Outside, the thunder drummed across the clouds and then lightning flashed, lighting them up. 'I guess, it's getting closer,' said Johnny, as he strolled beside Jenny through the dark.

'Yes, I'm frightened, Johnny. It could happen at any time now. The 'Register of Berserkers, Lichen Throats, and Imps' is all but full. Frank said we only have a day or two left, and then we are all going to die.'

Jenny's heart pounded in her chest. *Everyone's dying.* 'It's Mum's birthday the day after tomorrow. I can't bear the thought, she won't have another one.' Her bottom lip began to quiver.

Johnny stepped in front of her. 'Shush, Jenny,' he whispered, staring into her eyes.

She stopped. She was not afraid, she didn't have time to be, and she trusted Johnny implicitly. Even when he grabbed a hold of her coat and eased her gently around, backing her into the shade of the shop doorway, she did not mind; in fact, she welcomed it. Confused emotions about Johnny had swamped her for ages. *Does he like me, doesn't he? Why is he holding my hand, hugging me, looking into my eyes like that?* But almost immediately Jenny would sense some distance between them, and she assumed he was just being friendly, until the next time. But now she knew her instincts had been right all along. She gazed up into his slate-grey eyes. *How pretty they are.*

Slowly he pulled her to him.

She could feel his skin, his gentle touch; the anticipation made her dither, his firm hands gripping, holding her still.

'You know why Frank…' stopped in mid sentence by the slightest touch of his finger gently pressing against her lips.

His lips made that shush shape again, but nothing came out.

Jenny could not take her eyes from his; excitement rushed below the surface of her skin making her feel weak, defenceless; then he pressed his lips against hers. It was intense, beautiful, deliciously insane. His soft, warm lips moved slowly, and it felt like they were melting into one other, they were made for this moment. Jenny's head began to spin, and her entire body tingled with adrenaline and excitement. Her arms wrapped around him, his around her. *But, no, wait.* She pushed Johnny back.

He looked surprised.

'I'm sorry, I can't do it,' Jenny told him, almost crying.

'What, the world is about to end? We're all going to die; what is the matter with you?'

Jenny stared down at the ground filled with disappointment and betrayal. 'Is that the only reason, you want me. To see what it's like to kiss me before you die?'

'Yes, no, of course, it isn't.' Johnny stepped closer, about to put his arm around her once more, and lure her back into his seduction.

She pushed him back immediately, stopping his advances.

'Jenny, what is wrong with you?'

'Nothing… now is not the time, that's all.'

Johnny sounded frustrated, 'There is no more time.'

She pulled her coat straight, gripped Johnny's hand, and then she leaned against him and stared into his beautiful eyes, smiling. 'There is time. Johnny. We have to save Sam. That is the only thing we can do. By saving Sam, we save ourselves then we'll have all the time in the world.'

Johnny smiled. He looked like he was agreeing, but she could still see apprehension or sadness there.

She held onto his hand tight, pulling him from the doorway into the street lights, giggling like a little girl.

The thunder rumbled in the distance, but Jenny did not care. She was happy holding Johnny's hand, swinging his arm back and forth, and they walked along the cobbled footpath towards her house.

Then she remembered what she was trying to say before she was overcome with passion. 'I was saying before, about Frank. Remember how he reacted when he thought the gateway to the witch's lair was in Mr Booty's flat. I think I know why he behaved so strangely.' She paused for a moment, but Johnny did not speak. 'I bet he was thinking he would have to give up the thing he holds most dear. He thought he had to kill Bersaba. So I reckon, he just talks the talk. I know he said he would, but his reaction told me he couldn't possibly do it.'

'But that would mean he owns Mr Booty's shop. He said the owner had to make the sacrifice.'

Jenny was confused. 'Oh, yes, I never thought of that.'

By now, Jenny and Johnny had walked up the hill, past what used to be his grandfather's house and turned the corner in Jenny's road. 'Well, that's my point. If Frank can't do it, then Mr Camponara definitely can't.'

Jenny was very worried because she knew Johnny was right. 'I hope he loves the house more than he does Ellie.'

'It makes no difference, he won't do it.'

.

CHAPTER EIGHT

King Doniert's Stone

Jenny woke the next morning thinking how sad life was, having just had her first real kiss and now the world was about to end. As usual, Jenny dressed in her bedroom. She put her school uniform on, titivated her hair, slapped on a splash of makeup and ran down for breakfast.

It was very quiet outside with no one passing as she sat at the little table by the window. Jenny did this most mornings: eating cornflakes and watching the television in the corner of the room.

Mrs Chatter brought in two cups of tea and sat opposite. 'I can't believe this weather. Storm's been brewing out there all week. I don't think I've known one to linger so long in all my days; it's just so depressing, and have you seen what they're saying on the news? It's absolutely tragic.'

'No, why, what's happened?' Jenny asked.

'It'll be back on in a minute. Another two boats have gone missing from Newlyn and one from Penzance.'

'Aw, no, that's so sad. I can't imagine what those poor families are going through, waiting to hear about their loved ones, wondering if they've been drowned or just lost radio communication.'

'O shush, Jenny, you'll have me in tears in a minute.' Mrs Chatter reached into her pocket, pulled out a crumpled tissue and wiped her nose.

'The lifeboat and the air sea rescue helicopter will have been out long before the news reached the television, so they must have gone down. Strange how they've not found any bodies floating on the surface though? Something's not right.'

'Oh, you talk so coldly sometimes, Jenny. Where's your compassion?'

Suddenly, the table began to shake violently. The chair rumbled beneath her and pictures fell from the wall, crashing to the floor. The sounds of plates clattering and smashing in the kitchen sounded even louder when in the next instant the television screen went black.

Jenny gripped the edge of the table, trying to stop it, but her arms shook back and forth, and so did Mum's. 'It's happening again,' she yelled into Mum's tear-filled eyes.

Mum put her hand on Jenny's. 'We're having another earthquake.'

'Oh my… the whole house is shaking. I've never felt one as strong as this before.'

'Don't worry, Jenny dear. Just stay where you are; it will be over in a minute.' Mum sounded very calm and that made Jenny feel a whole lot better. After a few minutes, just as she had said, the rumbling disappeared and everything stopped moving. 'Well, that was an unexpected surprise.' Mum smiled and Jenny smiled back, but inside Jenny worried the sea witch had something to do with this one too. These days it was hard to think anything unusual was not brought on by her.

Mrs Chatter wandered over and bent down behind the television. She pushed the plug back against the wall and the red light came on putting the television on standby. 'There we are, see; no harm done; it just came loose from the socket.'

'Do you want me to help you clean up the kitchen?'

'No, dear, you get yourself ready for school.' Mrs Chatter pushed the button and the news came back on as Jenny was about to leave the room.

'We've just had some breaking news about massive devastation hitting Cornwall.' Jenny stopped and quickly turned around to the voice coming from the TV. Mum was transfixed to the screen. The reporter said, 'The Prime Minister has just come out of No. 10 to issue a statement.' The picture changed to Downing Street, a number of microphones on stands, a horde of reporters and the man himself dressed very smartly in a grey-blue suit and tie.

The Prime Minister said, 'It is with deep regret, I have to announce that an unprecedented catastrophic devastation hit the southwest of England just a few minutes ago. As you know, the area has been plagued by a number of earthquakes in recent days, and more rain than the area normally gets in two years has fallen in a matter of weeks. We don't yet know what caused the earthquake, but we think it is perhaps an aftershock from the loss of St Ives, which slipped into the sea yesterday.'

Jenny gasped, 'The tsunami yesterday, it was caused by St Ives?'

The Prime Minister lifted a white handkerchief from his breast pocket and rubbed his nose. 'We have yet to determine the number of casualties, but please be prepared. This is the biggest single disaster to ever hit our country, and our thoughts and prayers go out to all those who have lost loved ones. This Government will do everything in its power to help the people caught up in this tragedy, and we will, of course, keep you posted as things develop. Thank you for your time and for now we have nothing more we can tell you.'

Mum slumped into a chair. 'St Ives, gone… No, they must be having a laugh… It's not possible.'

'They're not, Mum. I saw a tsunami sweep across Bodmin, and I bet that's what caused it. Oh my, Cornwall has changed forever.'

Mum began sobbing into her hands, but Jenny ran into the hall, there was no time to lose. She put on her coat and picked up her bag. 'See you later; I've got to go.' Mum swept into the hall after her. 'Oh, Jenny, be careful out there. In fact, stay home; you don't have to go to school today, stay with me.'

Jenny gave her the biggest hug and smiled, hiding her fear. 'I've got to; try not to worry, everything will be alright.'

Mum stared at her ashen faced; then she took a deep breath, trying to calm herself, bringing back that stiff upper lip she always wore. 'Yes, I'll see you later, dear. Have you got everything… your lunch?'

Jenny smiled and nodded, throwing her small brown bag over her shoulder.

'Be careful. Have a good day at school, and I'll see you soon.' She hugged Jenny again.

Jenny almost cried with emotion then held it back. *Might never see Mum again, oh, what a horrible, thought.*

☆　☆　☆

Closing the door, she stepped into a very dull, grey morning. *Shouldn't have done that, I need to control my emotions better. She'll be worrying now.* But Jenny was not going to school. If the world was about to end, what was the point, and she wanted to see if Larson had discovered anything more during the night.

She walked into the shop. Mr Booty was serving a customer a bag of apples. 'Baking today, are we Missus?' he said, handing them to her.

'Yes, Mr Booty, I always bake on Wednesdays. Hey, terrible news about St Ives…'

'Yes, I've just heard it. Hmm, well, I'll tell you what, why don't I give you those apples, and you cut me a slice of pie when you're done.'

The old lady smiled. 'Oh, thank you. That's very kind, I'm sure.' She placed the apples into her big trolley bag and shuffled out, wheeling it behind her.

The door chimed and closed; then Mr Booty said, 'People just get on with it… Do you wanna go up?'

'Yes, please, Mr Booty.'

He pulled open the door behind the counter. 'Off you go then. Mr Larson is in the lounge having a spot of breakfast.'

Jenny rushed through the dark and up the stairs. True enough, Larson was sitting in his chair, blue-and-white striped pyjamas, flat cap on his head, with a slice of toast and a cup of tea on the little table beside him.

'Morning, Frank. Have you seen the news?'

'What?'

'St Ives: it's gone, slipped into the sea apparently. They've only just released it. I guess they had it on lockdown yesterday, you know, in case it was terrorists. Any luck with the, you know what?'

He took a sip of his tea. 'Not goin' to school this morning?'

'No point.' Jenny scrunched up her face and stared down at the carpet. 'Did you feel that earthquake this morning? I reckon, it'll be our turn next. It's got to be her who destroyed St Ives.'

'Um, I know what you mean.' There was a pause for thought then Larson continued, 'I've put the hairy stuff back in the wheel hub. It must be there for something, but I don't know what. It feels like real hair.' Jenny stared at it for a moment on the table; then she dropped her bag to the floor and sat down. 'I've found something though, and if you're not going to school, maybe you would like to come and check it out with me?'

'Why, what is it. Not more berserker trouble?'

Larson smiled then reached over and picked up the main part of the hub with the broken spokes sticking out. He pointed into the hole. 'There's an inscription in here; maybe you've heard of it, *Doniert rogavit pro anima*, which translates as…'

'Doniert begs prayers for the sake of his soul,' Jenny completed.

Larson smiled. 'So you know about the Doniert Stone?'

'Yes, of course, I do; it's a part of our heritage.' Larson handed it to her and she peered in. '*Rex Cerniu*, King of Cornwall, Doniert, the last King of Cornwall.' Suddenly, Jenny had the most terrible thought. 'The Doniert Stone, it's in the parish of St Cleer.' Jenny was thinking that St Cleer was only the most dangerous place she could possibly go to. Every single person living there wanted to kill her.

Larson's eyes met Jenny's, his face full of concern. 'Yes, I know. You don't have to come, not if you don't want to.'

Jenny winced at the idea. 'No, that's okay. I want to go with you.'

'Right, that's good. I'll get dressed and we'll be off.'

Jenny rubbed her hand across the rough edge of a gritty grey tomb stone. She squatted behind it, careful not to be seen. All around her, ancient slabs and crosses stood out of the ground at strange, derelict angles. Many of them had chunks missing, eroded by time, accident and vandalism. *It's like a scrap yard for the dead in here. No one to care for them anymore because the people that did are probably long gone themselves.* She cringed squeamishly at the thought of dead people decaying beneath her feet. *Yuk.*

Larson met Jenny's eyes, and she worried. His flat cap was visible above another gravestone, a short distance from her. 'Can you see it yet?' she whispered to him.

Larson shook his head then moved on to the next, his knees bent like an old ape, his long coat scraping along the ground.

Jenny did the same, running like a trench soldier from one grave to the next, ducking down, waiting a moment and then setting off again when she was sure it was clear.

Suddenly, her eyes lit up: *The Doniert Stone.* In fact, it was two stones and she crouched at the base of the first one, which was called the Other Half Stone. Jenny ran her fingers along the grey pitted eight-cord plaits, which decorated it. She had read about this and knew it was the front. The sides were blank, and Jenny wondered why the work had never been finished. At the top, it had a cross-hair groove. The book said this was where a wooden cross slotted into it, but it was long gone. 'Look at the mortice, Frank,' Jenny breathed.

'Yes, I know about it, and I know what it's for.'

How exciting, I guess Frank's many years have taught him a lot more than the history books. I wonder what it is. Jenny scurried across the ground to the second stone. Kneeling down, she wrapped her arms around it: *the last king of Cornwall*.

The taller stone was five feet further on and closer to the stone wall, which surrounded the church. Jenny knew that on the other side of it were the road, houses and people. It was daylight; how could she possibly check this out properly without being seen by someone?

Once again Jenny ran her eyes over the beautifully designed interlaced patterns. She moved around to the side, touching the words she had previously only read in books, *Doniert rogavit pro anima*. 'Why does Doniert beg for our prayers to save his soul? He must have done something really bad, don't you think.'

Larson was right behind her now – the two of them still very aware that they must not be seen. Jenny felt Larson's hot breath touching her face, and he spoke very quietly beside her ear, 'He did, Jenny – two stones for two kings.'

'What?' Jenny said, alarmed. This was well outside her comfort zone. It was scary enough knowing she might be caught any minute, but to find out that the history books have been wrong all along was beyond belief. *Doniert and Dalgarth are not the same king? If it wasn't simply another name for the same man, then what had happened, and why were they buried next to each other?* Jenny began mulling over the possibilities. She had not read this anywhere; how could Larson know? Was he there? *Was it possible that these two crumbling monuments were built for two magnificent kings? That would mean Dalgarth died before Doniert, of course, because the inscription says so,* The Last King of Cornwall. *And it must be Doniert's monument that Larson is interested in because that one has the same inscription as does the inside of the wheel hub.*

'There's no time to explain now, Jenny; that's another story, for another day. The mortise still stands, and we need to get the wood for the cross hairs from beneath the altar.' Larson turned around and once again set off across the graveyard, but this time towards the church with Jenny running low between the overgrown grasses and derelict stones behind him.

'What are we doing, Frank, if those people see us?' Jenny was thinking, certain death for both of them; probably drowning in the ancient holy well, which stood near the church gate.

'Just keep the noise down and we'll not get caught.'

Jenny reached the old church wall and hid in the shadow of the door. *Oh my God, where is he taking me?*

Larson slowly, cautiously pushed the door open. It creaked very loudly. Jenny looked back, fearful that someone may have heard it, and then she stepped inside behind Larson.

It was dim, lit up only by candles flickering in the light breeze from the open door. Rows of twenty and five deep stepping down gradually, the highest row at the back, the yellow flames dancing on lengths of white wax pushed into a large black iron rod stand. Jenny was mesmerised for a moment; then Larson gave her a nudge. 'Come on, it's this way.'

On the other side of the door, to the left, Jenny passed a stone font filled with holy water. In front of her, rows of wooden benches were separated by an isle down the middle and faced towards the altar at the far end of the room.

Behind the altar, high on the far wall, a massive round window was filled with stained glass. Light shone through it, sending a spectrum of colours down onto a white cloth-covered table.

Larson marched down the side, determination in his step. The place appeared silent and deserted. He turned right at the end of the isle and climbed four steps onto the altar. 'Quick, Jenny, keep up.'

Larson sounded sharp, and Jenny knew from his tone, he too worried someone might come in.

He waved her over and immediately bent down below the altar cloth. Jenny did the same. 'Can you see it, here and here,' he pointed at two lengths of wood and the thick metal plate which held them together. Larson clambered from under the table and jumped to his feet, like a young man would. 'Help me, Jenny. We need to lift off the top.'

Together, with one on each end, they slid the top to the side then carefully placed it on the royal-blue carpet. It was so heavy Jenny could barely hold its weight. Larson stood back, surveying the wooden base; then he stepped towards it, and gripped tight around the longest beam.

To Jenny's surprise, the beam moved upward, but she could see it was very heavy by the strained look on Larson's face. 'Are you okay, Frank?'

'Yes, I'm fine. Now you come here and hold this up, and I'll release the other end.'

Jenny felt the full weight in her arms. 'I'm not going to be able to carry this – it's too heavy.'

'You won't have too. Just hold it still for a minute.'

Larson grabbed the other end and heaved upwards. Jenny could see it was taking all his strength; then it moved. He continued raising the beam above the rest of the table, and then moving it to the side, he rested it and the weight was taken from Jenny's arms.

'Phew, that's a relief, but how are we going to get it outside?

'Don't you worry about that, Jenny, I can manage it. Larson stood up straight, taking in deep lung-filled breaths. After a minute, he said, 'Go check the door; make sure nobody's coming.'

Jenny nodded and ran off down the aisle, past the font and stopped by the door. It was still clear, not a soul around. *Oh my, what are we doing here? Whatever is Frank doing, it can't be worth it. We're certain to get caught, if he's thinking about humping that great big piece of wood across the graveyard.*

Jenny stared down the aisle at Larson. His moaning and wincing drew her eyes to him. *Poor Frank, I can only imagine this must have been what it was like for Jesus, dragging his cross through the streets of Jerusalem.*

The old man dragged his feet slowly towards Jenny, his face pained by the full weight of the wood across his back. For any normal man this would have been impossible, but Jenny knew Larson was no ordinary man. As he drew closer, he stared into her eyes, his determination was frightening, but she knew now why he needed her. It was to check the way was clear. It would be impossible for him to defend himself, with all his strength used to carry the weight of the wooden beams forward.

Jenny ran out into the daylight, quickly searching around for signs of life. It was still deserted and she waved him out of the ancient church and across the graveyard.

She was barely able to watch as Larson toiled, the wood cutting through the grit and dirt until finally they were back at the Doniert Stone. He dropped the wood onto the floor and fell down beside it, completely washed out.

Jenny rushed to kneel beside him, watching, helplessly worrying as his chest heaved unnaturally. She stared into his pale face, straight and gazing down to the earth. 'Are you alright, Frank?'

At first, he said nothing, but eventually after a couple of minutes, Larson said quietly, 'Well, we're still here, aren't we?' He looked up, forcing a smile.

'Yes, but we could still get caught. All it would take is for someone to walk past that wall, and we're done for.'

Larson nodded, talking between shallow breaths. 'Better get this done then, hadn't we?' He climbed slowly, arthritically to his feet, gripping the Half Stone for balance. Lifting one end of the solid wooden beam up, he placed it in the centre of the mortice cross hair. Jenny watched curiously as he lifted up the other end above his head and slotted it into the much taller Doniert Stone.

Jenny thought it looked like a giant fork, the prongs travelling right across from one stone to the other. Now she knew why two sides of the Doniert Stone were blank. The stone was finished. Two great pieces of wood rested on the smooth surfaces. The fork handle stuck out the other side of the Other Half Stone.

Larson took a deep breath and drudged over to the far side of the Other Half Stone. 'Right, I'm going to need your help.'

'What is it for?'

'I'm going to show you now. When I slotted the wood into the mortice, I released a catch in the top of both stones. This one', he said, slapping the Other Half Stone, 'will rotate, and the Doniert Stone should lean over the opposite way, making it stand upright.'

'You mean, it is supposed to be in the ground on that angle.'

'Yes, of course.'

'Oh, I thought it was leaning because it had sunk into the earth on one side. Well, you would, wouldn't you?'

'No, it has always been like that.' Larson pushed against the fork handle. 'Come, Jenny, help me push it round.'

She pressed her shoulder against it with all her might. Pushing, heaving, Larson too, his feet sinking into the soft soil and moss, his arms pressed out like bull horns against the wood.

Suddenly, it began to move.

Jenny gasped, excitement consuming the fear that had filled her mind. *What was going to happen next, and what am I about to discover?* King Doniert's Stone straightened vertically, leaving a large, dark gaping space between it and the ground.

'Right, Jenny, it's up to you now. Go quickly and see what's down there. I will hold the stone and stop it closing, but be quick.'

Jenny stared up into Larson eyes. His face appeared strained, his eyes filled with vigour. 'Slip your hand into my pocket; there is a torch. Quickly, waste no time; I don't know how long I can hold it.'

Jenny gathered the torch and ran the short distance. She stopped, hesitated, afraid. Where once the Doniert Stone had stood, there was now a square black hole and stone steps disappearing into it.

OMG, Frank wants me to go into the hole, but what if he can't hold it. I'll be trapped in the dark forever.

'Quickly,' Larson breathed.

Horrified, Jenny stared back at him.

His eyes bore into her, 'You must go.'

Bravely, she pressed the torch button and rushed down the steps into the dark.

Immediately, blackness and musty moss smells took her breath away and she began drifting into fantasias thoughts. *What is down here? What will appear from out of the blackness?* The torch gave off a small beam which lit up what was in front of it, but bearing down all around her was the thick blackness. *Try to focus*, she told herself, annoyed that thoughts of things leaping from dark corners was not only stupid, but also clouding her purpose.

In front of her, whitewashed walls and pictures of people from Doniert's time or maybe even earlier. Pictures of trees, men riding horses with bows and arrows, and hunting hawks covered the surfaces. *I bet nobody has seen these since the monument was put up hundreds of years ago.* She was thrilled by the thought, *for my eyes only*, and then fear crept back in. There was a river, a man lying in some water and an old woman, wearing a black robe, sitting beside him. *Was this his mother?* Other men and horses appeared to be staring at him also. *Doniert drowned in the river Fowey, a hunting accident,* Jenny recalled from a book she had read and she was sure this was what she was looking at.

But Jenny didn't linger to ponder on the questions the images posed. They would seal her doom for sure. She knew she could be permanently trapped at any minute. *If Larson's strength fails him or if somebody comes into the graveyard, that will be the end of me, trapped in darkness in Doniert's cold, damp tomb.*

Frantically, Jenny shone the torch around the chamber, bouncing the light off all four walls and the ceiling, her eyes searching for something, anything that might help her cause. Suddenly her skin tingled – a cold shiver. Had someone just touched her on the shoulder? She turned quickly, but there was nothing. *Must have been a breeze*, she tried to impress, but how could there be? The silence was all-consuming. She had barely noticed the birds singing, but now how she missed their sweet sound.

Jenny paced out along the wall, the torchlight flicking back and forth from the ground to where she was going. It was about fourteen footsteps; then still hugging the wall, she turned right, walking another ten short strides. Looking across the room, light shone on the steps and a little way along the floor. On either side were pillars of blackness; then Jenny noticed, in the middle between her and the steps, a mound of earth on the tiled floor.

A mingled pile of decayed wood and white dust lay on the

ground, like a fresh grave. In the middle of it, something straight and long ran the length of the mound, glinting in the torchlight.

Jenny approached it cautiously, her chest tightened and dithering, her quick, short breaths whispered into the silence. Slowly she reached down to touch it, excited by what she had found and at the same time frightened.

Dust and bones, this must be King Doniert. Some of his skeletal fingers still gripped tightly around the glinting pole. Jenny ran the torch along it. It was a spear made from a shiny metal of some kind. Jenny thought it unusual: there was no rust, and it appeared to be in excellent condition. Jenny had always thought spears were made from wood and only the tip was metal.

'Quickly, Jenny, get out of there,' came Larson's voice, muffled by angle and distance.

Jenny gasped. *Was he losing his grip? I have to get out.*

She grabbed the spear, tearing it from Doniert's dead hand. His fleshless fingers crumbled, as she did so; then to her horror she noticed something on the wall, which made her stop dead in her tracks.

The picture on the wall in front of her was that of a boy. In his hand, he held the spear and on his back was the tattoo of a bird. She looked around the chamber through the torchlight. The same symbol was all around the upper reaches of the walls. *Why hadn't I noticed them before?* Vultures and they appeared to be flying down onto her. A shiver ran straight down her spine, as it had before when she felt someone pressing down on her shoulder. This time she ran. *This is the spear in the picture, but who is the boy?*

'Quickly, Jenny,' Larson shouted again, but this time he sounded even more desperate.

Her heart thumped out of her chest at the sound of his voice, and she flew petrified up the steps, praying the Doniert Stone would not close on top of her.

Out into the daylight, relieved, she fell onto the earth just as Larson, unable to hold on any longer, released the wood. It slowly rotated back and King Doniert's Stone sealed his tomb once more.

Larson fell onto his side, in a heap.

'Oh no, Mr Larson, are you alright?' said Jenny, running to him. She threw the spear to the ground and knelt, yanking at his shoulder, trying to make him move.

His body lay still on the earth, his eyes closed, as if sleeping, and his skin, unresponsive to her tugging, remained white, like death. 'Please, Frank, wake up, wake up,' Jenny cried, fearing she had lost him. The strain too much for his poor heart, he was dead. *He can't be dead. I'll never be able to stop the witch on my own, even with Johnny; it's useless.* 'Come on, Frank, I need you,' she breathed into his hairy, pointed ear.

Suddenly, just as Jenny was thinking all was lost, Larson opened his eyes and moaned, 'I guess, I must have fainted for a minute.'

'Yes, you did.' Jenny smiled down at him, squeezing his cold hand. 'I thought you were dead.'

Larson smiled back. 'Why, Jenny, you were worried about me.'

Jenny felt her face flush, embarrassed. 'No, not at all.' She could never tell him how fond she had become of him. Not after he left Sam in the cavern to die. She could not understand it herself, liking someone who did that to her friend. It was all a bit too weird. 'What would I have done, all alone out here, with the people of Saint Cleer, everywhere, trying to kill me with you lying there unable to drive me to safety?'

Larson smirked. 'Oh, I'm sure you would have been just fine. You're more resourceful than you think, Miss Chatter.'

Jenny smiled back, pleased.

He rolled off his back onto his knees, and then with Jenny's help, he arthritically struggled to his feet. Brushing down the front of his trousers, he suddenly stopped, catching sight of the spear. 'Well, what have we got here?'

Jenny bent down, picked it up and handed it to him. 'It's King Doniert's spear,' said Jenny proudly; then she waited eagerly, whilst Larson inspected it.

'Where... How?' asked Larson, his eyes crawling up and down the shaft.

'There was a pile of dirt and ash covering a skeleton, and it held the spear on top of it, in the middle of the chamber.' Jenny looked around nervously. 'Do you feel well enough to move now?'

Larson stared down at the earth, smiling. 'Yes, I'm as good as new.'

Jenny found that hard to believe, but she sensed they had already pushed their luck too far, and she was feeling very nervous about someone walking in from the road. 'Right, well, can we talk about this later? Someone's bound to come past soon.'

'Okay, back to the car then.'

Jenny was relieved to hear Larson say that. She imagined him suggesting they put the wood back in the altar table to cover their tracks. That would have definitely seen him off, as it was, his skin remained pale and he looked very frail.

Larson led the way. Back between the tomb stones and derelict crosses to the rear of the church yard. There the Land Rover was parked in a field, behind a hedge. The car had not been touched, and nobody was around.

Sam would have been proud of me, a mission that hadn't failed.

Larson steered the car along the edge of the field and out through a grey metal gate onto the tarmac lane.

'So tell me, Jenny. What did you see down there besides King Doniert's bones and his spear?'

Jenny watched the windows; she still didn't feel safe and knew that until they were closer to home, she would not be able to settle. She had just done the worst thing ever, grave robbing, and not just any grave, but the grave of her ancestral King.

She glanced up to Larson. His eyes fixed on the road ahead, but she could see he was waiting for her to reply with interest. 'There wasn't much in there really, not what you'd expect for a King – just dirt and dust and his skeleton, as I said.'

'That was his coffin, no doubt, made from wood, which simply crumbled away to nothing. At the time, it would have been interlaced with patterns and inscription, but like the crosses, which slotted into the stone, they rotted away and decayed also.' Larson reached into a central compartment, his eyes still on the road. 'Here, do you want one,' he said, offering Jenny a spearmint chewing gum.'

Jenny slid a stick from the packet, unwrapped it and began to chew.

'My mouth's a little dry after all that activity.' Larson smiled. 'So is there anything else you can tell me about the chamber.'

'Yes, there were paintings and inscriptions on the walls. Birds all around the highest corners, they looked like they were going to attack me. I think they were vultures, long necks and big beaks, and a picture of a boy holding a spear; he had a bird tattooed on his back.'

'Hmm, interesting… The bird, by the way, is a condor, from the family name.'

'The family name's not condor; it's Doniert or Dalgarth by association. I read that both Doniert and Dalgarth are the same King, but you said…'

Larson tittered. 'You believe far too much of what you read. Don't you know, they're only guessing? I mean, do you really think people would have placed two monuments for one King?'

Larson's idea was a little unsettling, and she had to admit it was something she had not thought to question. *I must start to question what I'm reading.* 'But how do you know more than the historians?'

He looked disappointed. 'Jenny, you already know the answer to that, don't you?'

Jenny felt her heart aflutter and she raced over the possibilities of what Larson was saying. *No, he can't possibly have been… can he?* Then the words she was thinking slipped quietly from her lips, 'You were there?'

Larson grinned. 'Yes, of course, I was.'

'The Danes?' said Jenny. She remembered Larson telling her that he was a Viking and his mother a sea witch, but never did he mention coming to Cornwall as part of the Cornish–Danish alliance. 'You joined the Cornish Kings when Doniert was a one-year-old?'

'The West Wales Kings,' Larson corrected her.

'Touché, Mr Larson.' At that time, Cornwall was called West Wales. 'Formal names, is it?'

'Okay, Frank. You fought the Anglo-Saxon King, Edgar? You were there, defeated at the battle of Hingston, AD 838? I find that hard to believe.' Jenny was thinking no one could defeat Larson.

'Yes, that is true; I was defeated.' Larson shook his head. 'It wasn't a fair fight. We were outnumbered more than twenty to one. It wasn't worth losing my head – run today, fight tomorrow.' His face looked sad. 'I lost some good friends that day. The young Prince Doniert and his twin brother Dalgarth were only three years old and didn't have a clue what the world they were thrust into was like.'

'So that's it then: two crosses for two Kings.'

Larson nodded. 'The boys and the Queen were moved to the castle, on the far side of the River Fowey. It wasn't safe to stay at Liskeard. Turned out for the best, seeing as we lost the battle at Hingston, only twelve miles away from where we are now.'

'And what's this got to do with the Condor?'

'It was the family crest. Rumour has it that every one of 'em was born with a birth mark which resembled the bird. Apparently that's why it became their emblem in the first place.

Hundreds of years later, in the fifteenth century, William of Worcester wrote about Cradoc, Condor 11, as being a direct descendant of Cornish Royal line. He was made Earl of Cornwall by William the Conqueror. Cheeky swine, as if it was his to give.

However, Cradoc's father, Cador, which means Condor in Cornish, was previously the Earl of Cornwall, but William deposed him.

It's also rumoured that after deposing Cradoc, William suffered terrible nightmares, visited by sea witches they said, so he did the best he could to make amends by reinstating the family through his son. Of course, most of this is rumour and conjecture.'

'But why were Doniert and Dalgarth buried at Saint Cleer?'

'This is where they lived, but there is only one king buried there and two monuments erected. The sea witch took King Dalgarth, the first born, at the River Fowey. There was no body, so they honoured him with the monument. When he died, Doniert became king, but his reign was short. He died soon after his brother, and a second monument was placed beside it.'

'Yes, that makes sense. So how did you know about the leverage beams under the Alter table?'

Larson took his eyes off the road for a moment. He looked excited by the question, even pleased Jenny had asked. 'I was never told about that. It must have been a secret kept for only the closest of Doniert's family or even just his wife and the man that made it. I found it in the book. A diagram and its location were hidden in the words.' He put his hand into his coat pocket and pulled out the A5 book, passing it to Jenny. 'Here, you look, see if you can find it.'

Jenny started flicking through the pages. Back to the beginning, slowly, more pages, frustration building. 'Where, I can't see anything!'

Larson tittered then taking the book he slipped it back into his pocket. 'I'll show you when we've got more time, and I'll tell you the tragic tale of King Dalgarth and his brother, King Doniert as well, but for now, let's try and stop this sea witch destroying Cornwall.'

Jenny peered out of the window. 'I would have found it if my Cornish was better.' They were heading along an unfamiliar road and she was sure something was wrong. 'This isn't the way home. Where are we going, Frank?'

'There's somewhere we need to check out before we head back.'

CHAPTER NINE

Caradon Hill

'We're heading over to Minion village.'

'But why?' asked Jenny. 'Haven't we done enough already?'

'Houseman's Engine House has been partially restored as the Minions Heritage Centre, and I'm hoping we can get into the Houseman's Shaft from there. It's a part of the South Phoenix Mine, where there are two shafts, Houseman's and Parson's. I've heard they're open to tourists now. If I'm right, both mines will be up and running again, along with the other seven or eight, which are scattered around Caradon Hill.

It's been bothering me for some time as you know, and I thought seeing as we're only three miles away, it makes sense we pay 'em a visit. Make sure there's nothing untoward going on.'

Jenny was unsure and afraid; she didn't want to go. *Why is it always down to us? As if we've not been through enough already. I've nearly been trapped in a tomb for heaven's sake, run over by a car, chased by berserkers. Frank doesn't seem to mind putting me in harm's way. Jeez, he even said, he'd sacrifice the few for the many, even his own daughter. I guess he wouldn't think twice about sacrificing me and now we're going underground again.*

Another thought popped into Jenny's head, the one she had when she suggested they check it out, the day before. *Sam… I know it's a long shot; the witch is causing these quakes and that means Sam's involved, but how's she doing it?* The thoughts passed through Jenny's mind in a second, but it all came back to one overriding factor: finding Sam and saving him from the sea witch. 'Okay, Frank, just to be sure, let's do it.'

Larson kept his eyes on the narrow country road, but a smirk appeared on his worried face. 'Good girl, Jenny, just to be sure.'

'You think opening up the mines has something to do with what happened at St Ives, don't you?'

'Aye, I do. I don't know how or why, but it's all too coincidental for me. The mines open, the earthquakes start, and now one of the most beautiful of places in Cornwall disappears into the sea, just before the book of Berserkers, Lichen Throats, and Imps is finally full.'

'The news on the television said there was a fault line in the rock and the earthquake separated it. It could have happened at anytime, and it simply slid away, like jelly off a plate.'

'They didn't say that, did they?'

'Well, something similar.' Jenny tried to smile, but the idea that so many people had died. It sent her a chill.

'I thought not, it would have sounded a bit blasé considering them folks have grieving relatives. You don't believe what they're saying do yer?'

Jenny shrugged her shoulders. 'I don't know… maybe.'

'Well, Bersaba said that wouldn't happen, not without something forcing the rock apart. The idea that a whole heap of rock, the size of the St Ives peninsula, could simply slide into the sea is damn near impossible.'

There was one of those awkward, silent moments, and then

Jenny said, 'Tell me about the last King of Cornwall... What happened to him?'

'Aye, okay, Jenny. We have time whilst we're driving... Dalgarth was the older, Doniert the younger by two hours. Dalgarth was King; it was his right by birth and the young prince Doniert didn't seem to mind. The brothers were very close and Dalgarth trusted Doniert like he could no other; therefore, it was only right it was he, he sent to escort his young bride, Kirsten, from Ireland. But Doniert fell in love with Kirsten and her with him. Now I don't have time to go into all the nitty gritty, but what I can tell you is this: Dalgarth died on the edge of the River Fowey, not far from where the boys grew up.

A woman sat by the water's edge, her black robes covering her head and back. When she turned around, I saw... Dalgarth saw a beautiful maiden. He told us to wait as he dismounted his horse. I warned him not to approach her, guards first Sir, I called, but he told me to stand down. I think he wanted to help her. I mean questions needed to be answered, why was she sitting on the mud flats with her robes soaked through like that? Why was she alone? He should have let me check it out first.

Dalgarth approached her from the side and she gazed up at him. What are you doing here, he asked? She smiled for a second. Then as the King touched her shoulder – it was like the springing of a trap – she flew up, grabbing him in one hand by the throat. She lifted him into the air.

Realising Dalgarth was in danger, I pounced from my horse, changing as I did so. You know how fast I can move once I become a wolf. I was younger then and even quicker. With all my being, I tried to save him. She drew out the spear from beneath her black cloak and threw it to stop my advance, but I was too quick and it flew past my ear. Sadly, I was not quick enough to save my king. The witch leapt into the Fowey taking Dalgarth with her, and we never saw him again.

Word went out to the people that King Dalgarth had a hunting accident and drowned in the Fowey. Herr'a, herr'a, the king is dead, long live the king.'

Jenny stared at Larson, he was living the moment.

'Doniert became king. He and Dalgarth's wife, Kirsten, arranged the funeral. A wooden casket, a grave and a fitting monument erected, as if his body was there. Everyone believed Dalgarth simply drowned in the Fowey and his body was laid to rest at his home in Saint Cleer, close to the court of Liskeard. Later Doniert married Kirsten. That's when my suspicions were first aroused. How long had he felt like this for Kirsten? I spoke with him on many occasions, but it wasn't until three years after Dalgarth's death that I found out. Three years of torment sent Doniert to the edge of insanity. One day I visited his chamber, and he fell at my feet, begging forgiveness. I was horrified.'

'Forgiveness for what?' asked Jenny, intrigued by Larson's tale.

'He confessed had made a pact with the witch, his soul for the life of his brother. He wanted to be the king of West Wales and he wanted his brother's wife. The witch gave him that and he accepted it willingly. It was the first time I had seen wall witches, that day swimming through the stones of the castle at Liskeard. That's why I was so shocked to see them at Sam's house. Anyway Doniert was done for. There was nothing anyone could do to save him. I don't think he believed he had a soul until it was too late; then he spent the rest of his short life worrying about it.

Before he died, he asked everyone in the country to pray for his soul. Ha, as if that could help him. He also asked that the inscription be put upon his gravestone, so even after his death, people would be reminded to pray for him. The poor man was deluding himself, desperate I suppose. I asked the family to rest the spear upon him. At least, in the afterlife, he would have something of hers to fight with in the underworld.'

'So you knew what I'd find in the tomb.'

'The spear, yes, but I have never been in Doniert's tomb. I didn't know it was possible to get in. I was hoping it would still be there, and barring grave robbers, I saw no reason for it not to be.' Larson screeched to a halt alongside a row of other cars outside the Heritage Centre. 'Anyway, here we are, didn't take long did it? We'll have to pop in and find out what the situation is. Now if anyone asks, I'm your father.'

Jenny laughed. 'My Grandfather you mean.'

'What, err, you think I look too old to be your father, do yer missy?'

'Der, yeah,' Jenny blushed a little at the thought. *No one will believe he's my dad; he's far too old.*

'Now, reach inside the glove compartment in front of you and pass me the watch.'

Jenny pressed the button and stared in. There was a folded map, some brown leather gloves, a cap similar to the one Larson was wearing and a tartan scarf. 'I can't see a watch.'

'It's there; try looking under the map.'

Larson was right, but it wasn't like any watch Jenny had seen before. 'Do you mean this?' she said, pulling out a thick black rubbery clock with a rubber wrist strap.

'Yes, that's it.'

Jenny gazed at it for a moment. The clock face was four times bigger than a normal gents watch, and instead of having a second and hour hand, it only had one, which pointed up on two and three digits. There were nine little markers, then the number one and again nine markers, and two, and so on. 'What is this? It looks a bit like a watch, but it's not, is it?'

Larson reached out his hand and took it from her. 'It's an altimeter. Here, look,' he said, pointing at the fingers. 'You can see we're two thousand three hundred feet above sea level at the moment. Sounds about right to me; Caradon is the highest point in Cornwall and the reason the television mast is here. Back home, at sea level, I set the clock to zero and it has gone up.'

Jenny met Larson's eyes, excited. 'Where did you get it?'

'It belongs to a friend of mine. He has one of them flying machines, you know; they look like a kite with an engine and propeller.'

'A microlight, you mean.'

Larson nodded. 'Yes, this is how he knows how high he is when he's flying.'

Jenny frowned. 'So what good is it to us?' *I hope he doesn't think I'm going flying on one of them things.* 'You've got a theory haven't you?'

'No, I'm not sure, but this will tell me how deep the mine is. It may go below zero, meaning it is below sea level. If we can get down the mine, we can measure the depth and make a note. I've got friends visiting other mines and doing the same. I'm hoping it might tell us something about what's going on around here. Maybe what happened to St Ives, we'll see.'

Larson slipped the altimeter into his pocket and stepped out onto a shale path leading up to the newly built Heritage Centre door. It also split off around the back of the building and up the hill.

'This is a bit of alright, innit. I bet they used some of the funding from the Duke to get this place built. Everything looks new and clean.'

'As you'd expect from a building that is less than two years old, don't you think, Jenny?' Larson pushed open the big mahogany door. It had tall narrow panels of glass in it, and on each side, two much bigger panes, giving it a very contemporary feel. Set against the ancient granite of the engine house, it was like two worlds welded together.

Inside the building, a smartly dressed lady, about thirty, with full makeup, smiled, as if she was pleased to see them. She stood behind a reception counter, like those you see in a library. 'Good day to you, how can I help?'

Larson touched his cap and smiled back. 'Good day, Mrs… I was wondering if we could get on one of your tours to see the mine working.'

'Yes, no problem. We have a guide taking people into the mines every two hours. The tour takes about thirty minutes; then you can have a go at panning if you wish. The children love it, ha, ha, ha.' She stopped and cleared her throat, trying to regain her composure. 'For you and your…?'

'Granddaughter, yes,' replied Larson, straight-faced.

'That'll be sixteen pounds fifty, please.'

Larson felt around in his pocket. Jenny saw shock appear on his face, but he exchanged the money for two tickets. 'At them prices they don't need to find any copper or tin,' he whispered in her ear.

'If you go back out the front door and walk around the building, you'll see a group of people waiting for the guide. He's going down in ten minutes. Good timing, Mr…?'

Larson ignored her prying. 'Yes, well, thank you Mrs.' He turned around touching Jenny's arm, hushing her out. 'Right, come on, deary; we don't want to miss the tour do we?' 'Did you call me Deirdre?'

'No, dreary,' Larson sniggered.

Jenny rolled her eyes so Larson could see; then she followed him out without a word.

'Don't want to be telling her more than she needs to know.'

'A bit paranoid, aren't we?'

'I might be, but I don't know who to trust anymore. The less we say, the better.'

At the back of the granite building a group of people chatted, and three children ran about playing. Jenny sensed an air of anticipation and excitement. Another two children stood by their parents; a girl about five was wrapped around her mother's leg. 'I don't think she's going to enjoy this.'

'Tourists,' breathed Larson.

Jenny noticed an element of distaste in his voice and instantly thought, *he's got a cheek calling 'cos he's an outsider too, or maybe he's talking about the little girl; her parents haven't got a clue, taking her down a mine; there's bound to be tears when we go in*. 'If you mean, taking her down? That might be a good thing,' she replied quietly.

Larson smiled. 'Hmm, maybe.'

Suddenly, a door opened at the back of the centre, and a man in his twenties appeared wearing a khaki-green jacket, pants and good, solid walking boots. 'Good day, everyone. My name is Richard, and I'm your guide on this tour of the Caradon Hill mines. Just a few ground rules before we begin. No smoking inside the mine; we might blow up, ha, ha, and stay together. I don't want anyone going off and getting lost; we might never find you.' He chuckled again, but no else did. 'The tour will last about one hour, and I'll bring you back here to the visitors' centre. Any questions?'

No one spoke.

'Okay, then without any further ado, let's get going.' He set off down the shale path in the direction of what Jenny hoped would be the mine entrance. After a few minutes, the man started talking again, which made Jenny think they must be close. 'The Marke Valley Mine is on the north side of Caradon Hill. It consists of Salisbury Shaft, West Rosedown Mine and Wheal Jenkin. It produced a good yield of copper and tin throughout the 1800s.'

A little further on, around a mound of recently cut grass, Jenny saw the dark tunnel entrance, cut into the side of the hill, for the first time.

Surprisingly the roof of the mine was taller than she expected. Jenny imagined crawling around on all fours like in the secret passage between Larson's cellar and the cavern where Sam had been taken. Her body shuddered for a moment, and a pain pierced her chest with a longing to see him once more. But she was able to stand upright and was grateful for that along with the duffle coat, which kept out the dank and chill.

Lights ran along the wall, but they gave off a dim light equivalent to eco bulbs when first switched on. There must be reasons for this? Perhaps low lights mean low temperature and less chance of an explosion from methane gas.

The man at the front didn't say. He was talking about the history of the mine. Larson and Jenny remained at the back, which luckily was their obvious place, as they were the last to arrive. Jenny's ears kept filtering out the man's voice, sending her back to into her own thoughts with a light tremble, as she contemplated when Larson would make his move.

The child at the front of the queue kept crying. Jenny expected it in an eerie place like this. The child's parents tried desperately to quieten her, the mother's voice trying to talk all calm, but behind it a firm I'm-ready-to-explode tension, which everyone else was trying to ignore.

They all spread out and Jenny saw a large round hole in the ground. It was surrounded by a thin metal barrier to stop the tourists falling down, no doubt.

'This is one of the holes where the ore is hoisted up. In the early days, two men used a simple rope-winding system like you see over a water well to bring up a bucket, but later they used horse whims. Eventually, it was done mechanically, using power from the engine houses, as this one is.'

Above Jenny's head there was another hole. She leaned over the barrier to see if she could see daylight through the top of it. A thick rope dropped past her, through the shaft, disappearing into the hole by her feet.

Suddenly, the rope started moving. The guide looked just as surprised as everyone else. 'Careful now people,' he said. 'The whim is moving, and the ore is coming up.' A big circular bucket filled with chunks of broken stone appeared from the hole; it passed through the tunnel and disappeared again above their heads. 'Right, that was interesting. There's not much ore left down here. I think about two loads a day is about it. Let's move on.' He looked very happy it happened whilst Jenny and the others were there, and it seemed to put a spring in his step, as he turned around and led the party deeper into the mine.

'Boy, he's easily pleased. Must feel like he's giving us our money's worth, ay,' whispered Jenny, sarcastically.

Larson bent down to Jenny's ear. 'We need to get down there.' He pointed into the black cylindrical hole in the ground.

'Why?'

'Because men are working down there – that's where the action is.'

'But how, shall we jump into the bucket when it comes back?'

'No, we'll climb down the rope, of course. It could be hours before the bucket goes down again. Two loads a day, the money's definitely coming from the tourists. Sixteen pounds bloody fifty… I'll go first.' Larson wasted no time, straddling over the railing. He held the metal barrier with one hand and reached out grabbing the rope tight then he jumped across, wrapping his legs around it. 'Come on, Jenny, we've no time to lose.'

His impatience barely gave her a chance to consider her misgivings. *What if there is somebody at the bottom of the rope? What if I fall, I don't know how far down it is? How am I going to get back up? Oh crap, here we go again.* She climbed over the railings, and Larson started to shimmer down, disappearing into the thickest blackness.

Inside the hole, there was nothing but black rock all around her. Jenny could no longer see the rope she was holding, it was so dark. She gazed up wondering if she had the energy to pull herself back into the tiny circle of light above her head. That terrified her more than anything else, the feeling of being trapped. No way up and no idea how far she had to ease herself down on a rope she could no longer see. She wrapped her legs around it even tighter. *What happens if the bucket comes down? The rope I'm on will go up and eventually the bucket will hit me on the head, and I'll fall to a certain death.* 'Frank, are you there?' breathed Jenny.

His voice flowed back in a gentle whisper. 'No talking. If they hear you, we are done for. Just keep moving down the rope.'

Thank God, he's still here. The only sound Jenny could hear were her chest heaving in and out, and her hands and feet shimmering down the rope.

She descended as quickly as possible. Eventually there was yellow light below, similar to what she had seen before the bucket passed into the roof, and there stood Larson waiting for her. 'Only a few more feet, Jenny,' he said.

Suddenly, she felt his hands around her waist, she released the rope and he placed her feet gently, silently on the solid earth between two track rails. She turned and their eyes met for a second in the subdued light. Dark shadows cast across Larson's face and his eyes burned orange. This was where he belonged, in the thick of danger; she could see that now. He looked so alive. He dipped his hand into his coat pocket, checking the watch for a second; then he slipped it away.

'What's this?' whispered Jenny, pointing to the ground.

'It's the track for the carriage. It will be near the mine face by now. In it is an ore bucket, which is filled with raw stone blown and hacked off the lode. When the buckets full, it's pushed along the track to the whim, here. The empty bucket is unhooked and the full one attached, and then it's hoisted up out of the carriage and through the roof to the surface. The empty is thrown into it and wheeled back to the face.'

'So somewhere up there in the black is the carriage?' she said, pointing into the dark.

'Yes, but it could be some distance away.' Larson touched the rock wall. 'Can you see the line of different-coloured rock?' Jenny stared up at him and nodded. 'This is the lode line. It runs in seams and the miners have to hack, chisel and blow it away until it finally runs out.

All of this where we are stood now was once the lode, but it's been broken up and lifted to the surface for crushing.'

'Crushing?'

'Yes, it's crushed so they can separate the metal from the rock.'

In the distance, voices echoed along the tunnel mixed with clattering and banging sounds.

Larson pulled Jenny into the wall behind him in response. 'Busy people; hey, Jenny?'

She stared up at him without a word. *He is enjoying this.*

'Come on; let's see what they're up to.' Larson was just about to head off when suddenly he stopped. Something had caught his eye and he bent down immediately to touch it.

'What is it, Frank?'

'Hmm, very curious is that,' he said, running his finger around its smooth surface.

Jenny squatted beside him with a keen interest.

'Here on the lower lode line, between the two distinct colours of rock, a round metal fitting has been inserted into the rock.' Larson tugged on it hard. 'I can't move it; it's stuck solid.' He stood up and moved two metres down. 'There's another one here and look, Jenny, another. I've never seen anything like these before.'

Jenny was starting to feel even more afraid. Being captured by the men was scary enough, but Larson's strained features were starting to freak her out. *What is he thinking? Whatever it is, it must be really bad.*

'We should have gone back. I should have brought Bersaba. She would have been useful with all this rock business, her being a geologist and all.'

'What?'

'Stay here, I'll be back in a minute.'

Jenny instantly put her hand on Larson's arm. 'Where are you going? What do you mean? You're not leaving me here?'

'Just stay quiet and hide in the crevice over there. I can see from here it's wide enough for a little thing like you to slide into.' He pointed to a dark shadow in the rock on the other side of the tunnel by a supporting beam. Jenny did as he asked and tucked out of sight. 'No noise now.' Larson crept down the tunnel towards the men's voices and he quickly disappeared in the black.

Jenny was feeling more nervous than in Doniert's tomb. *What if he doesn't come back and I'm captured by those men. What will they do to me? I'm sure we'll never see daylight again, not if there's something sinister going on down here. Oh my, what was Frank thinking when he saw the couplings in the rock? That's what they are, couplings. Frank knows it, I know it, but what are they for? Why would anyone go to the trouble of attaching them into the rock like that? Frank knows more than he's letting on, I could see it in his eyes, fear… What is that I can hear? The clattering of a shovel and the smashing of a pick, I think.* Then a man cried out as if he were in pain. *A man crying, but only for a second, that can't be good. Something terrible has happened to him.* Jenny gasped. *Someone's coming, I can hear them running this way, boots are getting louder, pace is getting quicker.*

'Arrg!' Jenny nearly jumped out of her skin when something touched her arm.

'Come, we must leave at once… this way,' said Larson, excited and full of furore. He grabbed Jenny's hand and raced back down the track away from the whim to where the men's voices were now silent. There were more couplings in a line all along the wall, but these had thick yellow pipes connected to them, which went up into the shaft's ceiling.

Then, Jenny's eyes fell upon four men laid out on the ground. Dark shapes unmoving, as if they were dead. *It must have been them I could hear talking. What has Frank done to them?* Larson looked straight ahead, down the dimly lit tunnel, focused and determined, not concerned about the men at all. He still gripped tight onto Jenny's hand, her fingers hurting, her bones crushed and her legs barely touching the floor as she flew past. Very quickly her chest began to burn, then the muscles in her legs too. She screamed out, breathless, 'Stop, Frank, please let me rest', but Larson flew down the passage, as if she had said nothing and his life depended on it.

Suddenly Jenny knew why. Hoards of men roared from behind her and then a distinct voice shouted, 'I'll get yer, you no good vagabonds. You won't escape from us; I'll kill yer for being down here', and other voices started shouting vile words, much worse.

The passage came to a sudden end with a high black wall, but in front of them was a wooden ladder which went up some twenty feet to a crooked circle of white. 'It's another shaft entrance. Quickly, Jenny, up you go,' shouted Larson. 'Don't stop and don't wait or you'll be done for. Not even I can beat all these men.'

Jenny raced to the top of the ladder, chest burning, body aching, out into the open air. She stopped and glanced back down petrified into the hole only to see Larson's face pained and trying to kick a man from his leg.

'Don't stop, Jenny, keep running,' he cried, his fingers gripped firmly around the sides of the ladder. The man shouted out, falling back into the blackness; then with a thud it went quiet.

Jenny couldn't stop the hysterical screams which poured involuntary from her mouth. She turned and raced down the hill, faster, faster, her whole body shaking in fiery pain. A second later, Larson grabbed her hand, once more sending electricity along her tingling skin. She instantly flew along much faster, down the fancy shale path and onto the car park. They skidded to a halt at the back of the car and Larson immediately released his grip.

Jenny ran to the passenger door. Larson fumbled frantically with his keys on the other side then it was open and they both jumped in. The key slotted in the ignition, he turned it, the engine rumbled into life and they shot off like a Formula One racing car away from Caradon Hill, before the angry miners could get to them.

Jenny burst into tears. 'So what was all that about?'

Larson sighed and reached into his pocket, pulling out a handkerchief. 'O, come now, it wasn't that bad.'

She snatched the hanky from him and began dabbing her eyes. 'Not that bad? They were going to kill us. It doesn't get any worse than that. We escaped by the skin of our teeth.'

'Well, maybe… I guess we saw something we weren't supposed to.'

'I don't know, sometimes you're incorrigible.'

CHAPTER TEN

The Dangers of Cracking

It was later that evening when Jenny was called to Mr Booty's shop. It had been a full day already, and she barely had time to eat her tea and sit in the big chair in front of the fire, mulling over all the things that had happened. Suddenly, there was a loud knock on the door. *Saint Cleer, Doniert's grave and then Caradon Hill. Hadn't Larson had enough for one day?* Jenny felt fit to burst with all that had happened. She let out a big sigh. 'See you later, Mum. I'm going out with Johnny for a bit.' She closed the front door behind her. As she turned around, Johnny pinched a kiss from her lips.

'Hey, you,' she smiled.

Johnny looked alive, his eyes wild with excitement.

Thunder rumbled through the grey rolling clouds above their heads, reminding Jenny that time was short. *No time to sleep now, no time to settle, no time for fun. I'm sure Frank isn't sleeping at all.* She stared into Johnny's slate-grey eyes. 'So what does Frank wants us for now?'

Johnny linked her hand. 'I dunno, Jenny. Dad, Frank, Mr Booty and Bersaba are all having a meeting in the flat, and Dad sent me to fetch you.'

'Oh, right, I see. It must be pretty important then.'

'Yeah, I reckon so.'

There was a moment's silence, and Jenny pulled up her hood and quickened the pace. Moisture dampened her face and her hair was already wet. It wasn't raining although the looming clouds stretched out their crooked grey fingers and threatened too. It was the dank; it felt thicker than ever before. Every breath tasted like cool liquid in her mouth, and her white socks were drenched from the unavoidable puddles. 'Look, Johnny, everywhere is so wet. The ground is completely sodden. I don't know how much more it can take.' The harbour car park glistened with it, and Jenny stared beyond the estuary to the hill road, horrified. 'I've never seen anything like that before; it's a dirty brown river running down the street.'

The torrent of water gushed over the harbour wall and into the sea.'

Johnny suddenly looked glum. 'I know. If it gets any stronger, it will be taking the cars and houses with it. We need the rain to stop for about a year to let it all dry out a bit.'

'Well, that's not going to happen; by the looks of those clouds there's going to be much more water falling on us. Maybe that's the sea witch's plan, to send so much water down the road that we'll all get washed in with it and drown.'

Johnny sighed, 'Nothing we can do.' Then he turned, meeting Jenny's eyes. 'Where did you go to earlier? I called for you.'

'What, Mum didn't say?'

'She said you weren't home from school yet. It was okay, she didn't look concerned.'

'No, well, it was only four when I got back, so she was none the wiser about where I'd been.'

'And…'

Typical: Johnny, always wanting to know where I am, what I'm doing, who I'm with. Jenny quickly quelled her feelings. 'I went with Frank to Saint Cleer, and then on to Caradon Hill to check out the Minion mine. There's something really dodgy going on there.'

Johnny looked angry. 'Why didn't you call for me? You know how dangerous Saint Cleer is for us.'

'Apparently, Caradon is too. Let's face it, Johnny, nowhere is safe anymore. We could be killed, right now, just walking down the street.'

'I know but…'

'I don't know why Frank didn't ask you to come along. He didn't that's all. If it bothers you so much, then ask him yourself. To be honest, it's a good thing you didn't come. The two of us barely escaped with our lives; with three, someone was bound to get caught.'

Suddenly, there was another boom above their heads. 'It's Thor throwing down his hammer again.'

'Yeah, well, he's supposed to be on our side, with Frank being a Viking and all.'

Jenny didn't think he was funny.

She opened the door; the shop was empty. Jenny felt very strange, like walking into someone's house uninvited. The bell rang but still no one came. 'You'd think Mr Booty would be here; anyone could walk in and take what they wanted.'

'He might not be bothered.'

Jenny didn't wait, marching through the shop and racing up the stairs into the lounge.

'Hi, Jenny, Johnny, nice to see yer again; pull up a seat and we'll get started,' said Bersaba. She was sitting on the couch with a cup in one hand and a note pad in the other.

Jenny glanced around the room. Johnny's dad stood by the kitchen door, warming his hands on a mug. Mr Booty stood next to him, doing the same, and Larson sat in the armchair in the corner as always. Her eyes met Larson's and he smiled up at her.

'Hi, everyone. Have you seen the weather out there? There's a river running down the road.'

'Aye, well, it's to be expected,' replied Larson, in a quiet tone.

'I believe you've had an interesting day,' said Bersaba, much more upbeat and distracting.

'Ha, you could say that.'

Bersaba smiled. 'Yes, my father's told me all about it. A very productive day too, I think.'

Jenny frowned. 'I, I don't know about that; we didn't find anything, except –' She stopped herself. She didn't know what they had found, pipes and things sticking out of walls.

Bersaba stared at the note pad for a second. 'Yes, we have other people who also went into the mines today, and the information coming back is very interesting, to say the least.'

Jenny looked at her glum. 'Is this going to take long? I'm very tired, and I've got the most dreadful headache.'

'Mr Booty, can you get young Jenny a glass of water and couple of tablets, please,' said Larson.

Within seconds, Mr Booty was handing over pills and forcing water down Jenny's throat. 'Whoops, sorry about that. You've missed a bit.' He was referring to the water which was running down Jenny's neck and onto her blouse.

'Never mind that,' she said wafting her hands around. Mr Booty retreated. 'Look, things are really bad out there. I've never seen so much water in all my life, and I don't think we're any closer now to stopping the sea witch than we were last year.'

'Listen, Jenny; we think we've found something very important today. We think we know why St Ives slid into the sea.'

'But how's that going to help us?'

'We think she's going to do it again, but this time on a much bigger scale. St Ives was like a tester, to see if it would work. Now she knows it does, and from what we have found out today, it appears she's almost ready to put her plan into action.'

'What plan?'

'Cracking… she intends to crack the rock along its seams.'

'That's impossible; no one can do that.'

'Yes, well, we believe she can.'

'How,' Jenny asked.

Bersaba ripped two pages from her pad and held them up flat in front of her. She blew hard on them, and the top piece flew forward, settling gently on the carpet. Her fingers still held the bottom sheet.

'Yes, but the papers weren't one piece; they were already separate.'

'We think that's what the couplings are for. You saw them inserted into the rock in the mine. We think they are jets for firing high pressure water into the rock. If they all fire at the same time, the rock will fracture and separate along the lode line. In order to make it slide into the sea, the rock separation will have to be angled so that gravity will force the top to slide away from the bottom.'

'No, that's impossible.'

'Jenny, we've checked the data. The depth of the mine you were in was eight hundred and sixty-three feet below the surface. The mines on the southwest coast, Pendeen for example, are over two thousand feet deep, and they also have these couplings in the rock. As the mines move further this way, they rise higher, but none are higher than the Minion Mines at Caradon.'

Bersaba stopped, took a sip from her cup and Larson took over. 'What we believed happened was the sea witch summoned up the tsunami to flood the mines around St Ives. She forced the water, which had now completely filled the shafts around there, into the jets, and by reversing the engine pumps to suck in instead of suck out the water, coupled with the witch's power, she was able to crack the rock on a downward fracture line, causing St Ives to slide into the sea. The earthquake we felt this morning was St Ives rumbling away from the land.'

Jenny took a moment to absorb and try to make some sort of sense out of the information that had just been put in front of her. There were questions that had to be asked. 'Why have we been messing about around in graveyards and looking in books if all we have to do is shut down the mines?'

'It's not that simple,' said Larson.

'Why is it not? All we have to do is go to the police and show them what they are up to down there then they'll close the mines and we'll all be safe, no more cracking.'

'Who paid for the mines to be opened?' asked Bersaba.

'Em, em…'

'You know this. You and Johnny were there on the hill above the campsite when we first decided we needed to check out the mines.'

'The Duke of Cornwall,' said Jenny.

'And who is the Duke of Cornwall?' Larson interjected.

'The Queen's son, our future King,' she replied again.

'So who do you think is pulling his strings?'

'The sea witch,' Johnny and Jenny said together.

'I've said it before and I'll say it again. It is pointless involving the authorities – they take too long and they can't do anything about it. We have our own people; we'll stop the mines from being readied.'

Jenny's mouth was gaping wide open. For the first time, she realised there were a lot more people involved in this than just the six of them. She cast her mind back to the dreadful day that Sam's little sister went missing.

We sat around the dining table in Sam's house and Larson declared, there is a war going on and it's been going on for hundreds of years. His voice was full of furore when he said it. Before the telling book is full, the boy must come or all will fail. The book is pretty much full, the last page all but complete. Then Jenny had another thought. *This plan couldn't work, no way; Caradon Hill is the highest point in Cornwall.* 'There's one serious flaw in your theory. Caradon Hill is over three thousand feet above sea level; a tsunami won't be able to cover it; the sea will flow around it and on towards Plymouth, like it did the other day. It's not going to flood the mines, and if they're not flooded, she can't inject water into the rock.'

'Yes, we thought that too. I'm not sure how she's going to get around that one, but she must have something in mind. If the pumps are turned off, the mines will flood, eventually.'

'I think the sea witch will want to have full control when this happens. I don't think eventually will be good enough for her.'

'No, neither do I,' Bersaba agreed. 'And she will find a way.'

'Well, that's it then. We'd better pack up our things and get out of here. If the Duke of Cornwall wants to lose a county, who are we to argue. I'll go and tell Mum we're moving east. Kent is supposed to be very nice.' Jenny climbed onto her feet, distressed.

'Sit down, Jenny. You're not going to leave,' said Larson.

'Oh and why is that then. We can't stop what's about to happen, so we might as well go.' Jenny was sounding very upset. 'Too much talk and not enough action – that's the problem. Nobody ever does anything about these things. They talk and then it happens anyway. Well, I'm telling you now, Mum and I are not sliding into the sea.'

'No, I'm not either,' said Johnny.

Jenny grimaced at him.

'You're not going to leave; stop kidding yourself,' goaded Larson.

She placed her hands on her hips, defiant. 'And you're going to stop me, are you? I'd like to see you try.'

Larson smiled. 'I won't have too. You'll do it yourself.'

'And why, why would I?'

'Because you won't leave Sam, that's why.'

Jenny slumped onto the carpet, resting her chin on her hand. She knew Larson was right. She couldn't leave, but what about Mum? She doesn't even know what's going on. Jenny knew Mum wouldn't leave without her, and Larson was right that wasn't going to happen. 'So what are we going to do, Frank?'

'I've told you, I know people, an army of people, and we will destroy the injectors before the sea witch has time to use them.'

'How, now they know that we have seen them? They're not going to be left unprotected anymore. I wouldn't be surprised if every berserker, lichen throat and imp in the country isn't there right now guarding the mines.'

'I agree.'

'You do?'

'Yes, that's why we had to coordinate our visit to the Minion mines with everyone else. Because I knew that once their security had been breached, they'd shut up shop. We can't wait and hope Sam will save us any longer. We have to attack those mines and remove or at least destroy all the injectors.'

Jenny smiled. 'Yes, when are we doing it, tonight?'

'Ha, ha,' Larson glanced at Mr Booty for a second, and then back to Jenny. 'I love this girl; she's so impatient.' His face straightened again. 'Tonight, I'm travelling southwest to make plans with our leaders. Tomorrow night we attack.'

CHAPTER ELEVEN

Agnes

Sam listened intently from the green metal door, his fingers gripped firmly around a handle to stop him being washed away. It was very dark and misty, and huge waves crashed against the bow, spurting spray high into the air and spilling out across the deck. The front of the ship dipped headlong beneath the treacherous sea, and then seconds later she rose up again, high into the thick grey mist.

Sam looked up as forked lightning cut through the mist, like a jagged silver knife zigzagging behind frosted glass. He felt a tremor of excitement rush along his skin.

The noise was so horrendous that it was very hard to hear the conversation going on inside the wheel house. The mighty waves and wind sounded like a car crashing and then skidding on pebbles, as the ship was slammed and the spray spurted over.

It was around 11 pm when the trawler, *Agnes*, rounded the Lizard Point. By midnight, she was almost home and entering the bay, with Sam on board.

'It's been a bad 'un, Captain,' someone said inside the bridge.

'Aye, it has that. Two days out in the North Atlantic... Not even enough fish to cover the men's wages. I can't send 'em home to their families we' yat.'

'I wouldn't worry. They know what they signed up for, a cut of the profits, that's all.'

'Aye, a cut, but a cut of nothing is nothing.'

'Well, let's try our hand here before we go in. We ain't fished these waters for over two years. Stocks will have replenished by now… What do yer say, Captain? Another couple of hours ain't goin' ter matter… might even be worth it.'

The captain sighed. 'Okay, we'll give it a try. Wake up the men and get the beams back over the side.'

Sam stepped back into the shadows and mist as the door opened and a large man of stocky build stepped out onto the deck. He staggered along the side of the boat and past Sam, completely unaware he was there.

Slowly, Sam opened the door and stepped inside, closing it carefully behind him. The sound of the crashing waves dimmed, and the engines hum and warmth became prominent.

The trawler's bridge was dimly lit in an orange glow. Dark shadows marked out the shapes on the instrument panel, which looked like a mixing desk in a recording studio and ran the length of the room's width. The captain was just as Sam remembered him: dark wavy hair falling from beneath his black woollen hat, a strong rugged jaw with shadow stubble, a red rust jumper under a thick grey nylon apron, and long wellington boots. He stared out through the large glass panels into the mist and waves, holding onto the wheel.

'Hello, Bob,' said Sam.

The Captain jumped and turned, shocked by Sam's voice. 'What the…'

'I know. I bet you weren't expecting to see me?'

'Young Sam, is it you? But how? What?'

Through the bridge window, a deck hatch opened and three men climbed out. They started milling around outside in the mist, their dark forms swaying and staggering like drunks, trying to stay on their feet whilst untying ropes and connecting chains. Sam almost laughed out loud, as the men moaned and cursed when the sea poured over them.

'I wanted to be a fisherman. Set my sights on working one of the trawlers, *Agnes* or *Just*, with you. Thought I'd come and ask for a job when I got a bit older, but that's not going to happen now.'

The Captain stared, his eyes alight with amazement and tentative fear. 'I never knew that, Sam. You still can, now you've come back to us.'

'No, I'm afraid not.' He looked down at his bare feet and the water dripping from his pants and down his legs; then he stared back into the captain eyes, solemn.

The captain pulled his thick black jacket together with his gloved hands. He shuddered and then grasped the wheel again. 'You've been missing for over a year. Where've you been all this time? We thought you were dead for sure; and how've you ended up on my ship?'

Sam's dark-brown eyes glared at him for a second, reliving the moment. *Where have I been?* His mind raced back. *A dim torch lit cavern, chanting sounds, the witch, five strands of weed, a bubbling cauldron and fire reflecting on a scabby, barnacled face. It disappeared, became a beautiful face, a loving mother. She saved my life. He remembered being dragged into the sea and to the witch's lair by Hades' gate. Jenny's beautiful face, crying, her delicate fingers reaching out as she was dragged away and* The Sea Witch *exploding in the harbour.* A pain stabbed him in the heart. He was back with Bob Calvert, Captain of *Agnes*, pressing on his chest. He took a deep, shocked breath. 'None of that matters, now. Don't dredge here, Bob. Lift your beams and go home.'

The captain sniggered. 'I'll fish where I like, and no snotty nose kid's going to stop me, even if he has been missing for twelve months or more.'

Sam grinned at him. 'I never saw you as a fool.'

Bob frowned.

'Lift your beams and go home or…'

Suddenly, Sam fell forward, crashing into the instrument panel; then he rolled off to the side and onto the floor. Staring up, he saw Bob held in a tight grip with an arm across his chest and a knife to his throat.

Sam raised his arms, desperately trying to get to his feet and shouting, 'NO.' But it was too late. The knife slipped across Bob's throat and red poured onto the deck next to him. Bob gurgled and frothed, then slid to the deck, his dead eyes staring blankly at Sam.

Where Bob had once stood, the dark shape of Peter Von Strictum licked the sticky, warm blood from his blade.

Sam glared at him and yelled, 'You didn't need to do that.' Using the panel, he pulled himself to his feet with vengeful intent.

Peter smiled back menacingly. 'I know,' he said, coolly; then he started laughing, as the front of the boat nose dived beneath the waves once more.

'You're a real asshole, Von Strictum,' Sam shouted, furious with him.

Peter's face changed, becoming instantly dangerous. He grabbed Sam's collar and dragged him up to his face, snarling. 'You need to get with the programme, Camponara. It's not a holiday camp.'

Sam gripped his arm tight and yanked free; then he ran out onto the upper deck, alarmed. 'Hey, you men,' he shouted over the sound of the roaring sea and crashing waves. They all stared up at him, shocked. 'Abandon ship if you want to live.'

The crew stood silent for a moment, staring, as if trying to decide if Sam was serious.

'Abandon ship, I tell you,' Sam called out again, terrified for them.

The men started muttering, barely audible over the sound of the sea, but Sam got the gist of it – 'What's he doing here? Who's that? Stowaway…' Laughing, they waved their arms at him and then turned their backs and continued to let out the chains which held the beams, one each side of the boat, until they were dragging along just above the seabed.

Oh Jeez, they're all going to die. Sam ran to the edge of the boat, following the chains down to where they disappeared into the thickening mist.

A hand pressed down on his shoulder. It was Peter smiling. 'What the hell, it doesn't matter in the greater scheme of things, does it?'

Sam knew what he meant. *Not long now and the whole of Cornwall will be gone.* 'No, I suppose not, but I know these men.' Sam gritted his teeth and glared. 'I knew the captain, too.'

'Arr well, c'est la vie,' said Peter, shrugging his shoulders.

Sam smiled. 'You're right; such is life – nothing matters.'

'I am right, Sam, and life will be much better when the witch has changed things around here. We'll all be down there together, Dad and Fritz; um, it'll be much better.'

He must be completely insane. Von Strictum and Fritz will be fish food just like the rest of us when the witch has what she wants.

Suddenly, the ship came to a complete stop, throwing Sam and everyone else on board forward onto their faces. It whined and creaked, as if the metal had bent, separated and rubbed, shuddering beneath his hands and feet.

He crawled up and glanced over the side. His heart stopped with what he saw. *So it begins… berserkers.* Crazy people, painted in blue and black, climbed up the chains towards the ship.

The aft upended, driving the bow deep under the sea, as if something massive was dragging it down. The three crewmen cried out in fear and scrambled up ropes towards the ship's stern.

'What's happening, Joe?' shouted the grey shape of a man through the mist.

'I don't know. I guess, we must have snagged something on the bottom,' another voice replied.

'Can't have; the safety would have kicked in.'

There was a heavy thud and one of the men yelled out painfully.

I guess the berserkers have got him. Sam didn't want to see anymore and he dove off the side into the mist. Icy cold water instantly surrounded him. He swam down deeper and deeper until below him a grey mass appeared. He knew straight away what it was, the blurry shape of the sea witch. She was clutching the beam chains and dragging the ship down into a watery grave.

Agnes was the second trawler to go down that night. Sam had tried to save her. She held a special place in his heart, a representation of the life he had desperately wanted for Jenny and himself – a Viking warrior like Frank Larson – how proud she would have been. Sam away at sea with his wife waiting, longing for his return, but now that future could never be.

Sam swam down through the murky depths to stand beside her, the witch, upon the sand. Her beautiful face was alive with pleasure;

a gaping, cracked smile and dark-yellow glinting eyes staring at him. He smiled back, grabbed a hold of the chain, and helped her pull it down.

The Aegis Shield

Jenny sat at the small wooden dining table by the front window. She was up a bit earlier than normal because today was a special day; it was Mum's last birthday.

'How old are you now, Mum, fifty-nine?' Jenny laughed.

Mum was walking in carrying a tray with a plate of toast, two eggs in egg cups and cups of tea. 'You cheeky thing, I'm nothing like fifty-nine. How old will you be when I am?'

'I think you're just checking to see if I remember how old you are.'

Mum smiled and waited a moment; then she said, 'Well?', expecting an answer.

'I know how old you are. I'll be twenty-six.' *Twenty-six... I wonder, what I would have been doing at the age of twenty-six? Married... maybe, to Johnny or Sam, probably? Which one? Err, Sam... Johnny... Sam, Johnny, Sam, Sam, Sam. He's gone stupid.*

'Are you alright, dear?' Mum's stare, looked a bit worrying.

'Oh, yes, I'm fine.' Jenny smiled at her with flushed cheeks, then she remembered what she should be doing. 'Here, I've got this for you: happy birthday, Mum.' She lifted a present from her knee, hidden beneath the table cloth.

Mum reached across the table and pecked her on the cheek. 'I wonder what it might be.'

Jenny was pleased. Mom sounded genuinely excited, feeling it, moving it around in her hands, shaking it and then smelling the paper.

'Come on, for goodness sake, open it.' Jenny was getting impatient.

She carefully eased up the tape and folded back the wrapping.

'Rip it open!'

'Well, I'm thinking if I do it carefully, you can use it again next year.'

'Oh, Mum; we're not that poor.'

'No, Jenny, we're not poor at all… that is lovely, just what I needed. I'm so pleased.' Unscrewing the top, she put a bit on her wrists and rubbed them together. 'A bit more behind my ears,' she said, lightly dabbing; then lifting it right up to her nose, she breathed deeply with her eyes closed. 'Oh yes, roses; it's just beautiful, thank you.'

Jenny smiled and rubbed a bit on her own neck. *For goodness sake, it's only perfume. You would think I'd given her the crown jewels. It is nice though.*

Outside, the rain was lashing down and the thunder was louder now than on the previous days. It kept her awake for most of the night, but she knew sleep was virtually impossible, anyway, with the strange goings on in the Caradon mine and Armageddon around the corner.

The next minute, Johnny ran past the window, his school bag held above his head, keeping the rain off.

Bang, bang at the door.

'He's a bit boisterous this morning, can't wait to see you, 'ay?'

'Ha, ha, very funny,' said Jenny, smiling and running to the door. She opened it and Johnny stepped in quickly, dripping wet and pushing her back gently.

'Let yourself in why don't you.' Jenny was not really bothered, but Johnny had never come in without being invited before. *I hope he's not taking liberties because of what happened the night before last?*

He kissed her on the cheek and she smiled, a bit taken aback. 'Sorry about that, but this weather is awful. The storm clouds are edging along the beach now. What happens when they come over the town?'

'I don't know, Johnny.' Jenny was very worried again. 'Maybe we're all going to drown in a massive flood – you know like the tsunami we saw from Caradon Hill, or maybe we're going to slide into the sea like St Ives.'

Johnny put his bag down and shook off his jacket. 'Narr, I don't think so. Frank's not going to let that happen. Anyway, get your coat on; we're not going to school today.'

'Didn't intend to, not much point. I'm going into battle tonight with Frank's army.'

'No, this is serious.'

Jenny's temper was rising. 'I am serious. I can't think of anything more so.'

'Dad went with Frank and Mr Booty over to Sam's house earlier. They've brought Mr Camponara back here to the flat, and they're going to persuade him to burn down his house.'

'OMG, wait here a minute; I've got an idea.' Jenny ran off up the stairs and quickly returned with the Aegis shield.

'I'd forgotten all about that,' said Johnny. 'Look, it's shaped like a thunder cloud.'

'I know and now we know why. It's been under my bed ever since Sam gave it to me, years ago.' Jenny hastily placed it by her feet, took her coat from the stand and put it on. She picked up the shield again, carefully holding it in her arms and against her chest.

'Bye, Mum, got to go. I'll see you later,' she shouted through the house.

'There's no time to lose. Larson and Mr Booty, along with my dad, must have decided you were right. They have to find a way past into the…'

'They'll not succeed, not without the Aegis shield.' She stepped out into the torrential rain and howling winds. Johnny slammed the door closed behind him, and they ran down the cobbled alleyway to Mr Booty's harbour shop.

'Why, Jenny, what are you thinking?'

Rain dripped off her hair and down her face. She gazed into Johnny's eyes and smiled. 'You'll see,' she said, opening the door. 'Follow me, Johnny, or by God, I'll bash you with this thing,' she said, waving it at him then she marched through the shop.

'Okay, keep your hair on. I was coming anyway.'

'Oh, were you?'

'Yes, but why are you in such a rush; no one's going anywhere?'

Jenny entered the back of the shop taking long strides across the dimly lit store room. 'I'll tell you why I'm in such a rush. Mr Camponara is possessed by the sea witch, so no matter what Frank or anybody else does to him, he will not be persuaded to give up that house. This', she displayed the Aegis shield to him, 'will stop her from clouding his mind. It blocks her out, only then might he listen.'

Past the boxes, Jenny opened the door leading up the stairs into Mr Booty's lounge. 'Hello… Frank, Mr Booty, are you up there?' Jenny shouted up the stairs.

There was no reply.

'Hello,' Jenny sang out again.

Silence.

Then Jenny heard someone moaning. *Mr Camponara?* 'Quick, Johnny.' She raced up the stairs, her heart thumping like fury, her mind whirling, afraid of what she might find. At the top step, she turned, threw the door back and piled into the room with Johnny right behind her. 'Oh my God, what are you doing to him?'

Mr Camponara had his top half stripped bare and his arms tied to the back of a dining room chair.

Standing around him, like three big bully boys, were Frank, Mr Booty and Johnny's dad.

Jenny immediately threw the shield down onto the couch and marched over to Mr Camponara. 'We're not animals,' she said, reaching down, untying his bonds.

'I wouldn't do that, if I was you, missy,' Larson told her.

Johnny stepped forward, but his father glared at him. He stopped and retreated back near the door, instantly.

Larson reached out, gripping Jenny's arm. 'I told you to stop.'

'Why are you doing this to him?' she cried, and Mr Camponara started pulling and tugging frantically at the chair, trying to get free.

'Jenny, we've tried talking to him'

'You've taken his shirt; you're treating him worse than a dog.'

'Aye, well, if that witch is in there, I want to see her coming.'

'But he's Sam's dad; he deserves better!'

Larson stared at the carpet for a second and Jenny sensed he was ashamed; then his vigour returned. 'He won't listen. None of it matters to him, and he tried to shoot us and told us to get off his property. Now we've no choice – we're going to beat the witch out of him. Desperate times need desperate measures.' Larson's voice was filled with urgent fear, and Jenny could see he was at a loss with what to do. He raised his huge hairy fist, dangerously.

'But I've brought this,' said Jenny in a high tone, rushing to pick up the shield.

Larson's eyes opened wide; then stepping back, he ran his hand over his head, knocking off his flat cap. 'Of course, the Aegis shield. Why didn't I think of that?'

Johnny's dad frowned at him. 'Is this the…'

'Yes, it's the one Grandpa P made for Sam,' Johnny told him.

Larson reached out. 'Bring it closer, Jenny, but be careful.'

Slowly, cautiously, Jenny was unsure what would happen if anything. She had seen how it helped Sam dispel his fears, but she had never seen it next to someone who was positively possessed by a sea witch.

After all his frantic movement, Mr Camponara stopped, his chin fell onto his chest and an eerie silence was everywhere. This frightened Jenny more than anything. Something was going to happen, it had too. The sea witch was so powerful. There was no way she would let them take Mr Camponara back without a fight. Jenny started worrying the witch might possess her instead or Johnny or someone else in the room, leaping from one chest to another, any chest so long as the Aegis shield was not attached to it.

Closer, closer, *oh my, take it from me won't you*, fearful the witch might leap at her from out of Mr Camponara's bare flesh chest. She had before. Sam told her the witch leapt out, screaming at him, from Schooner Stevenson. Jenny stared intently at Mr Camponara, as she edged nearer. *Just let that flesh move one single inch.*

Larson cautiously took it from her in both hands. She stepped back a little way. He gripped it tight, and then suddenly pressed it firmly against Mr Camponara's bare flesh. Larson's face, especially his eyes, looked absolutely terrified.

He's never seen anything like this before, just by the look on his face, I can see it. He talked about fighting, Normans and Saxons, wielding swords, years of turmoil, every day, his life about to be snuffed out, but he survived. You would think nothing would frighten anymore, but it does, this does.

Mr Camponara let out the most awful cry; then he began to choke and wretch, his head thrusting forwards and backwards. His ankles and arms, still bound tightly to the chair, which rocked and creaked violently.

Larson held the Aegis against him at arm's length, his eyes glaring.

Jenny's hands came up to her mouth, trying to stop her screams, and Johnny fell back onto the couch in an attempt to get away.

The window shot up and a gale blew in, howling around the room. It whipped across Jenny's face, icy cold and damp.

'What is happening,' she yelled over the horrendous noise of howling winds and witch's cries.

Larson still pressed the Aegis against Mr Camponara's chest, his body straining to hold it there, battling against hurricane winds and something unseen. It couldn't just be the wind alone; something else was trying to force him back.

Jenny fell onto Johnny as the wind screeched past her ears.

Johnny held her there as she tried to get up. 'Get off me,' she shouted, elbowing him in the stomach. Winded, he released her and she ran to the window, sticking her head out, panting for breath. She realised immediately – outside, the cobbled streets, the harbour – it was completely different.

Everywhere was calm and tranquil. Clouds still hung over the bay, but the winds and rain has stopped. She stared back into the room. Wallpaper was tearing from the walls, the lamp crashed to the floor and the wind continued to whip furiously around the room. She had to take another look. *Outside, calm; inside, a raging violent storm; it just doesn't make any sense.* All the bad weather was isolated inside the room.

Suddenly, Mr Camponara threw his head forward and a torrent of water blasted out of his mouth. Larson brought up the shield to protect himself, and the liquid bounced off it onto the floor. It ran across the carpet, snake-like towards the window.

Jenny squealed and leapt up onto the couch, as it ran up the wall and out through the open window, leaving the room with a salty, seaweedy smell.

The icy chill stopped, and Mr Camponara's chin slumped onto his chest and rolled to the side. His eyes closed.

Johnny started fumbling with his coat button, and barely able to get his words out said, 'Is he d-d-dead?'

Larson sighed and shook his head. 'No, the poor man is finally resting.'

Jenny instantly thought about Sam's mum. All the anger she had for her, because of the lack of concern she showed for Sam when Jenny went over to the house, instantly melted away. She grieved for her, and crashed back onto the sofa. 'Where is she?' cried Jenny.

'Who,' asked Larson, shocked, his voice quivering?

'Sam's mum. We need to give her some peace too.'

Everyone stared at Jenny. No words. There were no words, but Jenny knew they all understood. Sam's mum and dad, they have the most beautiful house she had ever seen, but they live in hell.

CHAPTER THIRTEEN

The Most Beautiful House in Cornwall

Mr Camponara pulled on his shirt. Droplets of sweat appeared on his brow and he shook feverishly. 'What the hell happened to me?'

'Here you are, Mr Camponara; sit yer down,' said Mr Booty, offering him a cup of tea. 'You've been through quite an ordeal.'

'I have?'

'Yes. Why, don't you remember?'

'Mr Booty.' Larson glared at him, stern and for a moment there was an anxious silence. 'Right, come on, we have to get off,' he said, all rushed.

Jenny stared at him confused and frowning; then she realised what was happening. *Mr Camponara has to care or it won't work.* 'Yes, quickly everyone into the car, we have to get going.'

Larson met Jenny's eyes and smiled. She took the cup and ushered

Mr Camponara off his chair bossily.

'But… but…' He reached out, wanting the tea.

'We'll make you a fresh one when we get you home,' Jenny told him.

'Oh, okay,' he replied, very confused.

Jenny helped him into the back of the car then walking around the other side, she said, 'Where's Mrs Camponara and Ellie?'

'Bersaba's got them,' he replied, very quietly.

Johnny was climbing into the back next to Mr Camponara. *Thank goodness, he's brought the Aegis shield.* 'Mr Larson, have we got everything?' Jenny was thinking, apart from the Aegis shield, they needed the giant ship wheel hub, the five strands of weed and Doniert's spear, along with fuel and matches. Why? She had no idea. *But they must be for something, and if we're going to Sam's house to open a porthole to the witch's lair, then we need to be prepared for everything.* She felt an uncomfortable tension on her shoulders. *A sub-machine gun would be nice.*

Larson replied from the driver's seat, 'Yes, Jenny, we've got everything. It's all in the back,' then turning the ignition, the Land Rover fired into life.

She smiled bravely, hiding her concerns as she jumped up into the middle. Johnny climbed in next to her. Mr Booty and Johnny's dad sat either side of Mr Camponara in the back.

'Where are we going?' asked Mr Camponara, very confused.

'We're going to save Sam,' Larson told him, as the car hurtled down the country lane.

Mr Camponara smiled, blankly. 'Oh, that is good. I've not seen him since…'

Jenny stared at him, worried. 'What's wrong with him, Frank?'

'He just needs a bit of time. I suppose when you've been possessed for a long time and then you're not, everything is very confusing. He'll be alright, but we need to do this while he still cares.'

'Who… cares about what?'

Jenny ignored him. 'I thought that's what you were thinking.'

'We need to get to that house and fast.' Larson put his foot to the floor making the car zoom up the hill and around the bend even faster.

Within minutes, the car turned left, off the main road and onto the dirt track between the trees and Farndale's field. The trees finished and in front of them was the terrifying house on the edge of the rocks.

Jenny felt her stomach drop and a sickly feeling swept over her.

'Here, Mr Camponara, we're at your house.'

Sam's dad smiled. 'Arr, I do love this house.'

Jenny glanced at Larson, *that's a good sign*, and she knew by Larson's face, he was thinking the same thing.

Mr Booty turned and gave him an approving smile. 'Yes, we know you do, Henry. Is it alright if I call you that?'

'If you like,' he replied.

'That's good because it sounds a lot friendlier, and we're all friends here. Ain't that right, Mr Larson?'

The car screeched to a halt. Larson turned off the engine and reached around, meeting Henry's eyes. 'We are and we want to get your son back for you.'

Mr Camponara looked Larson over suspiciously. 'Sam?'

'Yes, he was taken by a sea witch more than a year ago. Don't you remember that day in the cave?'

He began to frown then his eyes became mad and fiery. He was remembering, bad thoughts, deception and murder. Suddenly, he began to scream and shout. 'It was you. You killed my son. I remember now: yes, you blew up the cavern and poor Sam was crushed to death inside.'

'Think, Henry. We waited in the rain, and when the rescuers brought out the bodies, Sam wasn't with them. The witch took him. She escaped with Sam before the pool was filled with rubble.'

Mr Camponara fell silent, thinking, thinking. Jenny sensed confusion, his eyes and his face like a gateway into his mind.

'We can get him for you,' said Johnny's dad releasing his grip. 'If you want him back, that is?'

Everyone waited, anxious for his reply then finally he said, 'What do we have to do?'

Jenny let out a sigh of relief.

'You have to cleanse the house. It has sea witches swimming through it, and they know what we are saying and doing, so you need to get rid of them.'

Mr Camponara frowned then laughed. 'Is this some kind of a joke?' His face straightened. 'If it is, it's not funny. Now move and let me out of this car.'

'It's not a joke, see, Henry. We can get Sam back for you, but you've got to clean the witches out first.'

'Then why don't you do it. You don't need me.'

'We would if we could, Mr Camponara,' said Jenny. Tears welled in her large speckled green eyes. It wasn't looking good at all and she sensed the only slither of hope slipping away. 'I would do it, myself, anything to bring Sam back, but it has to be you.'

Mr Camponara's eyes fell to the floor, and once more, Jenny sensed a debate going on in his head. After a few seconds he gazed up staring straight into Jenny eyes. She could see he was sad and for a moment she thought he was going to say no. A tear rolled onto her cheek, and she wiped it away with her finger.

Reluctantly, he said, 'Okay, what do you want me to do?'

There was a bit of cheering, a pat on the shoulder from Johnny's dad and 'Alright, Henry, here's what we're goin' a do,' from Larson. Jenny simply smiled reassuringly, knowing that was more important to Sam's dad than anything. 'I've got a can of anointing oil in the back. I want you to start in the bedrooms and pour some out, down the stairs, in the lounge, the kitchen and so on, and then meet me back here on the front porch.'

They all climbed out of the car. 'Anointing oil, aye, and you think that should do it?'

'Oh yes, Sam can't come back here until the house is clear of the witch's spells.' Larson dropped down the boot and reached into the back, dragging the petrol can forward. 'It's a good start,' he said, handing the can to Mr Camponara. 'There you go. Now as quick as you can, let's get this over with.' Larson looked at Jenny and she responded immediately. 'You go with him.'

She nodded and ran after Mr Camponara, into the house.

It was colder in the house than outside. The rooms were dark and eerily quiet. She flicked the switch, but the light didn't come on. She looked up at the chandelier above the dining room table. All the light bulbs had been removed.

Whispering sounds came out of the walls, *Who is this? What is she doing here?* And all the time, from the moment she entered the house, she had a strange feeling of being watched. A shiver ran across her skin, as if someone had lightly brushed their finger over her. Quickly, she ran to the top of the stairs, trying to keep up with Sam's dad; anything was better than being alone, even standing next to a deranged man with a petrol can, recovering from the biggest brainwashing spell ever.

Into Sam's bedroom, he placed the can on the thick soft pile carpet and pulled back the cap. It made a popping sound and the fumes scented the air with a sickly nose tingling odour.

'This isn't anointing oil? It smells like petrol with perfume in it?'

Jenny had a terrible feeling he wasn't going to go through with it. 'No, Mr Camponara, it's anointing oil, alright. I know it smells a bit like petrol, but that's what anointing oils are like. Now quickly, pour it out and let's get moving.'

He lifted the can and carefully poured out the liquid. 'The carpets are going to be ruined,' he said, annoyed.

'Yes, but that's a small price to pay, isn't it?'

Mr Camponara tittered, 'I can afford it. I'll buy some new ones.'

Jenny smiled back at him, mischievously.

He backed out of the room leaving a trail of wet into Ellie's and his own room, and down the stairs into the lounge and the kitchen before emptying the last drops onto the front porch steps. Jenny followed him out. 'Okay, Mr Larson,' he said, straightening up. 'It's done. Carpets are totally shot though. Never mind, I can afford some more.'

'But worth it to get Sam back?' Jenny said lightly.

'Oh, yes. So tell me how does this work? I've done as you asked. I've cleansed the house, but how will this bring Sam back?'

'We're not finished, Henry.'

'There's more? I thought you said we needed to cleanse the house?'

'I'm afraid so. This is going to be very tough for you. Worse than anything you can ever imagine, but it will be worth it in the end. You see, Sam made a wish on the witch's pendant. He asked that his parents get the most beautiful house in Cornwall, and the witch granted it to him. However it would take a very naive person to believe you can really get something for nothing in this world. From that moment he was doomed and you too.'

Mr Camponara fell onto the steps and Larson sat beside him. 'You mean the competition Sam asked me to enter. It wasn't real?'

'No, it was an elaborate hoax. A way to give you what Sam had wished for. The money enabled you to make this into the most beautiful house in Cornwall. Once in motion, there was no stopping it.'

'So what are you asking?'

'We know you don't really care about Sam at the moment.'

'I do, of course, I do.'

'Oh yes, you'll give lip service, mess up a few carpets to get him back, but what we need from you is the ultimate sacrifice.' Larson pulled the lighter from his pocket, flipped back the lid and rolled the flint. 'You must give it all back, every bit of it.'

Sam's dad stared into the flame. His eyes alight with terror radiating from his facial expressions. 'You want me to destroy my house?' He broke down crying onto his arm. 'I can't... Oh God, please don't make me do it.'

Larson reached his arm around Mr Camponara's back to comfort him; then he said quietly, 'Just take the lighter and throw it in.'

'I can't, Frank. I can't destroy everything I've worked for.'

Jenny looked up, away from him, desperate and filled with despair. *That's it then, it's over. I'll never see Sam again and we're all going to die.* Then she saw Ellie with a teddy dangling from one hand and Mrs Camponara holding her other. They stepped forward towards Larson and Sam's dad, and stared down at them.

Mrs Camponara's bottom lip dithered with emotion. 'You can do it, Henry. This was just a dream and now it has to be over.'

He gazed up into her eyes, a broken man. 'No, no, I can't.'

Larson still held the lighter out in front of him.

'You can,' she said firmly. 'It is easier to pass through the eye of a needle than for a rich man pass through the gates of Heaven. Henry, we don't need it.'

His desperate, glazed eyes fixed intensely and he said nothing.

'Do it,' she said again, grabbing the lighter from Larson and forcing it into his hand. She wrapped his hands around the cold silver steel. 'I will help you.' Heartbroken, she flicked up the lid then slowly moved her hands away.

Ellie ran to him, wrapping her arms around him, crying, 'Do it, Daddy. We don't need the house; we've got each other.'

His face was shaking, flushed and tears gushed from his glazed eyes. 'Oh, Ellie… Arrg,' he cried out, rolling the flint and throwing the fire down onto the porch.

Immediately, the fuel burst into flames and ran into the house. It ran up the stairs and disappeared along the landing.

Jenny and Johnny jumped back, shocked by the ferocity. Mr Camponara was dragged away crying by Larson and Mr Booty back to the car.

Trembling with fear and relief, Jenny knew it was to stop him having second thoughts and to stop him killing himself in the burning house. She watched filled with an emptiness of uncertainty as the flames lashed out through the windows like orange whips licking at the air. Was something going to happen and if so, what? Or was the house destroyed for no reason other than to release Sam's family from the witch's curse?

She felt Johnny's hand link into hers, soft and warm. 'Mr Camponara has done what was needed,' Johnny said.

'Yes, but the desperation in his face – it was almost impossible for him to do it. Destroying the thing he loved most in the world. The bitterness it will bring him, the guilt. I hope it doesn't destroy his family.'

'It won't, they'll get over it, and they'll find somewhere else to live.'

'I don't know, Johnny. You hear about families splitting up when they lose something most precious to them, don't you. They can't stand to look at each other because it reminds them of their loss, and the pain is too great.'

'This is different, it isn't real. When we get Sam back, everything will be okay, you'll see.'

Suddenly, there was an almighty crash; the wall witches screamed, haunting the night sky, and orange cinders flew out of the windows and door. Frightened, Jenny ran back even further from the house. 'What was that?'

'It was the floors collapsing. Won't be long and the whole place will be gone.'

'Oh, I hope it is worth it?'

Johnny said nothing. Jenny knew he couldn't possibly know if burning the house down would help them find Sam.

The car door clunked and Larson walked over and stood beside them, watching the house perish. Glass broke in the windows, and the white PVC melted and fell to the ground.

Jenny turned, staring up at his old face. 'Do you really think burning the house down will give us a way to the witch and Sam?'

'Not burning the house, Jenny, but the sacrifice Mr Camponara has just made will.'

Suddenly, aware she was holding Johnny's hand, Jenny shook it free. 'So what are we waiting for? What's going to happen?'

Larson put his hands into his coat pockets and shrugged. 'I don't know, but something.'

Flames danced on the porch veranda fence; then it collapsed onto the grass. Not long afterwards, the roof fell in and it looked like it was almost dead. Black and charred, the house on the edge of the rocks truly was the most horrible house in Cornwall.

Very quickly the intense heat from the fire dissipated. Hours had past and Jenny started to shiver as a cold breeze blew off the sea and across the field. 'Brrrr, I'm going to sit in the car. It's been ages. The house has almost completely been destroyed and nothing has happened.' Very despondent and angry, Jenny walked away, leaving Larson looking extremely uncomfortable.

'But, Jenny, I was certain something was going to happen.'

She glared at him from the car. 'So what are we going to do now?'

'I don't know,' he replied standing there, looking helpless.

'Well, that's bloody great. The book is all but full, and there's nothing we can do to save Sam or ourselves.' Jenny was seething. She climbed into the car and slammed the door shut behind her.

☆　☆　☆

Sometime later, Jenny was startled by someone touching her shoulder and shaking it. She opened her eyes. 'Mr Larson?'

'Shush, Jenny,' he whispered, putting his finger to his lips. His eyes were filled with excitement and Jenny instantly filled with dread. 'I've found it.'

'What?'

'A way in, come and see for yourself.'

Jenny glanced around the car. Everyone was asleep, huddled together on the black leather upholstery. She climbed down from the passenger side and followed Larson to the house.

The flames had died out, now just smouldering black ash everywhere. The shape of a couch, in what was probably the lounge, was barely recognisable. Most of the house covered in piles of black and ash wood, which Jenny assumed had fallen from the ceiling and roof.

Larson stepped over what he could and pushed the rest aside, as he made his way across through the dining room. The stairs had completely gone, but when Larson stopped and peered down at the blackened planks, Jenny pictured Mrs Camponara lifting coats from the back of a door under the stairs.

'Here, come and see,' said Larson, waving her to him.

She ambled over the burnt wood and stood beside Larson, peering down. A large black square hole, partially covered with charred timber, met her eyes. 'What is this?' asked Jenny, disappointed. 'It's not a porthole. It looks like it has always been there, a cellar hatch, like the one in your old house.'

'Yes, it probably has, but the fire opened it to our eyes. It's magical.'

'Oh, Frank, what is this folly?' Jenny said, filled with frustration. 'We've just burned Sam's house down.'

She was about to march back to the car, when Larson said forcefully, 'Wait! I'll prove it to you. Hear me, Jenny, I kid you not, this is the way.' She stopped and looked up meeting the old man's eyes. 'Go down there and then you'll know I'm right.'

She stared down into the dark space, not totally trusting Larson, and with good reason. *He had contrived a scheme that got Sam caught by the witch in the first place. For the greater good he said. Sacrifice the one for the many. Was I to be his next victim, a pawn in a plan he had not yet revealed?* 'You go first and I'll follow,' Jenny told him.

'I would, but alas, I cannot. I am a wolf and the witch will sense my presence immediately. I wouldn't get past the first chamber. You young people, your smell is so much less than that of an old wolf like me. She won't know you're there, not until it is too late for her to do anything about it. That is why you must go, not I.' He reached into the inside pocket of his coat and pulled out a large black rubber-handle torch. 'Here take this with you, not that you'll need it. Once you're in, you'll see with your soul, not with your eyes.

Filled with fear, Jenny took the torch from him. 'For Sam, Mr Larson, to the ends of the earth,' she whispered. Her bottom lip started to dither and she felt cold and prickly all over; she was remembering their last moments together in the cave.

'I know, Jenny.'

Suddenly, wood moved behind her, and she turned quickly to see what it was.

'You don't have to go alone; I'll go with you,' said Johnny. In his hand, he held the Doniert spear and over his other arm the Aegis shield.

Further back, another voice, Johnny's father, said, 'I wouldn't dream of letting you two go without me.' He lifted up his hand showing Jenny the witch's wheel hub and the five strands of weed with a knot in it; then he smiled.

Larson put his hand on Jenny's shoulder. 'I would go with you, you know that don't you? It's only that I'd give you away if I did, and anyway, I have much to do up here.'

Jenny smiled. 'The mines?'

Larson nodded. 'Yes, as soon as you've gone, I'll be attacking at the Minion mines. I suspect every berserker in that book will be protecting them by now.'

'But there are thousands of them,' replied Jenny.

'I know; we'll do what we can to destroy the injectors. Who'd have thought cracking would be the end of us? But truly I believe you're our only hope now.'

A scary prospect, but Jenny was feeling much better knowing that Johnny and his father were going with her. Johnny wasn't such a coward after all.

'Save Sam and kill the sea witch. Good luck to you, Jenny.' Larson picked her up with both hands and dropped her into the black hole in the ground.

CHAPTER FOURTEEN

King Dalgarth

A wet wall of black parted like a ripped curtain. Sam's body cut through it and once more felt the cold, hard stone beneath his bare feet. In his arms, he held some broken decayed wood. A second later, another boy appeared beside him.

Flames flickered from the torches on the damp cavern walls and across the boy's dark rugged features. Sam stared at him for a moment with distaste. 'Following me again, Peter?'

'No, vi vould I do zat, zu mean nozing to me?'

'I was just thinking how you turn up pretty much everywhere I go within a matter of minutes.'

'No, I don't, and anyway, vink vot zu like, I don't care.'

'I will. Just stay away from me.'

'Or vot, vot will zu do Zam?'

Sam glared at him for a moment filled with furore and gritting his teeth.

'Ha, zee, there iz nuzing zu can do, iz zere?' said Peter, raising his voice. He bashed down on Sam's wet driftwood and it fell onto the stony ground. Peter sniggered and walked away looking very pleased.

Picking up the wood, Sam scowled, and then carried it to a man who knelt by the fire. His clothes looked very old, from another time, and his dark hair curled down onto his shoulders. Brown stubble covered his jawline up to his ears and his piercing slate-grey eyes reminded him of Johnny.

'Ah, you don't want to be worrying about him,' said the man. 'If the witch wants to know where you are, she can do that without using the imp.'

Sam smiled and sat down beside him. 'I know, but he always seems to be there; it gets on my nerves.' Suddenly, a woman's harrowing scream made Sam's skin crawl. 'Burr, I still can't get used to that, no matter how many times I hear it.'

'No, me neither and I've been here a lot longer than you.' They both stared into the darkness, where the sound came from, where Peter had disappeared. 'I couldn't walk into that. If I did, I don't think I'd ever find my way back.'

The man prodded the fire with a sliver of wood and embers flew up into the air. 'Hell's down that way, Sam, you stay clear. The imp's already a part of it, but you and me, we're not the same; we'll be consumed for sure.'

But I am an imp, doesn't he know that? Sam thought back to the day in the ICT suit at Ridgemont Secondary when he and Jenny searched for information about sea witches. He discovered how they guarded the entrance to Hades' Gate at the western end of the ocean. Never did he think he would be there, but now he was sure that was exactly where he was, trapped in the gates of hell forever. 'No, I'll not go down there,' replied Sam, shuddering at the thought, but he didn't dare mention what he knew about Hades and the witch's lair.

Suddenly, Sam was distracted, tense for a second, and his eyes shot to the black watery curtain. Two mackerel leapt through and flapped around on the smooth cold stone. Sam smiled. 'Ah, supper at last.' He ran over, collected the fish in his arms and returned to the man's side. 'Do you reckon the witch does that?'

'What?'

'Sends us the fish?'

'Maybe, who cares so long as they keep coming?' The man reached for the long silver knife held on his hip by a dark brown leather belt.

Sam put his hand upon his and their eyes met for a moment. 'I'll show you a better way to gut fish, no mess, no blood.' The man relaxed his hand, releasing the knife with curious, questioning eyes.

Picking up one of the fish, Sam put its head into his mouth and bit down holding it firm; then in one smooth movement he twisted its body with his hands and pulled. The fish head separated from its body and the guts remained attached.

'Aw, that's disgusting,' said the man, staring at the dangling innards.

Spitting the head out onto the ground, Sam laughed at his distaste. 'An old fisherman showed me that back home and now it's come in quite useful.'

The man laughed with him for a second then said, 'And where is home?'

'Just outside Looe, well, Warrington originally,' he replied, whilst walking towards the black curtain. He stuck the fish through it, giving it a shake. When he withdrew his hand, the fish was washed clean by the sea. Sam wasn't surprised; he had done it many times since he arrived. 'Right, let's get it on the fire.'

'Yes, I know Looe very well,' replied the man. 'I've never heard of Warrington though. Can you show me that again, and I'll cook this one for you.'

'Okay, no problem.' Sam smiled, pleased he was of some use at last.

The man set up some twigs on either side of the glowing embers, like two little wigwam frames to support a thin metal rod Sam had brought back from a drowning ship. The fish hung there across the fire spilling oils, making it hiss and sparking life in the form of orange wispy flames and puffs of oily smoke. 'So tell me, Sam, what's your story. How did you end up down here?'

Sam stared at the fire for a moment then back into the man's eyes. 'Not much to tell, really. One night my friend, Johnny, and I stole a boat called *The Sea Witch* to do some fishing. We weren't to know it belonged to her, were we? We didn't know she existed. Anyway, she took Johnny and said she would exchange him for a pendant stolen from her fifty years earlier. It turns out Johnny's grandfather had something to do with it. I went and found it for her. Some old geezer had it, up at Lamorna Cove. I took it from him and gave it back to the witch in exchange for my mate.'

The man frowned. 'And what's wrong with that?'

'Nothing, except before I gave it back, I made a wish on it.'

'Oh, I see, bad mistake. Something good I hope?'

Sam smiled. 'Not worth my soul, but hopefully it has made life easier for Mum and Dad.'

The man lifted the fish from the fire and handed it to Sam. 'Here, tell me if it's cooked.'

Sam took a bite. 'Hmm, yes, it's pretty good… So what about you?'

The man skewered the second fish and hung it over the flames. 'I have absolutely no idea why I'm here. I could understand it if I took something of hers, but I never did. Nor did I make a wish or offend any creature of the sea. It just doesn't make sense, why she would bring me here.'

'You must have done something??'

'No, I've not… nothing.'

'You must have, Dalgarth; you've just not worked it out yet, that's all.' Sam fell silent for a moment. *There must be reason? He looks like he's been here forever. The clothes he's wears are from a different century. He could be a tramp, but I doubt it? What use would she have for one of those? Oh no, if he were a tramp, he would have gone straight onto Hades table, and his body would be a berserker for sure.*

'Maybe she's holding me for ransom. Yes, that must be it; she's waiting to get paid and she'll let me go free like your friend.'

Sam sensed his spirits raised for a moment. 'Oh yes, I forgot, you're a king, aren't you? That will be it then, she's waiting for payment, and she'll let you go.'

Dalgarth stared into Sam's eyes for a moment. 'You don't believe me? I know you're mocking. His hand reached to withdraw the blade and his eyes became fiery with dangerous intent.

'Okay, okay,' replied Sam, smirking. 'I'm only joking with you. If you say you're a king then I'll believe you.' *The guy must be completely insane*. 'So how long have you been stuck down here?'

Dalgarth released the knife. 'I dunno. It seems like forever, but that doesn't mean they're not paying the ransom. It just takes time to gather it together. She'll want a lot of ransom for a king, don't you think?'

'Oh yeah, thousands of pounds,' *Humour him, Sam, humour him*.

'Pounds, what are pounds?'

'Oh, never mind… Tell me again, you're king of what country?'

'West Wales, of course.'

'Ay!' Sam looked at him, confused.

Dalgarth smiled. 'Looe, where you live, it's in West Wales.'

'I dunno, I guess, maybe.' Sam didn't know what to say. Dalgarth had the knife and he was unhinged. One wrong word and that could be it.

'What you thinking?'

'Err, nothing; what do you mean?'

'Your eyes, they give you away. What are you not telling me?'

Sam sighed and stared at the ground for a second. 'Looe isn't in West Wales; it's in Cornwall.'

'Well, that will account for them not paying the ransom. It's not that they're trying to put it together, they're no longer in power and never coming for me are they?' Dalgarth lowered his head. 'Poor Kirsten, I pray she's escaped. My wife, my beautiful, beautiful, wife,' Dalgarth sobbed. Suddenly he stopped. 'Hark, did you hear that… she's coming, she's coming.' Quickly, he scurried into a dark space by the wall.

Sam looked to his left, and there she was beside him, her long raven hair flowing over her elegant black-robed dress. He noticed her eyes immediately; what beauty they possessed, glinting and alive with passion. He perused her soft delicate face, down past her lovely round-tipped nose to plump, red, lush lips.

Only once before in his life had Sam seen lips like those, and that was on a black-and-white poster of Marilyn Monroe in the Looe Art Gallery window. He stopped and looked at it for ages. When it was sold, Sam sensed distressful relief.

An urge came over him to move closer to her, and then a black chair appeared and he sat down into it.

'Hello, Sam, did you enjoy pulling the ship down today?' A sneaky laugh cackled in her throat.

'Oh yes, it was the biggest one so far.'

She ran her long narrow fingers through his hair. 'Yes, it was, wasn't it? I thought we'd save the best 'til last. Tomorrow, I've got a real treat for you, no more boats, something much better.'

Sam stared up into her yellow goat-slit eyes, longing for the answer. *What is it? What could it be?* An excited feeling like the thought of opening presents, desperate to see what's inside and waiting for Christmas and birthdays ran through him all at once.

'Ah… ah… wait until tomorrow,' she said enjoying his eagerness. Suddenly, her face became stern, dangerous and her eyes shot to a dark space on the far wall. 'Dalgarth, you shrew, what are you doing over there, hiding in the corner like some slimy spy? Not spying on us are you? Oh, I bet you are.'

Dalgarth started dithering and shaking his head, unable to speak. His frightened face came forward some way and lit up in the fire's flickering flames. He cried out as if pained, but without a single sound coming from his mouth. A black appendage ran from the side of Sam's chair and stuck to the skin on Dalgarth's chest. It disappeared beneath his fawn-coloured robe.

Sam stared at him coldly. He could only imagine what the suckers on the other side of the black hose were doing to him. Something bad, for sure; the pain was evident in Dalgarth's facial expressions. *Excruciating* sprang to mind, but Sam didn't care. He remained emotionless to it. *How can that be? Have I become desensitised to everyone and everything. I know what I should be feeling. Horror, aberration, sick, but I feel nothing.*

Dalgarth, panicking, reached for his knife, pulled it from his belt and raised it into the air ready to strike the appendage. In contrast to his action, he looked up and stared across the cavern pitifully frightened into Sam's eyes.

The witch flew up to his face, leaving Sam sprawling on the

ground by the fire. 'You don't want to do that, Dalgarth, not if you know what's good for you.'

His eyes dropped and he looked away, slowly withdrawing his arm from the air and placing the knife back behind his belt.

All the time, the witch held her face right next to his, inhaling the scent off his skin. 'Now that's better… remember your place, little man.' She stared down at the appendage on his chest for a second; then she breathed heavily onto the side of his cheek. 'Oh, I can feel your royal blood coursing through my veins. It feels so good, ha, ha, ha, ha.' Her laughing stopped instantly, and she swung around, slapping him hard across the face. At the same time she released the appendage from his chest.

He fell in a heap on the rock-hard ground, dithering with shock.

In a second, she slithered back along the floor, whipped Sam up from the stone and placed him back on her knee in the black chair. Sam knew it wasn't really a chair; it was a part of her, the way she shaped herself, but he didn't care, never even thought about it. Logic said it must be a chair, and beyond that, Sam's mind was lost in oblivion by a cocktail of potions and spells, and the witch stroked him like he was a cat.

He knew it was for her benefit more than his. Glancing beyond the fire into the darkness, Dalgarth was still crouched on the ground, his protective posture expressing how he had just been violated, his back resting low on the wall. Their eyes met, Sam's and his, and he saw Dalgarth's hatred and revulsion for him.

The witch feeds off him. Sam didn't care. He rested his head upon her chest, allowing the witch to comfort him. 'Mother,' he asked, deluded. 'What is happening tomorrow?'

She stroked the hair from his face with her long finger. 'Okay, I'll tell you,' she said. A smile swept across her face and her eyes lit up. 'We're taking back what is ours.'

'We?' questioned Sam.

'Me then,' she replied in a low voice. 'There used to be more of us, but now there's only me.'

'Is your name Sthenno or Euryale?'

The witch stared at him suspiciously, creasing her brow. 'Why would you want to know that?'

'I only ask because I have read about them in school.'

'My name is not important, only what I do.'

'I understand, it's not important to me either; I'm just interested that's all.' There was an uncomfortable silence; then Sam changed the subject. 'So what are we taking back?'

'Some of the land, we're giving it to the sea.'

'But why?' asked Sam.

'The Earth throws it out to release the pressure inside. It's like puss spewing from a swollen boil, all that hot molten earth. It's ugly, uneven, creased and it rises up out of the sea, so I wipe it away and put it back under the sea where it belongs.'

'But more land is better, isn't it?'

'It's more than we need. A little is okay, but this is a world of water, and it's my job to keep it that way.' Suddenly, the witch looked up and sniffed at the air, agitated. 'Can you smell that, Sam?'

'No, I can only smell mackerel burning on the fire.'

She sniffed the air again, her face becoming taut and strained. Something was wrong.

'What is it?' he asked.

'Something that should never be here, a wolf,' she cried, throwing him from her knee and rushing off, splashing through the stream into the thick blackness.

Sam's body lay sprawled out on the stone next to the crackling fire. For a moment, he didn't want to move. *A wolf, how can that be; there are no wolves down here?* He lifted his head, dazed, only to be confronted by Dalgarth standing over him.

'I don't know what you are, but you're not like me. I thought you were, but you're not, nor are you an imp, or a berserker. Yes, I've seen them all, but never one like you.'

Sam felt the force of Dalgarth's boot beneath his ribs, knocking the wind from his body. He curled up in pain trying to catch his breath. For a few seconds, he feared he would never breathe again; then his diaphragm contracted, stretching his lungs, filling them with air.

'Why did you do that?' cried Sam, through gritted teeth.

'What the hell are you? She nurses you like a baby – it's disgusting.'

Sam lowered his eyes, sobbing on the ground. 'I don't know what I am… I just don't know anymore.'

CHAPTER FIFTEEN

The Pit at the Bottom of the Bay

'Wait for me,' breathed Johnny through the darkness.

Jenny turned quickly, shining the torch up into his face. She smiled put her arm around him, and they hugged for a second. 'Sorry for rushing on, but at first I thought if I didn't, I would turn around and go back.'

The torch lit up part the rickety staircase past Johnny and the others to where she entered the lair. Once not so long ago, there had been a large square of white, but now there was only thick blackness.

How far down she had travelled, it was impossible to tell. Blackness has no depth, and Jenny hoped that Larson had put some good heavily-charged batteries inside the torch. The idea it may go off at any minute terrified her. 'Look, the porthole has closed; there's no way back now.' Jenny felt Johnny's shudder as he stared back, but she was more at ease with that. There was no option now: she had to go on and they had to find Sam.

The staircase sloped around the muddy wall and cold, damp splinters from rotten wood rubbed off between her fingers. Worse still, the old wooden banister rail moved in her hand as if it was coming away from the ground.

Above her, damp earth quickly changed to stone then smooth rock. She touched it with her hand. 'The wall, it feels wet.' Then the creaking, moving wood beneath her feet became solid stone steps also.

'It's no wonder Sam was picked by the witch. His house was built right on top of her lair,' said Johnny.

Jenny concurred, 'He didn't have a chance, but we're going to find him and bring him home, aren't we?'

Johnny didn't reply.

She didn't like that. *He wasn't confident they could do it, or surely he would have agreed.*

Mr Pothelswaite, who followed close behind Johnny, said, 'If you believe what *The Book of Black Magic and Revelations* said, and you believe Sam is the boy in the picture, then you might think it was his destiny to move into that house.'

Jenny continued to walk very carefully down the large stone steps. They reminded her of the steps leading down to the boats from the harbour. 'Perhaps it didn't have to be that house. Any house would have the steps leading to the witch's lair, as long as the owner was willing to give it up to save someone she had taken. Having said that, I believe Sam is the one, and I think I've worked out some of the riddle in the book.'

Johnny's voice sounded excited by her words. 'What do you mean, Jenny?'

'Sam comes from Warrington.'

'And?' Johnny replied, sarcastically.

'Sam come war, a wedding band, which is a ring, and a heavy weight, which is a ton: War-ring-ton.'

'Oh yes, it is Sam. He's the boy in the book, isn't he?'

'Well, it sure looks that way.'

Suddenly, the torch flickered then went out. Everything disappeared into the blackness, and Jenny gasped terrified, pressing against the cold, stone wall. *Oh my God, I can't see anything. How can I go on? I can't, I can't.* She started to shiver all over and her bottom lip quivered. 'Help me, Johnny, please help me; I can't see anything.'

'I don't know what to do. I can't see either,' he replied in a terrified tone.

'Don't panic,' whispered Johnny's father. 'Keep one hand on the wall and the other on the rail… Okay, now slowly turn around and feel your way back up the steps.'

Jenny was about to do just that when she was filled with determination and furore. 'No, we can't go back, we have to find Sam, now more than ever and anyway the hole it has gone.'

'No, Jenny, we have to go back. How can we go on when we can't see anything? What good would we be anyway? The hole, it might still be there,' said Johnny.

'Well, you go back then, but I'm going on.' She threw the torch down over the side, more through anger than anything else. It seemed to take ages before it made a quiet thud sound.

'What was that?'

'It's okay; it's only the torch; I threw it over the side.'

'That sounded a long way down,' said Johnny.

'I don't care, I'm not going to fall and I'm not giving up.'

'But, Jenny, someone might have heard it.'

'Well, at least we know it's not a bottomless pit, like your grandfather said.' She made her way down the steps, feeling each one carefully with her shoes. It was taking ages and every ounce of courage not burst into tears. Unexpectedly, Larson's voice came into Jenny's head like a cool breeze whispering through the cavern. *See with your soul, Jenny… Yes, of course, I had forgotten that. I don't need a torch; I can see without it.*

She couldn't – her eyes searched around, but the blackness was overwhelming.

Larson said I can see without a torch, so why give me one if I didn't need it? It doesn't make sense. Closing her eyes tight shut for a second, she started to picture the banister she was holding, the meandering path leading deeper and deeper under the sea and the cavern roof and stone wall, which had once been earth at a higher level. *I guess it was a comfort thing, something to get me on the right track. Would I have walked away from the porthole without it? I don't think so.*

Jenny opened her eyes and there it was: everything in monochrome, but well defined. She turned around quickly. Johnny was still behind her. She knew he would be. For all his moaning, he wouldn't leave her all alone, she knew that. 'Can you see, Johnny? Close your eyes for a second and think about where we are, and then open them again. You've just got to give your eyes time to adjust.'

Johnny closed his eyes for a second, and then opened them again. Jenny saw a broad smile spread across his face.

'Are you okay, Mr Pothelswaite? Can you see too?'

'Surprisingly I can, yes, better than through the beam from your torch too. Now I can see everything'

'Move aside, Jenny; I'll lead us down.' Johnny sounded brave and enthusiastic, ushering her out of the way.

She smiled up at him. 'Oh, you will, will you?'

'Yes, it makes sense. I've got the Aegis shield and Doniert's spear. The sea witch won't know we're coming if everyone's behind the shield, and if I see something nasty, I'll stab it.'

Down, down, deeper into the black and grey passage they went. A salty, seaweedy smell became more prominent over the mustiness Jenny recognised earlier. 'I think we're under the sea, Johnny.'

'Yes, me too,' he agreed. 'How long do you think it will take us to reach the bottomless pit in the bay?'

'I don't know. Let's just keep going,' Jenny told him.

'Well, I can't believe all this exists… I'll tell you what though, it does give me hope that we might find Sam after all,' said Johnny's father.

'Shush, Mr P, please don't say it – you might jinx us.' Jenny dared not to think anything beyond the next step. She had seen the witch's power that day in the cavern near St Cleer. She'd seen Sam too, his eyes glazed over, totally possessed. Even if she did find him, how could she possibly save him from that horrible creature and from himself? *One step at a time, that's all I can do. To the ends of the Earth, Sam, that was my promise to you. Would you have done the same for me? Yes, I'm sure you would.*

Johnny was moving much faster now, almost skipping down the steps, but as quietly as possible. Still there was the tapping from six feet, which worried Jenny; it might give them away. The steps finally finished onto a stony incline. It was nowhere near as steep as the wooden stairs, but still, it felt like she was walking down a mountain path.

Droplets of salty water fell from the ceiling like tears, reminding Jenny she was in a passage with a lot of water on top of her.

'What are we going to do when we get to the bottom, Mr P?' asked Jenny, hoping he and Mr Larson had put together a plan.

It was soon dashed.

'I dunno, Jenny. I guess, we'll just have to see what we come up against, and then figure it out.'

'But the plan is to save Sam, right?'

'Yes, more than anything, but if we can stop the sea witch at the same time, that'll be even better. Crikey, if we can't, we may not have a home to go back too.'

Jenny was relieved to hear him say Sam was his main priority. She remembered how he had said, I'll follow that lad into hell if needs be. Well, that might be about to happen, but Larson had another agenda. He would sacrifice anyone of them to get at the sea witch, but now she felt sure Johnny's dad was not like him.

A few paces further on and Johnny cried out, 'Oh Jeez', sending Jenny a wave of electricity through her skin, and he came to a sudden stop trying to back up. His spear and shield clattered onto the ground, and Jenny gasped as she stumbled into Johnny's back.

Something, someone appeared from a crevice in the wall. Out of the thick blackness, burning eyes, a bald head and painted Celtic pattern skin held Johnny by the throat. It lifted him from the ground and started shaking him violently. Johnny yelled with each jerk.

Immediately, his father pushed Jenny out of the way and she fell against the wall, shocked. The word 'berserkers', slipped from her lips, but everybody already knew what it was, and he rushed at it to save his son.

The berserker's head shot to his direction with piercing yellow eyes meeting grey slate in the darkness. Still it held Johnny by the throat, but now very still. *It's a standoff.* Johnny's father held up the wooden hub, as if he was going to slam it down on the berserker's head at any second.

Jenny was petrified for him because she knew no amount of pain would stop a berserker once it flipped. There was no way he could win. It would simply toss them all over the side into the abyss. *So is this where it all ends, right here, before we even see the sea witch or Sam?*

She sprang back onto her feet, determined. *If I'm going to die, it won't be without a fight.* Suddenly before she could reach it, the berserker fell to the ground, by Johnny's feet.

Jenny pressed forwards, peering around the side of Johnny's dad, to see what had happened. 'Chief Inspector Brindleblack, what are you doing here?' she gasped.

In his hand, he held a blood covered knife. For a moment, he appeared shocked by what he had done, and then he smiled. 'I guess the time I spent with the Special Forces wasn't a complete waste after all.'

Mr Pothelswaite patted him on the shoulder. 'No, I guess not. Well done, Chief, I don't know what I'd have done, if you hadn't shown up, but what are you doing here? We thought you died in the sea, two years ago?'

Immediately, Jenny's mind went back to the night Sam gave the pendant to the witch. Chief Inspector Brindleblack cowered on the deck at the front of the little mackerel-fishing boat and the men on the other vessels started shooting at her. The witch ignored them, taking the pendant and cackling rapturously as she lowered back into the icy water. Sam and Jenny hid behind the Aegis until all the shooting had stopped. When Sam lowered the shield, Brindleblack had gone.

He wiped the knife clean on the berserker's filthy, torn shirt and placed it in his jacket, inside his breast pocket. 'No, the evil bitch dragged me over the side. Most of the time I spend down here, but occasionally I get out.'

Jenny was very confused. He sounded like a proper jail bird. 'But why haven't you escaped, up the stairs where we have come from?'

'I didn't even know they were here; in fact, I'm certain they weren't. I get to move around, pretty much wherever I want down here, and I can assure you there were no stairs until now.'

'It must have been Sam's dad who opened the porthole. His sacrifice made it possible. Larson was right.' Jenny felt a shrill of excitement at the idea of an anti-spell working against the witch. She stared up at Johnny's dad. 'So what are we going to do now?'

But Brindleblack interjected before he had time to speak. 'Well, I don't know about you, but I'm gettin' the hell out of here, up that incline… a porthole to the surface you say.'

Jenny reached out, grabbing his arm. 'You can't, Detective Brindleblack. Please, we have to save Sam.'

'That's okay. You can do that… you don't need me.' And he went to move off again.

'Oh yes, we do. We wouldn't have got any further than where we are now if it wasn't for you. You can lead us to him. You said yourself about how you move freely down here. Show us where he is.'

He leant against the stone wall and stared at the ground. 'This place gives me the creeps… Look, it won't do you any good. He's not like us. In fact, I don't know why she hasn't squished me a long time ago.'

'What do you mean?'

'Sam's one of them now. We can't help him.'

'He's not. I don't believe you,' Jenny retorted, holding back the tears.

'He is, I tell you. You cannot save him.'

'Then take us to him and be on your way. We won't need you

after that in any case, and the steps will still be here for your get away.'

'Yes, just do that one thing for us,' interjected Mr P.

There was a moment's silence and the atmosphere felt thick with fear as they waited for an answer.

Suddenly, a woman screamed, a terrible shrill of a scream, the sound travelling from inside one of the passages a long way off. Nevertheless, Jenny thought she recognised the voice, and a heavy lump dropped in her stomach at the thought. *Oh, Bersaba. What are you doing down here?* 'Poor Mr Larson,' fell from her lips, and everyone stared at Jenny, sensing his loss, feeling for his pain.

'She's a brave lady, Jenny,' said Mr P.

A tear ran onto her cheek and her bottom lip quivered as she uttered the words, 'She was a brave lady.'

Mr P nodded. 'Yes, she was,' he said in a low voice. 'She gave up her life to lead the old hag away from us. She knew the witch could smell her coming. Now let's not waste the time she made for us. Let's finish the job.'

Brindleblack took in a deep breath and clenched his teeth. Jenny assumed the policeman in him had stirred and he said, 'Okay, I'll do it.'

CHAPTER SIXTEEN

The Minion Mines on Caradon Hill

The rain was falling harder than ever. Strong torrential rain poured from angry, dark clouds. Larson hated it, being patted all over and soaked through to the skin. Even his head felt wet, the rain penetrating his flat cap, but he had to get a better look. What was going on over at Minion?

He stared through binoculars from the hill at St Cleer across the land ruined by the tsunami and up to Caradon Hill, the highest point on Bodmin Moor.

People corrupted by the witch moved around on there – hundreds of them, maybe thousands, black antlike creatures scuttling back and too around the hill below the engine house level.

The sun was about to set and things were going to get much darker, too dark to see anything from so far away even for him.

'What do you think they're doing?' asked Mr Booty, who was equally as wet and staring through his own watery binoculars.

'They don't appear to be doing anything, just patrolling and guarding the place from people like you and me, I shouldn't wonder.'

Mr Booty laughed out loud. 'People like you and I. We ain't no people – you've been settling in for too long I think…You ain't never going to be one of 'em.'

Larson stared at Mr Booty for a second. 'What you saying?' Mr Booty didn't reply. 'I'm shocked. I thought you fit in better than anyone. Serving people every day in the shop; I've seen you laughing and joking with them. It was me. I struggled most of all, that's why I chose to live alone in the woods. I was always worried they could see who I really was, but hey, none of that matters now. I have a fondness for 'em. We was one of 'em too in a different life, and we still fight for a common purpose. This land is equally important to you, and me, as it is to them.'

'Do you think they know what is about to happen?'

'Not the people around here, but I'm convinced some do, the people who make the decisions, the Duke of Cornwall for example. He set the mines running again at great expense to himself, and you'll notice how few military and police there are around here? You'd think the place would be swarming with 'em after what happened over at St Ives. That decision must have come from the top, so I reckon the Government must be involved.'

'But why… who would allow this to happen to their own land?'

'It's greed, Mr Booty, no more than that. The men at the top lining their own pockets. They know what damage is being done by cracking the rock. They don't care. They'll simply hop on a plane and live out the rest of their lives in gravy. It's the poor souls left behind that pay the price, losing their health, everything they own and grieving over lost kin.'

Suddenly, as the last of the daylight disappeared, Caradon hill exploded. An orange, yellowy flash, and then rock and dirt hurtled into the air. Larson and Mr Booty instantly dropped to their knees unable to take their eyes from it. Beneath their feet the ground started to rumble.

'What is happening?' shouted Mr Booty.

Larson hands tried to steady him, spread fingers disappearing beneath puddles of muddy water, which were all around him. 'It's the aftershock from the blast.'

'Is this it then? Is this the end of us?'

Larson stared into his friends eyes, unsure. 'I don't think so. I expect it will get much worse.'

A few moments later the ground stopped moving and Larson stood, desperate for a closer look at what damage has been done to the hill. The smoke and dust quickly settled, damped down by the heavy rain. Binoculars to his eyes, he could hardly believe the devastation. Caradon Hill was no longer the highest point on Bodmin. Larson stared down on a giant crater, and all seven mines were now clearly visible like turrets around a fortress.

'What has happened? Why have they done this?' asked Mr Booty.

For a short while, there was nothing to say. It didn't make sense. The little black figures were climbing onto their feet and moving, but now they were around the top ridge of a huge crater.

'They must have known what was about to happen. That's why they were lower down than the engine houses, keeping intruders away from Caradon Hill.'

Larson stumbled, pressing hard upon his chest and would almost certainly have fallen to the ground if Mr Booty hadn't reached out and caught him.

'What is it?' whispered Mr Booty, filled with concern.

'I've lost her,' Larson cried. 'Bersaba, she's gone.'

Mr Booty lowered Larson onto a large wet rock. 'But you cannot be sure. How… how could you know?'

'I know alright. The witch has found her. She didn't stand a chance. Oh, what have I done?'

'Well, if she has, you did what you knew you had too. It's always been her destiny and yours. You made the oath with him up there and now you've had to pay the price. I warned you, didn't I. I told you not to pray for such things as children. I knew it would end in pain.'

'No, no,' wailed Larson. 'I could have refused. I should have sent her far away when I knew for sure what was about to happen.'

'You could not, and anyway, nobody knows what is going to happen from one day to the next. She could have run around down there for days without ever being caught. The witch might have been killed before…'

'The witch cannot be killed and still I made her go.'

'She chose to go; it was her decision not yours.'

'I, only because I told her she'd been sent to us for a purpose. It was I that put that in her mind from the day she could walk. Now she's dead, and worse than that, the witch has her soul. Oh God, why did you make me do it, why did you make me sacrifice my own child?'

Mr Booty slumped onto the rock and wrapped his arm around Larson's shoulder. 'Don't let Bersaba's sacrifice be for nothing. Let's stop this mayhem and do what we always knew we had too. I know she can't be killed, but she can be stopped, it says so in the book of Revelations.'

Larson looked up, staring across the dark valley towards Caradon Hill and the Minion mines. The cold had entered his bones and he shook from it, that and the rain and the shock of losing what was most precious to him. It struck his heart, a searing pain in his chest, and he spoke in short sharp breaths. 'Do you think Sam can do his part?'

Mr Booty climbed to his feet carrying a massive weight upon his shoulders. 'I don't know, Frank. We can only do ours and nothing more. We've got to stop them cracking the rock and sliding Cornwall back into the sea.'

'Yes, you're right, my friend. Bersaba's life will not be lost in vain. We must get inside that crater and stop them cracking it.' Larson rose arthritically from the boulder, helped up by Mr Booty, and together, they made their way through the knee length wet grass to the car.

'Do you want me to drive?'

'No, I'll be fine,' replied Larson, opening the creaky door.

The internal light came on, and from the back, Mr Camponara stared into his eyes. It quickly became clear to Larson that he had been watching from the car. 'Are you alright, Frank, what has happened?'

Larson tried to summon a smile, ignoring his questions. 'It's good to see you're feeling better.' He turned around on the seat and fired up the engine.

'Yes, I am. It's as though I've been asleep for ages and now I'm raring to go.'

The light went off again. 'That's good, see, 'cos you'll need to be alert from now on,' said Mr Booty.

'Oh, why is that?'

Larson's hands slammed on the wheel and then gripped it tight. The four-by-four bounced over what had become familiar ground, through the trees and out onto the tarmac road.

Mr Booty's eyes shot to Larson for a second and then back to Sam's dad, his face lit up by the lights on the road. 'It's time for us to fight back, Mr Camponara. The book of Berserkers, Lichen Throats, and Imps is all but full and we're going to try to save this place of ours.' He pulled a handgun from inside his coat pocket. After checking it over, he handed it to Sam's dad. 'Don't aim it at someone unless you intend to kill them. Head shots only, if you please. Anything less will not stop them.'

Mr Camponara inhaled a long, deep breath, and then took the gun and stared at it before meeting Mr Booty's eyes once more. 'So who are we going to kill then?'

'The berserkers on Caradon Hill; we'll be there in a minute or two, so you ready yourself.'

'Ah, now don't you be working him up, Mr Booty. You'll have him shooting at the first thing that moves,' Larson tried to joke.

Mr Booty slipped his hand into a side pocket and pulled out a handful of bullets. 'Here, now put these somewhere safe.'

Mr Camponara took them from him, hiding them away in his coat pocket.

'Gun's already loaded, so they're just for back up. And Frank's right, don't be letting me work you up too much. Be careful what you're shooting at, ha; I don't want to lose a leg or nothing like that.'

The car ground to a halt on a dark country lane. Larson turned off the lights and swung open the door. 'Come on, we're here,' he breathed, reaching down the side of his chair for the shotgun.

Mr Booty jumped out and immediately unbuttoned his long coat. 'How far have we got to walk?'

'Around the next bend, you'll see.' Larson clunked the door closed as quietly as possible and led them along the edge of the tarmac. There were no footpaths, just the road lined with bushes, prickly thorns and barely visible stone walls. On the other side of the road there were no walls at all, and dark shapes crept closer towards them. 'Holster that gun, Mr Camponara. It's only sheep having a nosy.'

Sam's dad didn't reply and the three men soon came around a bend in the road and were able to see past the stone wall. Larson stopped for a second, grabbing a hold of Mr Booty's coat. 'Up there,' he whispered. 'See the camp fires on the hillside?'

Small orange-white lights dotted Caradon higher up and around the hill until they could see no more. Larson had no idea how many berserkers had gathered around each one, but there were hundreds of little lights.

'We'll never beat all of them,' said Mr Camponara.

'We don't need to. If we can sneak past and destroy the engine houses with some of Mr Booty's dynamite, then it's job done.'

Suddenly, there was a rustling sound, and fifty or more dark human shapes appeared from out of the bushes and the grass.

Mr Camponara pointed his gun immediately and was about to fire, but Mr Booty quickly pushed his hand towards the sky. 'Whoa, now you hold on there, young fellow. That ain't no berserker; they're on our side.'

'What do ya mean? You didn't say anything about there being more of us. You should have told me. For God's sake, man, I could've shot someone.'

Mr Booty chuckled quietly. 'I doubt that. You haven't even taken the safety catch off, and Jethro's a lot quicker than you might think.'

The man closest to them stepped forward, holding out his hand. Larson shook it. 'Good to see yer, Yian.'

'You too, Eric. It's been a long time.'

'Please, call me Frank; we're amongst friends.' Larson shot a glance and a smile at Mr Camponara.

'I know the tale… that day in my house when you told me about Eric the Red and Madema your sea witch mother.'

'Call me Frank, anyways. I've grown quite used to it over the years and that way there's no confusion.'

Yian nodded.

'Is everything in place,' asked Larson.

Yian grabbed Larson's upper arm and smiled. 'Yes, everyone is in place from Looe to Wadebridge. We must be ready by ten o'clock. If one of the engine houses blows early, then the witch will be onto us and could still achieve her goal. We must stop them all at the same time.'

'But Caradon Hill is the vital one, right?' asked Mr Booty.

Yes, I think so. This one's at the centre of the county, and there are more mines close together here than anywhere else. If we stop the Caradon engines, then the others won't, or should I say, shouldn't be able to destroy Cornwall. Obviously, there will be damage, but it won't be the end.'

'Ten o'clock, you say?'

'Yes, Frank.'

'Mr Booty and I, we'll take the South Phoenix mines. It has two engine houses: the Houseman's Shaft and the Parson's Shaft.'

Yian nodded. 'I'll take some men round to the north side and destroy the Marke Valley mine. It has three engine houses: the Salisbury Shaft, the West Rosedown and the Wheal Jenkins.' He turned to Jethro, who stood beside him. 'You take the South Caradon. It has the Jopes Shaft, Rule North Shaft, Rule South Shaft, Kittows Shaft and the Sumps Shaft. Sumps is the deepest, going down some fifteen hundred feet, and it is imperative you destroy it.'

'No problem, Yian,' replied Jethro.

'Have you got enough dynamite?'

'Yes, we've got enough to blow up the Houses of Parliament.'

Yian sniggered. 'Hopefully, that won't be necessary.' Turning back to Larson, he said, 'When we have time to talk, we'll find shelter and reminisce on happier times for a while, my friend.'

Suddenly, Larson noticed a dark figure sneaking along the wall, at pace, towards them. He gripped his gun tighter.

Yian turned following Larson's gaze, and then patted him on the shoulder. 'It's okay; he's with us.'

The man was out of breath, resting his hands on his knees for a second. 'Yian, you need to come see this.'

'What?'

'I know why they blew the mines. It created a bowl and the rain's collecting in it. Already it looks like a small reservoir.'

Yian stared at the man with blank eyes, and then Larson realised what the man was saying. 'Yes, of course, the water will fill up the mines and the ground above, and the engine pumps, which are situated all around the top of it, will drain it off and force it into the rock.'

'No, I don't think so,' said Mr Booty. They all stopped and stared, waiting for him to explain. It wasn't often Mr Booty said anything, even in the old days when Yian knew him well. 'The earth has collapsed into the mines creating the bowl. Nothing can get out of there with all that weight on it and then there's all the water on top of that, tons of the stuff. But if the tubes attached to the engine-house pumps run through what are the now collapsed mine shafts and into the injectors you saw in the rock walls, the water from the bowl will be pumped directly into the rock, making it crack.'

'Yes, well done, Mr Booty. Without creating the bowl shape to capture the water in huge quantities, the rock could never have cracked, not here on Caradon.' Larson pushed back his coat sleeve and stared down at his wristwatch; it was nine o'clock. 'We need to get up there to take a closer look.'

Yian nodded. 'I look forward to speaking with you when this is over.'

They grabbed a hold and shook each other at the shoulders, and then up over the wall went Larson, Mr Booty and Mr Camponara. The men around them, Yian, Jethro, and the others seemed to disappear into the blackness and pouring rain, like ghosts fading to another time.

Trudging up the slippery incline quietly was almost impossible. The ground was completely saturated by the torrent pouring from the skies. It whipped at their faces like icicle knives. Larson was torn between searching for danger and using the rim of his cap to protect his face. He pulled his coat up tighter around his neck, carefully stepping over the bracken and slippery grass edging, which ran along stone walls separating the fields.

Larson, consumed by the idea he could bump into a band of berserkers at any minute, was starting to get nervous. He had come up against berserkers before in the cavern. Soulless, wretched creatures once they went into a rage, they killed anything and everything close to them. It made his skin crawl and he shuddered at the thought. The berserkers here were similar to the ones that killed his wife and fourteen-year-old son back in Helsingborg. They had travelled from Copenhagen some said, but to Larson's surprise, they did not travel alone. Fighting alongside them were hellhounds and imps. It was only when Larson saw them did his resolve start to diminish. He knew at that point this wasn't just men fighting men, even if they were crazy.

Something much more sinister was behind that force, something frighteningly evil. His village was destroyed that day, but he and many like him, those that survived the battle, had succumbed to the curse of being bitten by hellhounds.

That feeling was back, like acidic butterflies flapping around inside his gut. Up above him a silhouette of the first engine-house came into to view, standing out over the top of the ledge and a dark-purple sky. 'Stay alert now,' breathed Larson. 'We're very close and in amongst them for sure.'

Mr Booty slowly pulled his sawn off shotgun from beneath his coat. Mr Camponara and Larson stared at him for a second. 'I've been keeping it warm and dry,' he said, as if their eyes were questioning.

'Are you feeling alright, Mr Camponara?'

'No, Mr Larson, I'm pretty damn terrified actually.'

'Yes, me too,' replied Larson, trying to muster a smile.

He sneaked a few more paces and squatted by a metal farm gate, and then signalled his friends to get down. Beyond the gate was the car park where he and Jenny had stopped when they visited a few days earlier. It was completely barren of cars, and the visitors centre was in total darkness and unnaturally quiet.

Where is everyone? Larson knew they must be here, but where? He was feeling sick at the thought of running into them. *Was it a trap? They've allowed us to get this close, so they could surround us and pounce from all directions. No, berserkers are not that clever.* He inhaled a deep breath through his nose. 'Can you smell anything, Mr Booty?'

'Nothing,' he whispered back. 'Not even the grass. It will be the rain damping the dirty screbs' scent.'

Larson nodded and stared between the bars towards Houseman's Engine House. It was so close, he could almost taste the copper and tin inside, but something was holding him back. Was it fear of the inevitable or the idea he was about to be caged by berserkers on all sides. The fluttery feeling grew stronger.

'Come on, Mr Larson, it's going to be daylight at this rate,' urged Mr Booty.

'It just don't feel right.'

'You're telling me, it don't, but we've got a job to do, and it ain't goin 'er do itself.'

Larson gritted his teeth and slowly scaled the metal gate. It rattled ever so slightly, sending Larson a shivery chill.

Suddenly, a roar of angry voices choked the air and a swarm of bald, gangly human bodies flew out from around both side of the brick building. They were like thousands of dangerous, killer wasps, shooting out of a disturbed nest.

'Jeepers, Mr Booty, run for it,' shouted Larson, leaping backwards from the gate and running down the boggy field as fast as he could go.

Mr Booty grabbed Mr Camponara by the arm and raced after him through the darkness and away from the intended target.

Within seconds, the berserkers jumped the gate in crazed pursuit. Larson heard it rattle and shake, but he didn't dare turn to see.

Oh my God, we're not going to make it. 'Run faster, Mr Booty,' yelled Larson, 'the berserkers, they are gaining on us.'

'I'm going as fast as I can,' he shouted back 'But poor Mr Camponara, I'm going to have to let him go.'

Larson stopped instantly, his lungs burning like fire. 'No, Mr Booty, you cannot do that.' He turned swiftly grabbing Mr Camponara's other arm. His eyes alight with adrenaline and fear because the bald-headed creatures were almost upon them.

Mr Camponara moaned as if in pain, his feet barely touching the floor now the two men were dragging him along.

'I've got to stop… I've got to stop,' cried Mr Camponara. His legs gave way and for a short distance until the men could drag no more, Mr Camponara felt the front of his legs being dragged through the cold wet and mud.

It was useless. Larson let go of his arm and Mr Camponara's body flopped to the ground. He felt the furore he had earlier drain from his body as thousands of berserkers poured down the hillside towards them. All hope obliterated, he waited for the first of the berserkers to reach him.

For a moment staring into Mr Booty's eyes, he saw the same thing. No hope. They hadn't managed to blow up the engine house; the witch had surely won. Cornwall would slide into the sea and be lost forever. A huge sense of failure swept over him. *I've let everyone down and especially my beautiful Bersaba, who gave everything to save us. Maybe Jenny and Sam will succeed, Oh, well, I won't be around to see it.*

The first line of berserkers was only ten feet from them, ferocious and wild. Larson focused on the one closest to him. Black eyes set in a bald head, an emotionless straight face, and a curved metal-cutter, gripped and whooshing the air in dead fingers. It moved forward at the same continuous pace, as if Larson wasn't even there, but then its hand came up ready to swing a deathly murderous blow.

And for the first time Larson heard fear in his old friend's voice. 'Frank…' uttered from his lips.

'I know,' Larson replied in a faint tone. He closed his eyes expecting the heavy blow, sharp pain then what?

Suddenly, the sound of a shot. Larson instantly jumped and opened his eyes. The berserker dropped its weapon and slumped to the ground in front of him. All around the field, hundreds of black mounds rose up from the ground and turned into men firing automatic machine guns. The noise was horrific and deafening, and almost immediately, a high-pitched ringing echoed around Larson's head.

A moment's relief then dread. *I'm alive at least, but now the witch knows we are here. She'll also know we're onto her plan because we approached the engine house… or does she? How is information transmitted from here to her, and how does she tell the berserkers what to do, even if it's simply to kill anything that comes close?*

All these questions ran through Larson's mind in a second. He was in the midst of battle, and thousands of bullets shot across the field. He ran past the first line of them, fire and thunder reeling from the guns nozzles into the darkness, like a million exploding fire flies.

The berserkers still charged forward, jumping over the fallen and dead like rabid dogs, desperate to grab at them, their fingers reaching out and strained.

'You can fire that gun now, Mr Camponara, if you care too. Remember head shots only, if you please,' shouted Larson, trying to get the message to him above the almighty cracklings and rip of bullets.

'Mr Booty heard him too. He nodded and smiled and then blasted his first shot into the nearest berserker. Its head exploded and the body fell to the floor. Another followed quickly behind it, and all three of them let off round after round, whilst gradually retreating down the hill.

'Are they never going to stop,' cried Mr Camponara. 'They're still pouring over the gate like rats from a barrel?'

Larson could tell by his trembling tone, he was terrified. 'Just keep firing and make every shot count if you want to get out of this alive.'

Mr Camponara pulled his hand from his pocket. He opened it up revealing four small cylindrical bullets. 'This is the last of them.'

'Here take this,' shouted Mr Booty with furore in his voice. Swiftly, he pulled from beneath his long dark coat a small axe.

Mr Camponara took it from him and immediately lashed out at a berserker who was about to jump on top of him. He smashed it to the sodden ground and retreated a few more paces further back.

Larson smiled, his body tingling from the electricity. It ran all along the surface of his skin, making the hairs stand up. He swiftly clicked the gun barrels and stock shut again, and then blasted another berserker to kingdom come. In that moment, Larson was back in the old days; he had become Eric the Red, once more in the thick of battle. 'Ha, ha… When you're closest to death, you feel most alive don't you think, Mr Camponara?'

Mr Camponara stared at him for a moment, eyes alight emanating terrible fear.

Larson loved it, his face ever changing from smiles to fiery determination and then something caught his eye, filling him with dread.

On the top of the amputated hill and black against a purple sky, lightning flashed in sheets of white, followed by rolling, rumbling thunder. The huge black pumping arm started slowly moving up and down above the engine-house walls, and grey whirling smoke bellowed from its tall cone-shaped chimney stack.

CHAPTER SEVENTEEN

Wolf

Sam held his ribs, recovering his breath, and his head remained for a moment on the ground. Dalgarth strolled back and squatted by the fire. The light flickered from the flames onto his long dark hair and black eyes. 'So are you just going to lie there all day or what?'

'I might,' replied Sam.

'Oh, come on; get your backside over here by the fire. I didn't beat you that hard.'

Sam sat up and scowled at him. 'You're only saying that because you're afraid the witch might come back and see what you did to me. If you hurt me, she'll rip out your heart.'

'Maybe she will, and maybe that wouldn't be such a bad thing. No prospects here, cold stone floors and fish. I am used to someone making my meals – and proper meals too – not this crap. Venison, wild boar roasted over a spit, hmm, peacock, swan, goose and pheasant, so much glorious food I've had and now I live off this.'

Sam sat back down beside him. 'Oh, just stop it won't you; this is it, there is no more. Fish and cold caves are all you're ever going to know from now on, and you're no longer a king either. The witch is in charge, and it's time you got used to it.'

'I'll always be a king, for as long as I live. I am Dalgarth, King of Cornwall, taken hostage by a raggedy old sea witch, and one day I'll return to claim my rightful place.'

'So you keep saying. Well, I hate to break it to you, mate, but Queen Elizabeth is the ruler of our country.'

Dalgarth smiled, his eyes lit up and he appeared excited by the news. 'My wife, Kirsten, had a baby? Elizabeth, Queen of Cornwall, well fancy that.'

'What? No, mate, you misunderstand me. Queen Elizabeth of England; Cornwall is a part of England now.'

Dalgarth's face changed to anger in an instant. Clutching Sam's neck, he pulled him up to his face, dribbling and drooling, his eyes alight with fire. 'You'd better be joking, boy.'

Whoa, this guy is a real loony. He put out his hands, as if in submission. Dalgarth was a lot older, rougher and tougher and Sam knew it; a new tact was needed. 'Okay, I can see you don't find this funny, so I'll not do it again, I'm sorry, mate…'

'King.'

'I'm sorry, King. I won't make fun again. I'm sure your people will have you out of here in no time, and then you can go back to your wonderful rich life.'

Dalgarth settled, staring at the fish smouldering in the fire; then he looked up into Sam's eyes. 'But for now, just 'til that happens, you could go out and bring something really tasty back for me. You're not tied to this place like me, are you?'

Sam didn't hesitate. 'It's not going to happen. I never leave here unless my lady asks me too.'

'Ha, your lady,' said Dalgarth. He appeared confused or at the very least disgusted.

Sam started swooning. 'Yes, she is beautiful, don't you think?'

Dalgarth's face cringed. 'You poor deluded creature. She is the ugliest, most grotesque thing I have ever laid eyes on. How can you even put her in the same vein as a woman… Where is the wretch anyway?'

'Don't call her that, she's good and kind and gracious.' There was a moment's silence then Sam continued, 'I'm not sure where she is. She did say something strange just before I fell from her knee though.'

'Her knee? She hasn't got a knee.'

Sam climbed to his feet. 'I don't think I want to sit near you anymore. You're a complete loon.'

'I'm a loon? You're the one smooching up to the old hag.'

'What are you talking about? Old hag! I'm going to get real mad with you in a minute.'

'Oooo, I'm scared.' Dalgarth withdrew his knife part way from its sheath, and then slid it back equally as slow.

'I think I'll just get my own fire going over there. I don't need you.'

'Now don't be too harsh, Sam. Let's stop all this falling out and bury the hatchet.'

'I thought you might say that. Struggle to get you own firewood, seeing as you can't swim out there.'

'Okay, I give up. If you're happy, who am I to argue? What did she say?'

'What do you mean?'

'She said something strange?'

'Err, yes, she said *wolf*.'

'Wolf?'

'It must have disturbed her something terrible, considering the way she flew off upstream into the darkness.'

'But that was ages ago; I thought she might have returned by now.'

Sam met Dalgarth's eyes, questioning. 'You look at me as if I should know where she is… I'm not her keeper.' He stared into the darkness, trying to see if anything was there. 'I know you said we shouldn't, but what do you say we take a quick look around. I'm curious where Peter goes too.'

Dalgarth smiled. 'You said it, but hey, what the hell.'

'That's what I'm worried about.'

CHAPTER EIGHTEEN

The Houseman's Engine

'Look, Mr Booty, the Houseman's Engine, its turning.' Larson felt a sudden desperation to run towards it. It had to be stopped.

All around him men were crying out, pounced upon by thin, crazy, mindless bodies, but he didn't care. A sea of them stood between him and his goal, but how could he get past all of those creatures?

Worse than that, the berserkers started picking up dead bodies, holding them up and using them as shields against the relentless hail of bullets. They were no longer falling, but moving forward much faster, running over and stamping on the civil soldiers, as if they weren't even there.

These creatures are not so mindless after all. Larson's eyes lit up; it gave him an idea. 'Mr Booty,' he yelled, drawing his attention for a second. He picked up one of the bodies and slumped to the ground, dropping it on top of him. Watching through half-shut eyes, he saw Mr Booty and Mr Camponara do the same.

The berserkers raced down the hill with an almost inhuman roar. It was so loud, it drowned out the sound of gunfire, until eventually there was no one left on this side of the hill, who were able to shoot. They were either dead or seriously wounded. Larson feared the worst, but the roars soon faded into the distance, leaving just mellow tones of painful whimpering wounds.

Slowly he moved his head and gradually opened his eyes. Peering up from behind the berserker's corpse, the purple black clouds rumbled and rolled with white crackling electricity. Large drops of rain patted on his cold face, making him squint and blink. Cautiously, he looked around the dark hillside, eager to get moving, but not so fast as to draw attention to him. 'Mr Booty,' he whispered.

He waited a moment then a voice breathed back along the sodden ground, 'Yes?'

'Can you see anyone?'

'No, not standing.'

'Neither can I, I think they've kept going down to the road.'

'So do I.'

'Mr Camponara, are you alright?' asked Larson.

'Yes, I think so,' he replied, in a weak tone.

'Right, then let's get moving.' Larson rolled the body off to the side and climbed onto his feet. An acrid smell of gun smoke and iron hit the back of his throat, leaving a taste like chewed up spent firework in his mouth.

Mr Camponara stood up beside him shaking something off his hand. 'Awe, I didn't realise blood was so sticky.'

Larson smiled, unintentionally licking his lips at the thought then his cheeks flushed, slightly embarrassed. He pulled his cap down at the front, tightening it around his head and ears. 'Come on let's go.

We haven't much time.'

Above them was the stone wall and cow gate Larson had tried to climb earlier, and beyond that, the engine-house arm rose up and fell back in a black silhouette against the candescent sheet of cloud.

A crack of thunder… Larson jumped. Someone touched his leg, clutching his trousers. He stopped and stared down for a moment trying to contain his compassion. Sad, sorrowful, eyes gazed up at him, and a reaching arm beckoned. 'Sorry, son, I can't help you now,' said Larson, stepping away. Mr Camponara bent to his aid, but Larson spoke sharply and he stood. 'Leave him… we haven't the time.'

'But…'

There was a moment's hesitation; then Larson said, 'Okay, Mr Camponara. You see what you can do for him. Come, Mr Booty, we must fly.'

The two of them bent low like trench soldiers, hurrying towards the gate, and then without hesitation, they leapt over it and scurried across the car park to the side of the immense brick building. He pressed his hands against the cold stone and stared almost disbelieving his own eyes. Yes, Yian's man had told him what had happened here, but this is where the hill continued to rise up gradually above the engine house to the highest point in Cornwall, where a telegraph tower pointed into at the sky. Now there was only a ridge where the earth fell away into a huge bowl shape.

Suddenly, there was another wave of light running through the clouds and off into the distance. It reflected in the bowl where Caradon Hill had once been. 'Jeez, Mr Booty, the basin, it's almost completely full of water.'

'Aye, millions of tons of the stuff, and it's all going to be forced into the rock if we don't hurry.'

Larson's eyes shot around the lake ridge. Plumes of smoke were rising from all eight engine house which surrounded the bowl.

In the distance, gunfire and the roaring cries of battle started again. Larson's heart was aflutter again. He realised why the berserkers had moved on instead of returning to the top of the hill. They had defeated the men here and were now defending the engine houses from Yian's men on the far side.

'What we going to do, Frank?' asked Mr Booty.

Larson knew what he meant. They could never shut down all of the engines, and destroying this one wouldn't be enough to stop the rock from cracking. 'I don't know,' he replied, defeated. 'All we can do is finish this one and move on to the next.'

'Ha, ha, Zu ain't finizing anyzing, Eric.'

Larson didn't dare move. He felt something hard, cold, barrel-shaped pressing against the back of his skull. In front of him, Mr Booty gasped and his eyes widened emanating the way Larson felt inside. Worse still, he recognised the voice pointing the gun. 'You're not fishing today then, Azure?'

'What do zu mean?'

'*The Enchantment* or should I say *The Sea Witch*, she's your boat?'

'Ha, zu think zu are funny. I know it waz zu who blew up ze boat with the horrible children.'

Mr Booty jumped about on the spot. 'Well, that isn't strictly true, you know. That was probably my fault,' he said holding up his hands, shotgun dangling from his fingers.

Von Strictum glared at him. 'Shut up zu stupid old fool or you'll get zit first.'

A hand moved in from the corner of Larson's eye, taking the gun from him.

Larson turned slightly to see who it was. 'Ah, Fritz, I thought you died in the cavern.'

'I bet you wished I had.' His face became stern, and he bludgeoned Larson in the shoulder with the butt of Mr Booty's shotgun then his face changed, and he smiled, enjoying Larson's pain.

Larson winced, rubbing his sore flesh. 'Well, how did you escape?'

'We weren't there. Me and Azure it wasn't our time. We had taken the berserker from the giant ship's wheel down to the holding pen before you set off your bombs. Another few minutes and we'd have been back. Ha, you missed your chance.'

'I got your son though, right Azure? Peter, he's dead.'

'Wrong. Look, do you want to die or what?' asked Fritz.

'No, of course not, but he's not with you, so I assumed.'

'That'z because my Peter, he iz wiz ze vitch,' said Von Strictum, pushing the pistol hard against the back of Larson's head.

'How do you know, you can't be sure?'

'O yez, I can.'

'How?'

'Because he vosn't in ze cave.'

'Is that all? You think because he wasn't found in the cave, he wasn't there?'

'Yez, of courze,'

'Then you're a bigger fool than I thought. He could have been blown into a thousand pieces.'

'This is true, but I'm zure zu are wrong… I've hadz enough of zis…'

Bang! Bang!

Von Strictum immediately stopped speaking and slumped to the ground behind Larson. Fritz followed, hitting the floor like a bag of grain before he had time to react.

Larson turned staring down, hoping, praying Von Strictum was still alive, but the bullet had passed clean through the centre of his forehead, killing him instantly and Fritz the same.

'Why did you do that, Mr Booty?' Larson breathed angrily.

'Well, it was like this, see; the man had a gun to your head, and he was about to pull the trigger.'

Larson knelt down over Von Strictum, throwing his coat to the side and tearing at his shirt, revealing his chest. 'I wanted to know how he communicates with the witch. That's why I was asking him about Peter, but now he's dead and we'll never find out.' There was nothing there. He threw his shirt down and stood up.

Mr Booty slipped the Magnum back into his inside pocket, and then he met Larson with unappreciative eyes. 'Oh, and thanks for saving my life, err.'

Larson smiled and put his arm on his shoulder, shaking him lightly. 'I know you meant well, old friend.'

'I thought he was about to shoot you.'

'He might have…'

Mr Booty sighed, as if accepting he had done the right thing. 'So why were you looking at his chest?'

'I wanted to see if the witch was there inside him, trying to leave his dead corpse. Remember Sam's dad?'

'Aye, but there was nothing?' said Mr Booty.

'No, and that worries me because it could be that Von Strictum was not in communication with the witch at all, and the berserkers are simply programmed to attack anyone who gets too close to the engines.'

'It proves one thing: he was definitely working for the old hag. If he wasn't, the berserkers would have attacked him too.'

Larson nodded. 'Come on, let's do some damage to this engine.' He set off around the building, his dark physique hidden in the shadows.

Mr Camponara heard the shots and came running as fast as he could. He stopped and stared down at Fritz for a second; then he smiled and said, 'One hell of a shot', before racing off after them.

CHAPTER NINETEEN

Labyrinth

Sam lifted a burning torch from the wall and handed it to Dalgarth.

He stared at Sam with curious eyes. 'What, you want me to lead?' he said, pointing at his chest.

Sam smiled. 'Err, yeah, it's you who wants to know where Peter's gone.'

'You blaggard, you want to know more than I.'

'Oh, go on, just get going,' said Sam, pushing him in the back. 'Let's just see what's around the next corner.' He crept up gripping the edge of the rock. Dalgarth stood beside him without a word. The first thing Sam noticed was how surprisingly smooth and creamy it was. A cold film of water ran over its surface, down to a trickling stream which bobbled over small boulders and pebbles. He peered into it then something moved, giving him a start. A large crab, about the size of his hand, darted beneath the water and under a rock. Green weed danced around in the flow, and snails hung onto boulders for dear life.

Behind the creamy, jagged edge of rock was a very eerie blackness. It was impossible to tell how big or small the cavern was. The torchlight didn't reach the far side, so it could go on forever. The silence and the cold were very unwelcoming, and Sam felt a shudder run down his spine when he thought about stepping into it.

A part of him wanted to turn around and run back to the fire and the mackerel; it was safe there then Dalgarth reached out his arm with the torch.

Suddenly, a gruff voice shouted out, 'Hey, who's there – you scabby dog? I can hear you. Now show yourself before I cut out your gizzard.'

Sam gasped and his eyes shot around to where the sound was coming from. He searched for a few seconds; then three figures stepped away from the wall into the torchlight. *Why did the man say that, surely he could see the flames? He must have seen Dalgarth long before we saw him?*

Dalgarth stepped cautiously towards them, and Sam followed close behind. The man closest to him was no taller than Sam, with a balding head and long grey wispy beard. The two other men stood behind him touching his arm. They appeared anxious and afraid, but Sam couldn't understand why although he too was apprehensive. He was almost touching the man when he noticed something very strange. 'Look at their eyes, Dalgarth,' Sam told him.

'Yes, I know.'

All three men had a white film covering their pupils, like sheets hiding their eyes from the world.

'Are you possessed? Has the witch done this to you?' Sam asked.

The old man chuckled. 'Cataracts. I should have wished for eternal youth and good health, but foolishly I chose money.' He splayed his hand around, and Dalgarth stepped a few paces in the direction he was indicating. The torch soon revealed what the old man was talking about. The wisps of yellow torchlight reflected on a mound of golden coins. 'Not much good to me in 'ere, I can't even look at it.'

'No, I think I wished for the wrong thing, too. If only I'd wished for more wishes,' said Sam.

Dalgarth turned staring with questioning eyes, and the old man chuckled again.

'I'd have been able to wish us all out of here', Sam told him, 'and still have the most beautiful house in Cornwall for Mum.'

Dalgarth turned away waving the torch, searching the darkness. 'I thought you liked living down here with the hag?'

Sam was offended. 'No, why, what makes you say that?'

Dalgarth sighed. 'I thought you and that creature had something good going on.'

'Hey, you must be joking!'

Dalgarth put his hand on his heart expressing love, but his face looked disgusted. 'Hasn't she got the most beautiful eyes, you said?'

'Are you completely insane?' reeled Sam.

'Well, you said it.'

'I did not?'

'Don't you remember?'

Sam turned to the three old men. They had quietly shuffled back into a dark corner by the wall. A feeling of emptiness and overwhelming despair crept into him, leaving a strange empty feeling in his gut. Something was terribly wrong.

'You don't remember, do you?' mumbled Dalgarth.

Sam stared at him unable to answer. He searched through the spaces in his mind; climbing aboard *The Sea Witch*, warning Jenny to get off her before Peter or the witch arrived to do her harm. She was lucky that day, only just escaping. If Von Strictum had caught her she would most certainly be dead. His mind mudded; then he remembered Von Strictum sliding his knife along Bob Calvert's throat and his body slumping onto the deck; then through the wheel house window, he watched the berserkers killing all the crew. His mind mudded again, and he remembered Dalgarth kicking him in the ribs. He touched his side; it still felt sore. 'What is happening to me?' he said in a desperate tone.

Dalgarth's voice remained very cool. 'It appears that you are possessed when the witch is near you. Nothing I can do about that, but I'll tell you this, I don't like it when you're close to her. I don't like the other Sam; he's not nice at all, cold and unfeeling.'

Sam stared into the thick darkness. His eyes were much better than Dalgarth's in the dark, and he knew why. He thought about that day in Larson's cabin. The day Jenny plonked the biggest book he had ever seen on the bed next to him. The day Jenny turned the pages and read out the lists of names, searching for Larson's under the heading of Lichen throats and seeing his own name there. 'An imp, I am an imp,' he told Dalgarth.

Dalgarth sniggered. 'No, you're not. Peter Von Strictum is an imp, but not you. He changes into the devil's cat. You… you never have. I don't know what you are.'

Sam sensed a sudden panic come over him. 'I am, I tell you. Maybe I don't change. Maybe something went wrong or I haven't done something to make me that way yet, but that is what I am. I've seen my name in the book.'

'What book?'

'The book of Berserkers, Lichen Throats, and Imps,' cried Sam. 'I know what I am, and I can see much better than you in the dark. I've got eyes like a cat. I guess I was just afraid of walking into it, but now I remember, now I can see, I'm the hag's servant.'

'I don't know this book, never heard of it.'

Sam stared beyond Dalgarth, deep into the darkness. 'Come with me,' he said, grabbing Dalgarth by the arm. 'I'll show you.'

'Where are we going?'

'You'll see in a minute; it's only a few feet away.'

'But I can't see anything.'

Blackness was all around them, and the only light was that from the torch in Dalgarth's hand. It only illuminated his rugged face, arm, some of his rancid clothing and the ground around his feet. The smell of fish was much stronger here and Sam assumed that was because there was no burning wood smoke to dampen and blend with it.

Suddenly, he stopped and reached out Dalgarth's hand. Sam could feel him restraining, but not completely. It was that moment when you know someone doesn't altogether trust you. Sam knew Dalgarth had good reason to feel that way; he was after all a servant to the sea, the hag's child, and he could have been putting Dalgarth's hand into a fire, so to speak, especially as he had only recently beaten him up. He felt the icy coldness wetting his hand, and Dalgarth, instantly reacting to its touch, pulling back his wrist. 'It's a wall of water like the one in our cave.'

Dalgarth's arm relaxed and he reached into it, as if checking to be sure. 'Strange that, don't you think?'

'I don't like it,' replied Sam, stopping instantly to unexpected, unfathomable flapping sounds by his feet. It made him dance around on the spot, terrified for a second, and Dalgarth stepped back away from him, gasping with fear consuming his face. Sam realised what it was. On the floor by his feet, three good-sized Mackerel jumped around on the stone, and shuffling feet immediately came rushing towards him.

'Get away from those fish,' shouted one of the old men, as he and the other two entered into the torchlight and fell to the ground feeling around for the fish. One of them grabbed a hold of the poor creature, and baring his crooked, tombstone teeth in the torchlight, he sank his teeth into it.

Sam was instantly repulsed, and as he met Dalgarth's eyes, he realised Dalgarth had noticed it too.

'You're not an imp, Sam, no way. I told you I didn't think so. If you were, something like that wouldn't bother you… Umm, interesting. I sense feelings in there lad… Come on, let's get out of here.'

Sam nodded and smiled. 'I'll lead and you follow with the torch.' Silently he turned, prowling over the ground to the stream. Cupping his hands in the cold water, he covered his face, sipping it lightly. 'Let's move into the next cave,' he breathed with mild excitement in his voice.

'Are you sure? We could go back,' said Dalgarth sheepishly, pointing that way.

Sam was afraid the witch might be close by, but curiosity had the better of him, and he was keen to see what was in the next cave. It reminded him of the night he broke into Schooner Stevenson's house. Creeping around, terrified, and praying the people there didn't catch him. The hairs rose up on the back of his neck at the thought. That was the night he had found the witch's pendant, the night he made the wish and ruined his life. Still the curious part of his nature hadn't waned, overwhelming all his fears, and he was determined to go on no matter what. A mischievous smile swept across his face. He said, 'No, let's do it.'

'Okay, if you're sure.'

Sam peered into the next cave from the separating rocky edge.

Again, it felt smooth, like a stalactite, with icy water running gently over its surface to the ground and on to the rippling stream a few feet away. But it was nothing like the old men's place or his own.

They were living a torturous existence in the cold and damp, their only pleasure being the fish which strayed in through the curtain of sea. That was where the similarity ended. Sam's eyes scoured the cavern. It was only a few feet away from the old men's, but he could hardly believe what he saw.

In shadows of light and dark browns, recognisable shapes slowly appeared. A round coffee table with a three-seat sofa and a thick upholstered chair caught Sam's eyes first, then base cupboards, a cooker set between them, and a microwave on the worktop. It had been so very long since Sam had seen anything like this, and immediately, he thought about the house on the edge of the rocks.

He stepped into the cavern running his hand along the smooth surface until he reached the sink and taps. The back wall behind the worktop was uneven and rough, as you might expect of a cave, but the room was laid out like a kitchen/diner with the worktop finishing on the far wall.

Sam looked around to see Dalgarth still behind him. 'I can't believe we've been living like that when a comfy pad was only two caves down.'

'What is this?' asked Dalgarth, picking up the toaster.

'You cook bread in it,' Sam told him.

Dalgarth still had wide eyes and an open mouth. He put the toaster gently on the top. Sam ran water through the sink taps just so he could watch Dalgarth's reaction. Dalgarth didn't disappoint with a broad smile and a rush to touch and taste it. 'Fresh water,' he breathed, just like the stream.

Sam nodded. 'Yes, all the houses have running water like this nowadays.'

He quietly turned off the taps and stared around. The familiar curtain of sea hung on the adjacent wall like a huge black painting. He strolled over to it, unable to resist poking his head through.

As soon as the water covered his face, gills appeared on the side of his neck filtering the oxygen from the sea. He stared down into an abyss, but when he looked left through the murky water, there was a curving wall of grey rock, in it hundreds of squares of deep brown and black.

A school of silver flashes swam by, turning one way then another in an orchestrated, yet chaotic dance. *Why have I never seen this from my porthole? And why is it so much deeper here? I can see a sandy bottom from my cave, huh; I've even walked on it.*

Suddenly, there was a tugging on Sam's arm, pulling him back into the cave.

'Oh, man, you should see it. There must be thousands of these caves… It's a labyrinth of underwater apartments.' He turned around and gasped. Dalgarth still held the torch, but his other hand held onto the arm of Peter Von Strictum who was pressing a knife against his throat. 'Von Strictum, what are you doing in here?'

Von Strictum was bare from the waist up, glaring into Sam's eyes. 'Dis is my place anz I don't remember invitings zu in.'

Awkward! 'Err, sorry, we didn't know.'

'No, zu didn't and thatz the vay I like zit.'

'How come you've got all this stuff?' There was a moment's silence, and it quickly became clear, Peter wasn't willing to discuss it. 'We live in that hole. Does the witch think you so much better than me that she gives you this and me nothing?'

'Ha, ha, I guess she does. Az zu can see, I have all ze mod cons.' He waved his hand as if pointing out the kitchen and the lounge.'

'Look, do you think you can let go of me whilst you're talking.'

Peter scowled, gripping him tighter. 'Why zud I?'

'Well, I figure, if you were going to kill me, then I'd be dead by now, and I don't think the witch would be too happy about that, do you?' said Dalgarth.

Von Strictum pondered on the question for a few seconds; then he lifted the knife and pushed him away. 'No, maybe no… Come on ze here, Zam,' he said, grabbing him at the top of his arm. 'I vant to show zu somezing.' He led Sam to the other side of his cave, slipping his knife back into its sheath.

'Why have you got all this stuff?' Sam was unwilling to let the subject drop. 'Is this what you wished for and why the witch has you in her power?'

'Ze vitch doesn't have me; I chose to be zere. I'm not like zu, Sam. I didn't vish for anyzing.'

'Then…'

'I didn't vish for anyzing, I tell zu. Most of zu down here got what zu vished for and now live ze life zu deserve. Not zu, Dalgarth, I know your story, but most of ze ozers, zem next door, vished for gold; zey have it, stupid fools. Zu vished for a house for your parents. Zey have it, zo zu have nothzing down here. I didn't vish for anyzing, but all of this appeared for me. I guess the vitch knew vot I vanted wizout me zaying. I am happy wiz it.'

They strolled on a short way then from out of the darkness came the monotone shapes of three beds and beside cabinets, each with a lamp on it. 'As zu can see, I have everyzing I need to live a comfortable life here, and I've prepared for my farzure and Fritz to join me here also.'

'But why here? Why not back home?'

'Because home will no longer exist after tomorrow. I'm going to be zair when Cornwall slides into the zea, and I'm going to rezcue my farzure and Fritz.'

'But what about all the other people? You must know lots who are going to perish.'

'Not my problem. It vos bound to happen in ze end. I can't zave everyone, and I don't even vant too. Cornwall is going into the zea. People have had enough varnings, and if zey are that bothered about their stupid lives, zey vud have stood up or moved out a long time ago.'

'People have a right to live where they want,' replied Sam.

'Vhy do zey?'

'If they buy a place to live then…?'

'…zen vot… People don't own ze earth or the zea. Ve are all tenants and ze earth can kick us out venever it vants.'

'But this isn't the Earth kicking us out, is it? This is an evil being no different than any terrorist group committing a terrorist act, intent on destroying people and property.' Sam turned meeting Dalgarth's eyes. 'We have to stop this before she destroys Cornwall.'

'But how?' replied Dalgarth.

'You vil not succeed,' Peter told them.

Dalgarth stared at Von Strictum in disgust. 'You should be ashamed. Never did I think someone who carried the mark of a king would betray his people. You scum.' He spat on the floor by Peter's feet, reinforcing his feelings for him.

'What do you mean?' asked Sam.

'Him, he carries the mark. God knows how, but he does.' Dalgarth turned Peter's body and pointed at the birth mark in the shape of a condor between his shoulder blades. 'See here.' He loosened the belt from around his waist and slipped off his short robe; then he lifted his dirty white shirt over his head, throwing it to the ground. 'Can you see?' he said turning his back towards Sam.

Sam stared at it then at Peter. 'It's true, they are very similar.'

'Vot does dis mean?'

Dalgarth looked deep into his cold dark eyes. 'Much as I despise saying it, you and I are somehow related. You are a direct descendant of King Robin of West Wales.'

Peter smiled. 'No vay, I have ze royal blood.'

Dalgarth sighed. 'Only descendants of the true King of West Wales…'

'You mean Cornwall?' Sam interjected.

'I mean West Wales, Sam, the place where I was born…Von Strictum, you carry the mark of the Condor.'

Peter smiled and then his face appeared serious, even angry, and he clenched his jaw, inhaling a deep breath. 'Dis makes no differenze. Ze vitch vil take zit back tomorrow, and there iz nozzing zu can do about zit.'

Dalgarth picked up his shirt. 'Come, Sam, let's get out of here.' He took the flickering torch from Sam's hand and headed back towards his own cave.

Sam met Peter's eyes. There was no one he despised more, and the idea he, of all people, had centuries old heritage to Cornwall made his skin crawl. 'I wouldn't get too full of yourself. He's a crazy old fool, and you ain't nothing more than what you are, an imp with a posh pad.'

'Ha, ha, imp boy, I 'ave more vight and za better standing than zu; I ave ze voyal blood.'

'Then you are a traitor, Von Strictum.'

'Aw, Zam, zu zound like zu care, and you're not even fromz zaround there.'

Sam felt his face blush. 'I do care and so should you.'

'Ve'll zee how much when ze vitch returnz.'

A shudder ran through Sam's body. Peter knew. Shocked, he turned quickly, racing back towards the safety of his own cold, dark cave, away from him and his horrible words. *It cannot be true, can it?* Sam knew it was. *All my concerns, my caring about what happens gone the moment the sea witch returns.* Sam didn't want her to return, he liked who he was when she wasn't there. He liked the idea of doing something to help Cornwall, but when she returned he wouldn't care anymore.

Gripping the cold stone edge of Peter's cave, he stumbled and almost fell into the blind men's cell. He staggered on, over the pebbles edging the stream, desperate to get away, and all the time behind him, he could hear Peter's horrible taunting laugh echoing through the caverns.

CHAPTER TWENTY

Plymouth

'Mr Booty, Mr Camponara, this way,' Larson hurried through the darkness. He knew exactly where he was going, leading the way, his fingers barely touching the black stone wall of Houseman's Engine House.

'The man who gave tours around the mine came out to meet Jenny and me from here,' he whispered.

It was quiet and very dark, except for the breathing sound coming from the pump inside the stone building, and the creaking beam slowly moving up and down above their heads. It pivoted high up on the wall, and from it, a long metal rod plunged into the ground a few feet from them.

At the front of the building, big panes of thick glass faced onto the car park. Larson had run past them only seconds earlier. He figured to break in that way would be suicide. It was completely open and the noise from the shattering glass would most certainly bring the berserkers upon them again.

Suddenly, as Larson reached the big wooden door, set back in the stone, there was a huge explosion on the far side of the crater. It lit up the sky and reflected in the expanse of water. Caradon Hill had become an enormous reservoir, and the rain continued to pour into it from angry, dark, rumbling clouds, threatening to make it overflow.

'We must be quick, Mr Booty. Now that the first mine has blown, the police and marines will be here at any minute, and the witch will surely know what we are doing. Plymouth's only a short distance away by helicopter and from HMS *Raleigh*, no more than a few minutes.'

'Yes, but Raleigh's a training camp. They'll not send men from there,' replied Mr Booty.

'Oh, I wouldn't be too sure. They'll be marine's training on Dartmouth too; I bet they're boarding helicopters as we speak. We must hurry if we are to succeed.' Larson stepped aside and Mr Booty pulled out a pair of bolt cutters from beneath his long coat. He stopped for a second. 'Do you think there's anyone inside?'

'No, I doubt it. You wouldn't let a single one of them berserkers inside the place, would you? If you did, they'd be fighting and brawling, knocking everything over and breaking it, wouldn't they?'

'Yes, you're right, but it would save us a job. I guess Von Strictum or Fritz stoked the boiler and started the engines. I bet he's got the keys.'

Mr Camponara immediately stepped away, as if he thought about returning to the bodies.

'Arr, don't be bothering with that,' said Mr Booty, squeezing the cutters together. The padlock cracked and fell to the ground by his feet. He flipped back the clasp and pushed the heavy creaking door open with his heaving broad shoulder.

A second explosion went off just as Larson followed him into the room. 'Ha, just as I thought, the room is empty… Mr Camponara, watch from the door and be sure nothing gets in.'

Mr Camponara stopped and nodded. He turned, staring out into the darkness.

'There we go, see,' said Mr Booty, pulling four sticks of dynamite from inside his coat. He reached lower down and pulled out a coil of fuse cord. 'How much time do you want, Mr Larson?'

Larson smiled mischievously, taking it from him. 'I'll do that if you don't mind… The arm or the pump?'

'Jam it between the cylinder and the condenser, Mr Larson. The arm will be useless without them and we must be sure. No cylinder, no power.'

Larson nodded and then rushed down the steps. 'I think you're right, Mr Booty,' he said, forcing the four red sticks under the steaming-hot tank before unravelling twenty feet of fuse cord from the reel between his fingers. He cut it off with a pocket knife, and pushed two lines into the end of the explosives, trailing it off along the floor towards the door. 'Get the hell out of here… I'll be right behind you.'

Larson watched them disappear into the darkness then he stepped out and knelt by the door. 'I'm using the firebox, Mr Booty.'

'You'd better be quick.' Mr Booty reached into his coat and pulled out a yellow box.

Larson snapped it up and wound the wires around two points on top of the box. 'Take cover, fire in the hole,' he breathed, crouching on the ground, and then pressing his finger firmly on the red button, he instantly set off a huge explosion.

The wooden door, brick wall, and ground all shook. Larson sensed a rush of adrenaline surge through him, and the sound of glass tingled in his ears. He ripped the wires from the box.

'Where to now?' shouted Mr Booty, as the three bulky figures raced along the top of precipice.

On the far side of the lake came flashes from gunfire. 'The fighting is still raging over there,' said Mr Camponara, his voice trembling.

'Yes, that's a good thing. Yian's men are keeping them busy, so at least we can do our stuff here.

Suddenly, a long way off in the distance, far beyond Caradon, a flash much bigger than the sparks of gunfire was followed by a low boom. 'That's one of the great Onslow consol engines near Tintagel. It's fallen.' Larson smiled and his eyes filled with fiery excitement.

Everyone is trying to destroy them now, we are many.

Until now Larson was unsure who was willing to fight for this cause or even willing to believe it, but all that dissipated in an instant with the blowing up of the Tintagel mine engine. *I wonder how they are doing at Callington? If they can stop it happening there, maybe we'll have a chance.*

Suddenly, the uneven swirling roar of rotor blades flew low over Larson's head. He dropped to the ground, numb for a second, shocked by the suddenness of it. Rolling onto his back, instantly afraid, he knew in the door of the helicopter men, soldiers, were searching and pointing machine guns at anything that moved. The sound was instant and deafening. 'Oh my God. The Marine's have arrived,' he shouted to Mr Booty, still staring up through patters of icy rain. Larson watched the huge dark beast move slowly past, its silhouette set against the purple, flickering white sky as it floated overhead.

Boom! The Houseman's engine exploded, deafening sounds filling Larson's ears, obscuring the helicopter's vibrating whoosh, and filling the air with orange and yellow flames and black flying debris.

The helicopter wobbled and then veered away from it, over to the right. Probably the shock forced the pilot's hasty manoeuvre; then he appeared to gain control, levelling and hovering just above the ground on the edge of the lake.

'The berserkers will definitely come back this way now. Quick, Mr Booty, we must destroy as many of the engine houses as we can before they get here.'

'But we'll never destroy all eight of them, especially now that the army has arrived. They'll think we're terrorists and shoot us on sight.'

'I know, old friend, but we must do what we can.' He jumped to his feet, agile, alive and filled with furore. 'For Bersaba, Mr Booty.'

Mr Booty smiled and nodded through a serious, worried face. He reached into his coat and withdrew another five sticks of dynamite, throwing them to Larson. 'Let's do this,' he replied. 'Come, Mr Camponara, onto your feet. We must fly.'

Away from the soldiers they ran, along the edge of the lake, and very soon the dark shape of the next engine house came into view. Behind them, Larson noticed the chopper had taken to the air. A sudden chill ran over his skin. The soldiers were on the ground and would soon be after them. The thought of being chased excited him. *Don't change*, he told himself. Then he felt Mr Booty pressing on his arm.

'You okay, Frank?'

Larson stared at him unsure what he meant.

'Your eyes they're turning yellow-orange.'

'What? You mean he's changing,' asked Mr Camponara, moving away from him.

'Ha, ha, no, I'm sure he'll be fine. You will, won't you Frank?'

Larson never slowed even for a second. 'I'll try, Mr Booty.'

'Yes, I think you should because if one of them soldiers sees what you become they'll finish you in an instant.'

Larson smiled. *I wouldn't mind if they did, but who would finish this then?* 'They can try, Mr Booty, but I don't give them much hope. I might be old, ha, I'm still fast.'

Mr Booty appeared very concerned.

'Don't worry I'm not going to change.' He climbed the four large stone steps and pressed his shoulder hard up against the wooden engine-house door. It creaked and then slowly opened. 'Come inside, quickly.' Larson waited until they were all inside; then he forced the door shut.

Mr Camponara bent over, arms pressing just above his knees holding him up. His chest was heaving up and down heavily. Larson sensed his weakness, his loss of breath and struggled to restrain the overwhelming urge to tear into his flesh.

Mr Booty put a calming arm upon his shoulder.

Larson turned staring into his eyes; there were no words, but he knew Mr Booty was concerned. He also realised Mr Booty was feeling it too. A lesser man would have slain him there and then, but he had learned to resist the fix, but oh my, how tempting it is, an addiction he had managed to quell but never lost. Something drained of its energy was always tempting; he wanted to tear him apart, feast on his flesh, the sweet taste of sticky blood, but this was Sam's dad, the father of the boy in the book. He inhaled deeply then slowly released it. 'I'm okay… you?'

'I can hold it.'

Larson smiled. 'Me too. Let's blow this place before the soldiers get here.'

CHAPTER TWENTY-ONE

The Sea Witch's Lair

Jenny's heart leapt. She could hardly believe it, hesitating for a second before an overwhelming urge came over her to run to him, shouting, 'Sam, Sam.'

He turned around, his face shocked and his eyes filled with fear. 'No, Jenny, what are you doing here?'

At the same time Dalgarth stood up and slid away from the fire into the shadows.

Barely noticing, Jenny threw her arms around Sam's neck, kissing him on the cheek and hugging him tight. 'Oh, I've missed you so much. I told you I would come, didn't I.' A sense of joy and relief swept over her and the tension which had clung like a ton weight for so long instantly disappeared.

Sam pulled her to him, tightly hugging her also, and she knew then how much he had missed her too. Until that moment, Jenny hadn't realised just how heavy that promise, those words, *I'll find you,*

Sam, to the ends of the earth if needs be, had weighed upon her.

Now she felt light-headed and giddy, but it was to be short lived. Sam released her, holding her back by her shoulders. She felt him gently pushing her away, and she stared up at him, disappointed and fearful of what he was about to say.

'How did you get here? We're thirty fathoms down at least.' Suddenly, his face became even more afraid, and Jenny knew something terrible had entered his mind. 'The witch, she has captured you too and brought you here?'

Jenny smiled, with relief as much as anything. She thought he was going to say something far worse. 'No, we've come for you. We've made a porthole with steps to the surface.' Sam stared at her with questioning eyes. 'It's a long story, but all that matters is we've come to take you home.'

Johnny, Mr P and Detective Brindleblack all stepped forward.

How you doing, mate?' asked Johnny in a jittery tone.

Jenny knew why. Johnny was thinking about the witch turning up at any minute. She felt an anxious quiver in her stomach, but Sam distracted her thoughts, putting his arm out and patting Johnny on the back. He eagerly stepped closer. 'I've had worse days,' Sam replied, 'and I'm all the better for seeing you guys, but you must leave.'

'Not without you,' cried Jenny. 'I've been trying to find a way to get to you for more than a year.' Her eyes filled with tears at the thought of leaving him again.

'Yes, she's right; we're not leaving without you,' said Johnny, in a firm tone.

'But it's no good. I cannot go. The witch owns me now, and there is nothing we can do about it.'

'Oh, yes, there is,' said Johnny. 'That is why we've bought this.' He held out the shield hung over his arm in the shape of a thunder cloud.

Sam smiled. 'The Aegis shield?'

'Yes, it was Jenny's idea. She figured if the witch tries to possess you, then you can protect yourself from her by standing behind it. You know it works, you said it yourself, remember, back in my grandfather's house, the night we burned the boat and you gave the shield to Jenny.'

Sam took it from him and began running his fingers over the fish scales and goat's fur. 'Yes, I remember; thank you for bringing it.'

'I told you I would look after it for you,' Jenny said, quietly.

After a moment, Sam stared up at Johnny. 'And what is that you have there?'

But before Johnny had time to answer, Dalgarth stepped forward into the flickering light. 'It's the witch's spear. I've seen it only once before, the day I was captured and brought to this place. She threw it at one of my men to stop him from saving me. It was enough and she plunged into the sea taking me hostage.'

Jenny gasped, turning to the sound of his voice. Not only did the interjection of his voice scare her, but the words which came from his mouth were a shocking confirmation that what Larson had told her on the way to the Minion mines was true. 'You are King Dalgarth?' The words slid from her lips as confirmation of her knowing as much as much as question.

'Yes, I am,' he replied.

'Well, blow me. I can't believe it. Dalgarth, you old dog, you've been telling the truth all along,' said Sam, then he turned to Jenny. 'But how did you know?'

'Larson, he told me about King Dalgarth and his younger brother King Doniert.'

'Doniert, how is he?' asked a concerned Dalgarth.

Jenny looked into Sam's eyes for a moment then back to Dalgarth. 'He died hundreds of years ago, but your bloodline continues. He had a son and his son a daughter who married into the current reigning monarchs that are our present day royal family.' Jenny felt uncomfortable; she didn't want to say anymore. She didn't want to tell him it was Doniert who had sent the witch to capture him so that he could marry his wife and take over his throne. What good would it do anyway?

'But you said Larson told you. He was the man the witch threw the spear at. If he is alive, then how can that be?'

'Larson is no ordinary man,' Sam told him.

Dalgarth said nothing and Jenny quickly changed the subject. 'So we have the spear in case the witch comes back, and we have the shield to hopefully stop her from getting into your mind.'

'We also have this,' interposed Mr P, holding up the giant ship's wheel hub.

'What is it?' asked Sam.

'We're not sure, but the witch tied Jed to it the day he was sacrificed in the cavern.

Memories came flooding back into Jenny's mind. She felt Sam's body flinch against her and knew he was back in the cavern too. 'The wheel hub would have been pressing into Jed's back and the rotating bluish-white circle of teeth which cut into his chest had to have something to do with that.'

'I remember', replied Sam, 'Jed's body writhing in pain and the terrible, terrible echoing screams coming from his wife.'

It made Jenny's skin hot and clammy. For a moment, she thought she was going to be sick. Pulling away from the thoughts, not wanting to think about what happened to Jed anymore, she said calmly, 'This is the centre from that giant ship's wheel. Inside it has black hair, and although we don't yet know what it does, we thought it might be useful.'

There was an awkward silence before Sam said, 'Well, I have something useful myself', and he withdrew five emerald-green strands of weed with three knots tied in it from inside the cuff of his shirt sleeve.

'The witch's pendant,' Jenny and Johnny said together.

'Yes,' Sam smiled, looking very pleased.

'But how?' asked Jenny.

'The witch threw me from her knee.' His eyes shot to the floor as he said it. 'She was in a rage, and I caught a hold of it by accident, ripping it from her neck. She mustn't have noticed, and I was going to give it back when she returned.'

'Do you know how to use it?' asked Jenny.

Sam looked glum. 'No, sorry, but we do know it turns into a kind of wand for her. What were the words she used?'

There was a moment's silence then Jenny said, 'That's okay, at least she won't be able to turn us into stone, and I can tell you something very interesting about that hub and the weed.' Jenny paused for a moment, thinking about the inscription inside the hub. *Doniert rogavit pro anima (Doniert asks the people to pray for his soul). Dalgarth's brother, betrayer, he had it inscribed there but why? And what good will it do to tell Sam now? It will only open me up to even more questions from Dalgarth. Eventually, I will have no choice but to tell him his brother is the reason he is down here, and his brother's soul belongs to the witch.* She decided to skip over that part and continue to the more practical things that had happened. Gazing into Johnny's eyes, she said, 'Remember that day, above Mr Booty's shop, when we opened the wheel hub, and we pushed on the weed releasing the tension on one of the knots so we could look inside? The weed contained something like mirror shavings, and the wheel-hub shot across the carpet towards it.' Johnny nodded, but said nothing. 'Well, I'm wondering what might happen if we open the hub and release one of the knots, not completely, but enough to make the inside of the hub move towards it again.'

'What are you going on about, Jenny? We don't have time for this.' Johnny sounded exasperated and frustrated, as if he expected more from her. 'We need to get out of here before the sea witch returns; that's all that matters, getting away. Look what happened when we did what you were saying in Mr Booty's flat. A raging storm filled the room, it was flat calm outside, and the witch was with us, flying around and screeching like a banshee. It was opening the weed that brought her to us. I don't want to do that again, do you? We need to go.'

Jenny shuddered at the thought. 'Listen, I'm trying to make a point, but you're just not getting it.' She turned to Sam. 'Remember the story we read about the sea captains buying five strands of weed with three knots from the witches hundreds of years ago?'

'I do, but what has this got to do…'

'We were searching the school computer for what the witch's pendant might look like, and then we discovered Sir Francis Drake called on sea witches to help him destroy the Spanish Armada.' Sam nodded and Jenny continued. 'The sea captains opened the knots because they believed, if they did, the wind would blow. I guess by opening the knot, the witch came to them and blew into their sails. It makes sense, doesn't it? Opening the knot brought the witch to them, and she blew into their sails whipping up the wind and the swell.'

'Get to the point, Jen,' said Sam, 'because that witch could be back at any minute.'

Jenny sighed. 'It's no good us leaving; it would only be a temporary release, and what about Cornwall? It might not even be there when we get to the top step of the porthole.'

'Larson and Mr Booty, they'll sort that out,' retorted Johnny. 'We don't need to worry about that. We only came for Sam.'

'I don't think so, Johnny. We came for more than that, even if we hadn't realised it. It has to be us; we have to stop her – it's the only way.'

Johnny screwed his face up. 'But how?'

'Larson gave us these things for a reason, and at great risk: the spear, the shield, the wheel hub and the weed. We have the witch's pendant too, and I'm sure Larson never expected us to have that. If ever there is a chance for us to finish this, it is now.'

'I like your vigour, Jenny,' said Dalgarth, 'but we have one more thing, more important than all of those you've mentioned.' They all stared at him, eagerly waiting for the answer. 'We have each other and a common goal, a purpose.'

'Ha, ha, ha, zu bunch of tozzers.'

Jenny jumped, reeling around to see who it was. 'Peter Von Strictum,' she yelled, his dark gangly shape stepping out of the blackness.

'Dalgarth, zu spineless vimp; we've got each ozer, what a joke! You've got nozing, and very soon less than nozing, because zu are all going to be fish food.'

Sam shot towards him, stomping across the cave right up to his face. 'This is it, Peter, your only chance to be free, a chance to get rid of her once and for all. Join us and help fight the witch. This is no life, living in this cave forever.'

'Listen to zu. As soon as she appears, zu will become her zervant again, and zu will do exactly vot she vants. Did zu forget so quickly, Zam, zu are ze imp? If ze vitch gets to your friends before their souls leave zeir bodies, zey are hers forever, and zen they'll find out vot hell iz veally like.'

Jenny ran to Sam's side, clutching his arm. 'Don't listen to him, Sam; we have the shield – it will protect you.'

Von Strictum laughed, 'Ha, zkin and zcales, who are zu trying to kid?'

'Don't listen to him, I tell you,' Jenny cried. 'Use the shield. Don't look into her eyes, and you'll be okay.'

'She's right, Sam, and what do we have to lose in any case. We came down here to stop the witch and bring you home, so let's do this,' said Mr P in a determined tone. In his hands, he held the large strand of weed Jenny had been talking about. It was only part of it, hacked from the giant ship's wheel in haste, but it did contain the large knot Jenny and Johnny peered into that day in the flat. His hands gripped tight on either side of it, and he stared with wild eyes across the cave into Jenny's.

'Do it, Mr P,' she said, unwavering.

Mr Pothelswaite loosened the knot. Everyone stood hesitant for a second; then Brindleblack said in a quivery voice, 'I don't think that was a good idea', and he stepped back away from Mr P towards a black hole in the cavern wall.

'Go, if you want to,' seethed Jenny. A light wind brushed through her long auburn hair, like fingers parting each strand, and then she thought she saw something scuttling along the side of the cavern wall, hidden in the darkness and her heart missed a beat. *What could it be?* 'Get behind the shield, Sam.' Jenny grabbed a hold of it by its edge and pulled it up in front of his face. 'No matter what happens, you must not look at her.'

Brindleblack disappeared from sight and Mr P ran across the cave closer to Jenny, facing towards and staring down the dark passage where the pebbled stream faded into the darkness.

There was a slight scuffle. Dalgarth grabbed Von Strictum, spinning him around, and then holding him with his knife close to his face. Nothing was going to distract Jenny from the blinding passage, not even Dalgarth's stern voice threatening for a second with deadly intent.

'Zu wouldn't kill me, vud you? Not von of zur own descendants.'

Jenny put her hands softly on Sam shoulder. 'Are you okay, there?'

'Yes, but I can't see what's going on. What can you see?'

'I'm not sure. Something's moving, but it's too dark. I can't explain it.'

'It looks kind of like a transparent figure, a ghost,' added Johnny, his voice quiet, hesitant, unsure.

It slid off the wall, and a sudden sound of pebbles clattering sent a cold tingling across Jenny's skin.

'What was that?' asked Sam, trembling.

'I think she's just thrown a pebble at us.'

'So she's coming,' breathed Sam.

'Zu bet your life she'z coming. Ha, now zu are going to get it,' Von Strictum laughed.

'Shut up,' threatened Dalgarth, yanking his neck tighter.

'Zu are a fool, Dalgarth.'

'Shut up I tell you or I'll cut off your head.'

'Ha, zu are holding me because I'm allowing zu to, but unfortunately for zu, I'm bored with zor empty threats, so now I'm going to free myself. Try to stop me if zu can.'

Dalgarth gasped, his arm was still holding the same shape, as if it was around the boy's neck. His other hand was holding the knife up in front of him, but Von Strictum was no longer there.

Instead, by his feet, a black panther snarled up at him. Dalgarth jumped back and yelped as it lashed out with huge ivory claws.

Johnny immediately leapt to his side, brandishing the spear close to Von Strictum's head. He snarled again and for a moment prowled impatiently back and forth, his yellow eyes burning into Johnny's. Johnny jabbed at the air dangerously in front of him then Von Strictum turned and ran into the black where the witch's ghostly shape still shimmied slowly back and forth.

Suddenly, the sea witch shrieked and then sobbed for a second.

'I think she's just realised her pendant is missing,' Jenny whispered. Sam smiled.

His eyes were still dark. They hadn't glazed over the way they had that day in the cavern the day the witch took Sam away. 'The Aegis shield, I think it is working?'

'Yes, I think it must be,' Sam replied.

Jenny sensed a warm feeling at the thought of them being together, followed by apprehension and fear that it might be short lived, and she would lose him again. 'Just make sure you stay behind it no matter what happens.'

Sam nodded. 'I'll try, but what are we going to do? The sea witch ain't going to stay out there in the dark forever. She's just weighing us up. Soon she'll be coming in to get us, and I'm not going to be much help cowering behind this.'

'You're not cowering. If you weren't behind it, you would be against us too, and that would be even worse. And yes, I know she'll be coming for us soon; we summoned her here didn't we... any thoughts?'

They all looked at Jenny with blank expressions. An awful feeling of responsibility rested upon her, weighing her down again. *They're all here because of me. I led them into the porthole. They trusted me. I told them to summon the witch and I don't have any answers. Oh, Frank, what shall I do?* Every time Jenny thought about him, her thoughts returned to the same question. *Why did Frank send down the wheel hub, the spear and the weed?*

Suddenly Jenny gasped. Out of the darkness stepped a beautiful woman in a long black robe. The hood covered most of her head, but long black hair flowed over her robes onto her chest. Her lips were red and lush. Jenny noticed her eyes. There was no disguising who it was from them. Gangrenous yellow with goat-slit pupils stared towards her.

Jenny immediately looked away, afraid she too might be possessed by her beauty. 'Don't look into her eyes,' she warned everyone.

'She's back then?' said Sam.

'Oh yes, she back, and that creep, Von Strictum, is standing right beside her.'

'What are they doing?'

'I think they're just assessing the situation. She's probably wondering how we got down here.'

'Yeah, I bet that's shook her up a bit.'

'I think it must have.'

Suddenly, something whipped Johnny up into the air and slammed him hard against the cavern wall. She flew to him in an instant. 'I know you,' said the sea witch, running her nose along his face, breathing him in. 'You are the boy I released in exchange for my pendant. I knew I should never have let you go. Still you are here now.' She cackled horribly, gripping him tighter around his collar and squeezing the air from him.

Johnny yelled out, terrified and started jabbing at the giant octopus arm with the spear.

The witch instantly let him go, retreating towards the darkness and Johnny dropped to the ground in a heap. For a moment, it was silent. Mr P ran to him, helping him to his feet. 'Are you okay, Son?'

'Yes, I'm fine, Dad. Now she knows what she'll get if she messes with me.'

Mr P smiled, hastily dragging Johnny back to where the others stood waiting for something else to happen.

'Oh God, here she comes again.' Jenny wanted to get behind the shield with Sam. She felt completely helpless with nothing to protect herself with. The witch glided over the ground, her appendages once more leading the way, and at the same time, the black panther leapt out of the darkness towards her.

Jenny took in a deep, gasping breath, closing her eyes, knowing this was it. Peter Von Strictum was about to kill her, his long ivory claws protruding from huge black pads like eight curving knives about to cut.

Dipping down beside the shield and Sam, Jenny crouched into the foetal position. In the final millisecond, she opened her eyes. There above was the panther, about to land on top of her. Suddenly its arms changed direction away to the left, and its shape changed back into the evil boy with the black-studded collar. A glint of light, the silvery line of pointed metal flew past her eyes and Von Strictum caught it in both hands. He rolled onto the ground by her side; it all happening in the blink of an eye.

Jenny's immediate instinct was to jump onto him, but it was too late. Before she had time, the boy threw the spear back in the direction of Johnny. Jenny watched horrified as it hurtled towards

Johnny's heart. 'No,' she cried out. The thought of losing him was beyond anything she could bear. Her heart aflutter, the spear about to pierce him, Mr P jumped in front of it.

The spear ripped into his body. For a moment, he stood there, his hands holding onto it; then he fell to his knees. His chest had stopped moving, and his eyes glazed over in a film of tears.

Johnny dropped beside him, wrapping his arms around his neck sobbing, 'Oh, Father, hold on; don't leave us; we'll get you out of here.' Then the witch's face appeared beside him, soaking up deep nose-filled gulps from his skin. Johnny leapt to his feet, desperate, repulsed and screaming at her, 'Get away from him, you disgusting creature', but for that second, he could not move. It was as if he was glued to the stony surface.

The witch wrapped her hand around Mr P's neck stopping him from slumping onto the ground. Her eyes fixed on Johnny, and then she started laughing horribly. 'He was your father, hey; well, he's mine now.' She released him, and his limp body collapsed onto the ground.

This seemed to free Johnny, and he jumped forward grabbing hold of the spear, pulling it from his father's chest and turning it towards the witch.

At the same time, Sam hammered down the edge of the shield onto Von Strictum's foot. He let out an almighty howl. Sam threw down the shield and leapt onto him.

Jenny realising what was happening, picked up the shield and advanced towards the witch so that she remained between Sam and her. She turned around, only to see Sam fall from a punch to the jaw. He immediately sprang back up, grabbing Von Strictum by the black-studded collar and butting him in the face. Von Strictum yelled out again and blood oozed from his nose.

Suddenly, Von Strictum stopped, his body flinched and he croaked, as blood poured from the corner of his mouth. Dalgarth's head appeared from behind him, his hand coming up around his throat. 'You ain't no relative of mine,' he breathed before lunging the knife into his back for the second time.

'Sam, get behind me,' yelled Jenny, as she advanced towards the witch. 'Look, Sam, she's retreating.'

Sam turned around, meeting Jenny's eyes then he crouched behind her, leaving Von Strictum to his demise with Dalgarth.

The sea witch slowly backed away, her face filled with fire and fury. Unexpectedly, when she spoke, her voice was calm and smooth, and not fiery at all. 'I'll tell ye what, deary, I like you, so I'll make you a deal. Just put down the thunder cloud, and I'll let you live. I'll even let you go back to your mum, so what do yer say? Do we have a deal?'

Jenny continued to step closer and the sea witch continued to back away. 'Never,' shouted Jenny. 'I'll never make a deal with you.'

In that split second, the witch shot along the cave's craggy wall and out through the vertical water into the ocean.

'I've got to go after her,' Sam hollered. 'Johnny, throw me the spear.'

'No, Sam, you can't. What if she possesses you again?' Jenny was terrified, she was about to lose him.

'Don't worry, Jenny. I won't look into her eyes.'

'Then how are you going to…' But it was too late. Sam had caught the spear and disappeared through the wall of water, leaving Jenny feeling drained and helpless.

CHAPTER TWENTY-TWO

Five Strands of Weed, Three Knots

It was hard going, swimming with a shield in one hand and a spear in the other. Sam knew he could never catch up with her. Even without the drag from the shield, he couldn't swim anything near as fast as the sea witch. His only hope was that she would see him in the murky depths and come back to claim him once more.

Jeez, I wish I'd stayed in the cave with the others. Maybe that was it. Maybe that was our chance to escape, to flee this place. I must be crazy to come out into the sea. She's more at home out here than she is in the cave. I might as well have encouraged her to kill me a year ago, for all the good a spear and a shield will be. I'll have more chance of surviving if I wait in the cave. After all if she is going to come back for me here, she'll come back for me there. Ha, listen to me, as if I matter to her. There I go again, possessing myself. I don't even need her to be near me. What is this fascination with her? I think I'll swim back and wait. All she needs is a bit of time to pull herself together; then she'll most definitely muster up a plan.

Sam stopped on the silt, searching around. In the distance, the wreck of the trawler, *Agnes*, lay on the bottom, her nets strewn across the sea bed, one of the beams pressed into the sand like a stiff arm stopping her from toppling over.

I bet she's hiding in there, watching, waiting to pounce out like a back-alley murderer. The thought of her leaping out from some dark corner made Sam shudder. *I'd rather know when she's coming, so I'm not going over there, no way.* Suddenly, he had a thought. *The pendant! When Jenny wanted the witch to come, she told Mr P to open the knot slightly. Doing this obviously summons her to us; it worked for the boat captains, maybe she doesn't even have a choice?*

Sam searched his pocket and pulled out the five strands of weed with three knots. *I wish this had never existed. If it didn't, none of this would ever have happened.* His mind raced back to that terrible day, the day the sea witch dragged Johnny from the boat and into the icy black tar sea.

'This is the spawn of the one who took my pendant away. Is he still alive?' She asked. Sam saw himself nodding, terrified, in the cursed boat and thinking about Johnny's grandfather, and the tale about him and little Tommy Elcinarb. 'And can you get it for me?' asked the witch.

'Yes, yes, I can,' Sam told her, thinking he might live through this.

'You have until the next new moon, fifteen days from now, to get me my pendant, and if you do not return, this will be food for my urchins and crabs.' The sea witch held Johnny at the back of his neck; then she dragged him down into the bottomless pit in the bay.

Sam stared through the salty water at the wreck and sighed before taking the weed in both hands. He pushed open one of the knots, revealing the silvery substance inside.

'You've got something of mine, Sam, do you forget? You're not going to renege on our agreement, are you?'

Her voice gave him a start. He hadn't expected her to be there so soon. Quickly shoving the pendant back into his pocket, Sam picked up the spear and held the shield up in front of his face. 'I think it was you who reneged, not me.'

'You shouldn't have made the wish. If you hadn't, you wouldn't be here now.'

'So I can't have anything without losing everything for it. All I wanted was a nice house for my parents, was that too much to ask?'

'You wished for it. I gave it to you. What, you think someone shouldn't pay? Every day people go out to work for what they have. They toil and break their backs earning enough to simply eat. Why should you get it for nothing?'

'I didn't know,' Sam cried.

'Drop down the shield. Throw it away, naive boy. You belong to me. You've always belonged to me. Boys like you they all belong to me. Shit, if I get anymore, I'll be looking for a bigger place to keep you all.'

She's right. Why did I ever think I could get the house for free? Schooner Stevenson, writhing in his chair, the witch visible inside him, poking through his skin, I should have known then nothing is truly free.

'I really mean so little to you?'

The witch paused for second, as if debating the question or deciding whether to tell Sam what she thought. 'Of course, you are special. You are lucky. Thanks to Peter, he made you special.'

'Because I'm an imp, you mean?'

'Drop down the shield, and we'll forget all of this nonsense. Together we'll go on to have many adventures, we'll sink many fleets, take back lands, live a wonderful life and yours will be forever. Isn't that what you want? Isn't that what everyone wants?'

Sam had a sudden tingle of excitement and dread, all at the same time. 'Forever?' It was incomprehensible.

'Yes, look at Dalgarth. He hasn't aged a day since he came to me.'

'Came to you?' It was offensive to even think of it in that way. 'You snatched him from the edge of the River Fowey,' Sam retorted.

'I did?' the sea witch replied.

'Dalgarth told me.' Suddenly, something moved in the corner of Sam's eye. He turned quickly to his right, swinging the shield around to protect him.

'Forget Dalgarth, Sam; he's of no matter to us anymore.'

'No matter, what do you mean?'

'A means to an end, that's all. You're what matters now.'

A similar thing happened again, his eye catching a slight motion, and Sam spun to his left, protecting his eyes. His nerves were in tatters with wondering where she was going to turn up next. One thing Sam was sure of, she was trying to get past the shield and into his mind. 'Why are you so interested in me? Please, just let me go back to my own kind.'

'Nobody leaves once they're here. I offer only permanent residency to my guests, for your little friends too.'

Sam heard a slight cackle after she said it. 'No, no,' he cried. The thought was too much to bear, and all hope drifted away from him, 'But why?'

'Slippery tongues, Sam. Slippery tongues can do a lot of damage.'

'I won't tell a soul,' he pleaded. 'Just let them go.'

'Not going to happen. No one leaves.'

'Then I have nothing to live for. An eternity lost in oblivion, my friends all dead and gone, just Dalgarth and I living off fish in a damp cave.'

'Oh no, I don't need to keep him anymore. I did enjoy toying with him, leeching off his blood, but now that he's killed my imp, he's finished.'

Again Sam moved at the slightest thing. Again she tried to get past the shield and into his head, in a cat and mouse game of manoeuvre and counter manoeuvre. It made Sam feel alive with excitement and fear. His skin was feverish with adrenaline; he gripped the spear tight and the shield tighter still.

The witch hadn't mentioned the spear. *I wonder why? She should have immediately asked for it back, after all it was hers as much as the pendant.* He remembered only too clearly how she screeched with anticipation and then relief as Sam gave it to her two years earlier in the little boat. Now it was back in his possession, and he didn't want to let it go again. *Maybe she can't see anything that's behind the shield. Maybe she doesn't know I have the spear. The pendant is a different matter because I used it to lure her away from the* Agnes.

Sam had a sudden urge to check if it was still in his pocket, but he couldn't. In order to do that, he needed to free up one of his hands, and that wasn't going to happen, not when she was so close.

Around to his right, a long black tentacle appeared at the edge of the shield. It moved cautious, tentative at best, and from this Sam realised how afraid she must be. He imagined it was like putting his fingers through a window into a blacked room and not knowing if someone was there to snip them off. Sam knew how that felt.

Still it tapped along the sea bed like a blind man's stick. A moment later, a second one appeared on the right of the shield. It was some way from him, tapping on the sand, but Sam knew she was getting more daring, perhaps even impatient to get to him. Suddenly, a dark shadow blotted out the blue ocean above him and he gasped, horrified by what he saw.

The sea witch rolled through the water above his head, as if she was leaping over a high bar on an athletics track. Her hood slowly fell back, and her hair separated and moved snakelike in the salty sea.

He turned his eyes quickly before her face became visible to him. He knew, just one glance, they would be locked together, and he would be lost forever under her spell. But before he had time to turn the shield towards her, he felt a hundred suction cups latch onto his back. The shock of it stung his flesh. It made him drop the spear and the shield instantly.

They slowly sank to the silted ground by his feet, along with all hope. He yelled out in pain, squeezing his eyes tight shut as she dragged him up to her face. The grotesque creature had him in her clutches, and she pulled him right close, inhaling deep nose-filled gulps from Sam's skin.

'Open your eyes, boy,' she said in a stern tone.

Sam shook his head and squeezed them shut even harder than before. 'No, no, you're not going to possess me again.' But it was a hopeless situation; she had caught him, her knobbly fingers clenched tight under his chin, and very quickly his determination started to wane. *This is how Johnny must have felt when she dragged him up out of the sea; his eyes slightly opening, unveiling his obliteration.*

Sam was about to do the same thing, after all, what was the point in fighting; she had won. Nothing could save him now.

At that very moment, a feeling of immediate release came over him. The stinging on his back had disappeared, and his body was unsupported and heavy on the sea bed. The sense of the witch's stale breath close to his skin had gone also, and it was as if she wasn't there anymore. *But how can that be?*

Suddenly, Sam felt a tingle run through his arm and down to his fingertips. Someone touched him.

'Open your eyes, mate.'

It was Johnny's voice, but Sam was frightened to open his eyes; it might be a trap. If it was and her yellows goat-slit eyes were staring at him, he would be lost, destined to forever serve the witch in a possessed mind every time he saw her.

Instant relief and hope, followed by distrust, came rushing through him like a motorway pile up. *It could be the sea witch mimicking Johnny; she might have even taken his form?* 'Oh God, Johnny, is that you?' asked Sam, at his nerves end.

'Course it is. Now come on, we've no time to lose; she might be back at any minute.'

'But how, why?' asked Sam.

'The hag retreated when I pulled the shield up from the sand between us and her,' said Johnny, a big smile sweeping across his face. 'This shield, it's great, but how does it do that?'

'It was your grandfather; we can thank him for spending all those years researching this stuff.' Sam remembered the first time he ever went the old man's house; the medusa image on the front door. Jenny cut her finger on it and stormed off in a huff. Inside, a sea-witch carving on the wooden dresser and old, worn-out books piled upon the table. The old man splayed his hand over them. 'This has been my life's work,' he said, and then he gave Sam the Aegis shield.

'Johnny, thank God. I didn't think you'd come. I thought I was done for.' Sam shook on his shoulder vigorously.

'For a minute there, I nearly didn't. I watched the witch toying with you. I almost swam back to the cave.'

Sam stared at him puzzled, and then suddenly he realised what Johnny was thinking. 'Jenny, ay?'

Johnny gazed down at the sand then meeting Sam's eyes he said, 'For a while there, I thought she was my girl.'

Sam gripped him dangerously. 'What do you mean?'

'I wanted her, that's what I mean,' Johnny yelled back at him. 'But I was kidding myself to think that she could ever love me. As soon as I saw her face light up when she saw you, I knew it could never be. She's always put you first, Sam, even after not seeing you for so long and you an imp, too; she still prefers you. I just don't understand it.' Johnny shrugged off Sam's grip with a glum face. 'Women, ay. Who'd have 'em?'

Sam smiled, feeling a bit sorry for him. 'Still, you didn't leave me. You saved me from her once again.'

'It's no more than you did for me.'

Johnny was talking about the time Sam went in search of the pendant and exchanged it for his life on the night of the new moon. A shudder ran through Sam's body at the thought. 'Well, come on, we're not out of here yet, and that sea witch won't let us leave if she can help it.'

Johnny's face became fearful again. 'Here, Sam, hold the shield and this time don't let it go.'

'What are we going to do?' asked Sam, wondering how they could possibly escape. It was so open here. Flat sand all around them and the trawler lay on it, like a dead whale in the distance.

'It's a standoff,' said Johnny, picking up the spear. 'She can't see us behind the shield, I'm sure of that. It puts an invisible barrier between us and her. I was watching from behind that rock,' he said pointing, 'and it is clear to me, she can't come within three or four feet of it. It repels her. Even her tentacles tried to move around it, keeping their distance.' Johnny shuddered. 'She's not even human, is she? She looks human, but she's not. It's all a mask.'

'Well, that's something, isn't it?'

'What?'

'She can't see us,' replied Sam, trying to find some positives.

Johnny nodded, but his face remained gaunt and his lip started to quiver faster than the gills on his neck. 'Maybe, we should retreat back to the cave?'

'Yes, I was thinking the same thing. We'll have more chance in there.'

'You think?'

'Hmm, sarcasm.' Sam tried to muster a smile, but the thought of the witch possessing him again was overwhelming. 'Let's swim over to the coral and rocks; it's far too open here.'

When they reached the coral ledge, it was brimming with life. Small fish darted into crevices, out of sight, and strands of green weed swayed from side to side, slow dancing with the moving sea.

'Wait a minute,' said Sam, touching Johnny's arm.

Johnny stopped and stared at him with curious eyes. It was clear, by his body jumping around, that his only intention was to reach the cave, where Jenny and the others were, as soon as possible, but Sam had another idea.

'What if you take the shield and put it up in front of you. I'll stand on the sand and open the knot in the weed then you can jump out and stab her with the spear.'

'She's not going to fall for that.'

'She might? She won't know you're there until it's too late.'

'No, no, let's get the hell out of here,' cried Johnny.

Sam held him by the shoulders and stared calmly into his eyes. 'We'll not make it, Johnny; she's too fast. I think our only chance is to take a stand right here with our backs to the coral. At least that way, we'll see her coming.'

Behind Johnny the coral curved around in a horseshoe, with a ledge of rough ground shells above. It supported some long green weed, which draped down like tassels on a Hawaiian skirt and brownie-red sea urchins mingled between their roots.

As soon as Sam saw the fish disappear, he thought Johnny might be safe there, protected on three sides and from above with the Aegis shield in front of him. 'Here, tuck yourself in and pull the shield up in front of you.'

Johnny was hesitant to take it and stared out of the crevice with bulging, worried eyes. 'Are you sure we should do this?'

'No, I'm not, but what choice do we have?'

Johnny said nothing and slowly pulled the shield up in front of him. 'Don't look at her, Sam – please don't look at her.'

'I won't. Now stay very quiet.' He pulled the weed from his pocket and stared at it in his hand. Under the water, it glowed much brighter, fluorescent more than emerald. *The sea witch is sure to see it.* Just to be sure, Sam closed his eyes and squeezed the knot open. He pressed his thumb into it and released one of the knots.

'You stupid boy that is my pendant, not yours, and now you've wasted one of my knots.' The witch grabbed Sam by the shoulder and shook him violently. 'Now open your eyes, I tell you.' Sam remained stubborn, his eyes tight shut. 'I'm not messing anymore, boy. I'll cut off your lids, so you'll have no choice but to look at me, and you'll never be able to close them again.'

Sam yelled out, terrified, 'No, please don't do that – I'll do as you ask.' *Please, Johnny, do something now.* Suddenly, as Sam was about to look at her, she screeched out, as if in pain. It lifted Sam's heart immediately, filling him with vigour. Staring down by his feet, the witch's black cloak lay on the sand. His eyes quickly swept up to her chest, where the silver spear lodged in her heart. Johnny's hands were still firmly gripped around it, and he forced it further into her body.

The sea witch writhed in pain, trying to free herself.

'Don't look into her face, Johnny.' Sam grabbed a hold on the spear, also pressing down with all his might. Suddenly, there was pop and Sam felt the resistance go. 'Doniert's spear has gone right through her and into the sand.' The witch stopped struggling and lay motionless on the sea bed. Sam smiled, 'Wow, Johnny, we've done it and what a rush.' He released the spear slowly and stepped back away from her.

Johnny remained gripped, as if he was unable to release his hands from it. He had one foot pressed into her body and both hands forcing the spear down where his eyes remained. His body was physically shaking, and immediately a vision popped into Sam's mind.

'It's you, Johnny. You are the boy in *The Book of Black Magic and Revelations*. It's not me at all.'

Johnny looked up and smiled. 'Yes, I guess I am. After all this time and everyone thinking it was you, ha.'

Sam picked the shield up from the sand. 'Come on, mate. Let's get the hell out of here.'

'What about the spear?'

'Just leave it; we don't need it anymore.'

Johnny let go of the spear, and together with barely a glance behind them, they swam off towards the cave. 'So what do think; you know, now I'm the man. Do yer think Jenny might go for me instead of you?'

'Ha, you must be joking, mate, with that bald chest.'

'Oh, I wouldn't be so sure; I'm the saviour of Cornwall.'

Sam smiled. 'Yeah, yeah, yeah, come on, I'll race you back. Where is your shirt anyway?'

'I thought it might be easier swimming without it.'

'Oh right, can you keep it on next time?'

'Funny. There's not going to be a next time. I'm not doing anymore missions with you. Think I'm going to find myself some new friends.'

'Ha, I don't think so.'

CHAPTER TWENTY-THREE

Five Strands of Weed, Two Knots

Sam and Johnny stepped through the wall of water to be greeted by three anxious, timid faces in the dank cavern.

Jenny gasped then smiled shouting out, 'Sam, Sam, you're still alive.' She ran into his arms, throwing hers around his neck, sending him onto his back foot. 'I was so worried about you; I thought you'd both been killed.' Then she kissed him all over his face.

'No, it's the witch that's dead,' said Johnny, interrupting and pushing back his shoulders.

Jenny retracted and stared at Johnny alarmed. 'But the witch can't be killed?'

'Don't worry about that. We saw her die, didn't we Sam?'

'She's dead alright,' Sam agreed. 'Johnny spiked her in the heart with Doniert's spear.'

'It's not my brother's spear; it belonged to her.'

'Nevertheless, it went right through and came out of her back into the sand – she's dead,' Sam insisted.

Jenny took a step back, her face filled with terror. 'You're wrong. You've made a mistake, the sea witch can't die.' Her eyes jittered around, as if something terrible was about to happen. 'Quickly, we must get out of here and fast.'

Suddenly, startled by a loud slapping sound on the ground behind Sam, they all scattered to different sides of the cavern, searching for crevices and dark spaces to hide in.

There in front of them stood the sea witch. Her eyes burned like hell's fury, and she leaned towards them, her hands out, palms up, as if they had done something terrible to her. The black hood fell from her head, and snake like creatures, which were hidden there until now, hissed and snapped at the air in their direction.

'Now you're all going to die,' she screeched, 'but it will be no ordinary death for you. I am going to make each one of you suffer more than you ever thought possible.' She turned to Sam, 'And I'm going to make you suffer more than anyone else.'

'Where's the spear?' shouted Dalgarth.

'She must have pulled it out and thrown it away,' replied Johnny.

'What? You mean this,' she screamed wildly, dragging it out from behind her robes.

'Hey, you,' Brindleblack shouted at her.

She turned and glared at him. 'Isn't it strange how everyone turns against you when you're down?'

'You're not down,' Brindleblack shouted. 'But you will be.' He marched towards her, as if he had no fear.

'Right then, you will be the first to die,' she snarled, jabbing the spear between his ribs.

Brindleblack stopped, instantly shocked, his mouth gaping. She lifted up the spear, and he slid down it, right up to her determined, furious face. He cringed, gritting his teeth and screwing up features.

Sam tried to squeeze further into the wall, his stomach rolling in acid-burn revulsion, as the sea witch brought up one of her appendages, covered in suction cups and tiny jagged teeth, pressing them into his back.

Brindleblack screamed in agony – it must have been – for him to make that sound as every drop of blood was slowly sucked from his body.

'We've got to do something,' cried Sam.

But Jenny shouted across the cavern to him, 'There is nothing we can do. Pick up the shield and cover your face.'

Sam searched for it. *She's right, the shield. Where's the shield?* Then Sam spotted it lying on the ground between him and sea witch. He made a lunge for it, and she too jumped towards him, throwing Brindleblack off to the side. Brindleblack slumped on the ground dead, and Sam retreated quickly, careful not to look at her.

Dalgarth's eyes flirted from Brindleblack to Johnny, who stood beside him. 'What is that between your shoulder blades?'

'What,' asked Johnny?

'The mark on your back, it's a Condor… Goodbye lad,' said Dalgarth. He leapt towards her, knife gleaming in his hand.

Jenny screamed, but she couldn't do anything to save him. The witch picked him up and threw him against the stony cavern wall in a flash.

Blood spattered onto the side of Sam's face. He felt the warm, sticky substance and tried to wipe it away; then he glanced down quickly. Dalgarth's head rolled to the side, his eyes wide and black and his face emotionless, dead.

The witch glided over to him, and Sam retreated away as quickly as he could, still refusing to make eye contact. For a moment, she stopped, breathing Dalgarth in through her nose, and then her face darted from one to the other, as if she was deciding who to kill next.

Jenny ran screaming back down the cavern to where Mr P's body lay slumped on the ground.

The sea witch made a dart towards her, but Sam quickly caused a distraction, waving his arms and shouting, 'Hey, bitch, come and get me if you can.' Sam was close to the shield; he whipped it up and crouched behind it, stopping her from pressing on towards him.

'Johnny, catch this,' hurried Jenny, throwing the wheel hub to him. 'Unscrew it, but don't open it yet.'

He caught it and stared at Jenny for a second, unsure what to do; then he started unscrewing the hub.

Jenny ran up behind Sam and the protection of the shield as quickly as she could. In her hands, she held the green strands of weed taken from the giant ship's wheel. 'When I shout now, open the hub and push it into the wound on her back.'

'What?' Johnny yelled back, in a horrified tone.

Jenny ignored his response and breathed into Sam's ear, 'When I count three, drop the shield.'

Sam was equally surprised and alarmed at the idea of dropping his only defence against the witch. 'You must be joking.'

He felt her hand pressing gently on his shoulder. 'Just trust me, Sam. Here we go: one… two… three. Now, Johnny!'

Sam instantly dropped the shield onto the ground. The sea witch cackled and seizing her opportunity slid rapidly towards them. *Is this it, the end at last?*

Johnny leapt at her back, dodging the serpent creatures and

forcing the open hub into her. At the same time, Jenny stood up, forcing the knot open.

The witch's face turned from anger and exhilaration to absolute terror in an instant. She looked down realising something very strange was happening to her. A green orb about the size of her heart appeared under pressure, as if being forced from the wound in her chest. Black hair strands began to surround it. Suddenly it shot out, flew across the cavern and in through the gap in the knot.

Jenny quickly pulled the knot shut tight, and the witch's black robes fell, oozing a black, oil-like substance onto the rocky surface. The back of the hub had shot forward, also slamming hard against the weed and Jenny's hands, but when Jenny pulled the knot tight, it fell to the floor along with the sea witch's limp body.

'Where's she gone,' asked Johnny, looking down at the mess.

'She's not dead; she's in here,' replied Jenny, staring at the weed.

Sam climbed onto his feet, letting out a deep sigh. 'So is that it, then. Is she gone for good?'

'I think so, Sam, as long as we find somewhere to put this where no one will ever open it again.'

'I know, let's make a box for the weed, and we'll bury it with the Aegis shield on top.'

'I think that's a great idea,' Jenny agreed, 'but I think you've got one more thing to do before we go home.'

Sam looked at her bemused.

'Throw the witch's pendant into the fire. Schooner Stevenson should have done it years ago, but he didn't. Just to be sure, Sam, I don't want you ending up like him.'

Sam thought about him writhing in his chair as the witch burst out of his chest. It sent him a chill. He reached into his pocket and smiled. 'I forgot all about that.' Lifting it up in front of his face, he dangled it between his fingers, five strands of weed, two knots. For a long moment he stared at it. The urge to keep it was strong.

Jenny put her arm around his waist, and rested her head on his shoulder. It made him feel warm and wanted, and he revelled in the idea that they might have a long, exciting future together, now the sea witch had gone. He placed his arm around her shoulder and hugged her for a moment then he said, 'Johnny, come here, mate.'

Johnny stepped up beside him. Sam could see how sad he was and realised he must be thinking about his poor father lying dead on the ground close by.

'He was a brave man.'

Johnny nodded, barely lifting his head.

'Do you want the honour? After all, I can't think of anyone who deserves it more.'

'Yeah, go on then,' he breathed, taking the pendant. For a moment Johnny held it over the dying flames – then he released it.

The End

AUTHOR BIOGRAPHY

 My name is Michael Peter Ward (M. P. Ward) and I am a published author with representation from the Gilbert Literary Agency.

I have always loved putting pen to paper and when I read about sea witches it inspired me to do it again. I love writing fantasy fiction, but I always use elements of fact within my stories. I'm sure the historians will be up in arms when they discover the last King of Cornwall had a brother.

It was in Cornwall where I first had the idea for Sam to the Ends of the Earth. Summer 2006, I was reading about sea witches and at the same time I was holidaying in Cornwall. The place where Jenny and Johnny live does exist. When I first saw it, it engraved this dark and mysterious tale in my mind.

I now spend much of my time promoting my books through social media and school and Library visits. This year I have an author event organised by the Sandbach Library and I'll be reading to fifty secondary school students. Normally I read to about thirty so I'm a little nervous and excited to be sharing my stories with them.

Before I was a writer I worked in Schools with Primary children and acquired a BA(hons) in Primary Education. Now I spend as much time as possible writing and promoting my writing in schools and my previous endeavours have proved very useful to this end.

Thank you for reading my personal Biography. If you want to know more about me and my work you can contact the Gilbert Literary agency, visit me on twitter and facebook or email me at mike.wardsatsw@yahoo.co.uk

Lightning Source UK Ltd.
Milton Keynes UK
UKHW021815010319
338261UK00008B/237/P

9 780994 141743